A TALE OF TWO BESTIES

# SOPHIA ROSSI

raz0r
bill

Los Altos High School Library
201 Almond Ave.
Los Altos, CA 94022

An Imprint of Penguin Random House

razOr bill

An Imprint of Penguin Random House

Penguin.com

Copyright © 2015 Hello Giggles, Inc.

Library of Congress Cataloging-in-Publication Data

Rossi, Sophia Rivka.
A Tale of Two Besties : A Hello Giggles Novel / Sophia Rossi.
320 pages cm
Summary: In ultra-cool Los Angeles, can two freshman girls remain best friends despite a tidal wave of high school drama, or does growing up mean leaving some friends behind?
ISBN 978-1-59514-849-0
[1. Best friends—Fiction. 2. Friendship—Fiction. 3. High schools—Fiction. 4. Schools—Fiction. 5. Los Angeles (Calif.)—Fiction.] I. Title.
PZ7.1.R75Tal 2015
[Fic]—dc23

2015007090

Printed in the United States of America

1  3  5  7  9  10  8  6  4  2

Book design by Anthony Elder
Interior illustrations by Sara M. Lyons

Cover banner design by Fun Cult: Fun Cult is known for its original Glittering Fringe Banners, which you can use for both super-special occasions, as well as bedroom hangouts where you play records and eat pizza with your besties. Visit JOINFUNCULT.net

To all the Gigglers

# Foreword

I learned to read while I was living in the Seychelles, a group of islands off the east coast of Africa, when my father was making a movie based on *Robinson Crusoe*. I had left the familiarity of my Los Angeles home, my first grade class, and all of my friends for this tropical beach reminiscent of an explorer's desert island. Although it was beautiful, it was so different from home—with a very small population and just one tiny general store, it was nothing like the big-city culture I was accustomed to. I had my sister there with me, and did manage to make one or two new friends. But I still missed life at home and the friends that went with it. This new feeling was what led me to discover that I could escape into the stories in the books I was learning to read. Instead of feeling homesick, I could picture the characters and the places I was reading about. My imagination was thriving, and I finally felt at home.

When I returned to California, I got my first library card. I came to love the musty smell that accompanied the shelves upon shelves of undiscovered stories. From the fairy tales I knew from my early years to the page-turning young-adult novels I discovered as I grew older, books became my constant and consistent friends. From fiction to nonfiction, history to mystery, books of all kinds became my confidants, my teachers, and my entertainment, and they never, ever let me down. I took my books with me everywhere I went, and they silently soothed my bad days. I couldn't wait to get into bed and read every night, sometimes so engrossed in a story that I would sneak a flashlight under my pillow so that I could keep turning pages well past lights-out.

Books also become a way that I bonded with my friends. We exchanged our cherished and tattered paperbacks, and then wrote down our own stories when we were inspired. This was how I first became interested in going into the profession of storytelling, of playing other characters, of inhabiting other worlds. If you get tired of your own world, there's always a story waiting to take you away to someplace interesting.

Sophia's book, *A Tale of Two Besties*, is an homage to the books of our youth—and to our real friends, the ones who are as consistent as our favorite novels. I hope this book can be something you can share with your friends, and that will remind you of how lucky you are to have them.

Zooey Deschanel

**Lily (2:46 pm):** PuppyGirl. What if, instead of going to the first day of school tomorrow, we just hid out under the pier forever and made a living selling friendship bracelets and seashells? That is totally doable, right? Please say it's doable.

**Harper (2:47 pm):** Hang on, Gawkward Fairy! Do you really want to spend the last night before freshman year freaking out? Let's soak it in! Beverly Hills High won't know what they're missing when you go to Pathways!

**Lily (2:47 pm):** Stop. You're going to make me do one of those cry-face emojis.

**Harper (2:48 pm):** Like this one

**Harper (2:48 pm):** or like 😥

**Harper (2:49 pm):** Why are there so many face emojis? like do humans even have the capacity to make these faces?

**Harper (2:49 pm):**

**Harper (2:49 pm):** I bet it's the last one that is basically a picture of your face right now and also the rest of the time.

**Lily (2:50 pm):** "I STILL CAN'T FIGURE OUT HOW TO MAKE MY PHONE DO THAT!"—Your mom.

**Harper (2:50 pm):** Oh my god, right? "HOW DO I GET THE RINGTONE TO PLAY DRAKE but not the singing part only the part where he 'raps'?" Ughhh, okay mom.

**Lily (2:51 pm):** I <3 her.

**Harper (2:51 pm):** Not the way you <3 Tim Slater. Want me to say hi from the "Fairy" tomorrow when I see him in class? 😉

**Lily (2:51 pm):** Seriously: NOPE.

**Harper (2:52 pm):** Playing hard to get, are we? Or have you accepted what a serial weirdo our male buddy is?

**Lily (2:53 pm):** Man you seriously date someone for 2 months and they crush your heart by not being that into you and you never live it down?? I don't like him anymore, I just like those comics he draws for us!

**Harper (2:54 pm):** They are good comics, Gawkward Fairy. And that's not just me as my superhero PUPPYGIRL with my SUPER EMPATHY talking.

**Lily (2:55 pm):** Nice try, but the Gawkward Fairy has up her ultra gawkward shield. NOW I AM immune to all forms of kindess!! Let's face it: the saddest day of my life starts tomorrow and will last FOREVER.

**Harper (2:56 pm):** FOREVER? So dramatic. No wonder they are sending you to the Pathways School of Creative Angst.

**Lily (2:56 pm):** Now I'm actually crying face.

**Harper (2:56 pm):** Okay, that's it. Emergency BFF meeting. Same secret time, same secret place?

**Lily (2:56 pm):** Only if you bring a sacrificial goat and/or Pinkberry.

**Harper (2:57 pm):** duh.

*I, Lily Annelisa Farson, thirteen years of age and of sound mind and body, do hereby declare that the following is the whole truth and nothing but the truth, so help me Zeus.*

*Here is a list of things I love:*

1.  *Really loud thunderstorms (but in a safe "I'm indoors!" kind of way)*

2.  *Music mixes for and from friends and collages of friends and me*

3.  *My red chucks and sometimes my blue ones when my mom washes my red ones without asking* (see: **NARWHALS!**)

4.  *Crazy animals that shouldn't exist but do.*

5.  *Comic books (and not just the ones people think girls will like. ALL OF THEM. Even DC)*

6.  *BASICALLY anything in a thrift store.*

7.  *Sneezing. (It makes me feel powerful.)*

8/9.  *(Tied) Horses/Vanilla ChapStick*

10.  *My best friend Harper!*

*And here is a list of things I really, really don't like:*

1. *Peppers (sometimes I pretend I'm allergic for dramatic purposes only, promise)*

2. *Aggro-angry music, where someone just yells into a microphone like... Aggressive sounds are so aggressive.*

   RAAAGHHH!!

3. *Volleyball*

4. *My hair (too wavy)*

5. *The smell of airplane bathrooms. I've only been on one plane but it SURE WAS MEMORABLE*

6. *The Mansons—the cult and Marilyn*

7. *The lady at the mall who works at Day of Knights. It used to be my favorite shop until I accidentally broke a ceramic dragon figurine when I was 11 and she told my dad when he came to pick me up, even though I offered to pay for it. I was planning on being a loyal customer. So really HER LOSS.*

8. *PATHWAYS!!!*

9. *Hashtags (Remember when it was just the "number" symbol and nobody used it, ever, because it was super ugly?)*

10. *Traumas*

I scrawled my signature at the bottom of my note. Mom and I were keeping a scrapbook of my lists and journals, and she told me that she was even thinking of doing some capital-A Art based on them. There wasn't a lot of room left on the fridge, but I made an executive decision and replaced a postcard Dad had sent from his last trip to Brazil with my note, using our "Got Milk?" magnet to keep it in place right where Mom would definitely notice it.

"Are you ready, Lily-Jolie?" My mom has a way of sing-talking my name like she was an old black-and-white movie starlet. It immediately evokes nostalgia for a time and place that doesn't even belong to me. She was standing shadowed in the doorframe with the light behind her, looking like a classic beauty in her wide sun-brim hat and paint-splattered denim dress. On anyone else it would have looked frumpy, but on her it looked like couture. "We're going to be late meeting Harper at the Pier."

I stepped back to view the note within the larger context of the fridge. Did it draw the audience's eye? Yes, it did. But would the audience (my mom) understand that the last item—the dreaded Pathways Academy—was the most important? I hoped so. It was only eighteen hours, thirty minutes, and nineteen seconds until I descended into the darkness otherwise known as freshman year at a totally new school where I would know exactly zero people.

"Okay, coming!" I turned and grabbed my shimmery blue fairy wings off the back of one of our red, mismatched kitchen chairs and stuffed them in my backpack. Within minutes, Mom and I were in the car zooming toward the ocean, on our way to the Santa Monica Pier to say goodbye to summer. I closed my eyes and tried to smell the salt in the air.

Besides Harper, my mom is my best friend. She's always understood me, and even when she hasn't agreed with my decisions, she's supported me. Just one example: In third grade, when we were living back in Maryland, I had the brilliant idea of cutting off all my hair—really short, like Felicity in *Felicity*, which is this old show I found on Netflix and watched because they said it was made by the same guy who did *Lost*, which I was psyched about until I realized it didn't feature any smoke monsters. Anyway, I needed short hair to pull off a rattail, which I desperately wanted. Most kids' parents would have laughed in their faces and told them to get real, but my mom took me to her friend's salon in Baltimore the next day. She said my new look was *au courant*.

Now, speeding down the highway, I wiggled my toes and told Mom that I had heard something interesting the other day.

"What was it Lily-*Jolie*?" My mom's family is from France, where "jolie" means "pretty." It's not even my middle name, which is Annalisa, but it might as well be.

"It's just about how students who go to public high schools usually have an easier time of it, you know, academically, than kids who transfer to private schools. Same with getting into college. Because they have better extracurriculars, you know, with public funding? And I also read an article about how private school students are more likely to join a gang or do drugs than regular kids, because they are more susceptible to peer pressure. Like in *Lord of the Flies*, but with heroin."

My mom sighed. "Lily, we've been over this. You are going to Pathways."

"I know." My feet were fidgeting so much that the sole of my sandal was almost entirely detached from the actual shoe at this point. "But maybe if I transferred after first semester? If I really, really hated it, maybe . . ."

We pulled into the parking lot for the Pier, the Santa Monica amusement park only a quick trip down the boardwalk, which was made even faster when I wore my chunky purple rollerblades with the vintage stripes. The Pier is where Harper and I had our secret spot.

Mom turned off the car and took my head in her hands, wiping away my tears. I didn't even know I had been crying.

"Oh Jolie," she murmured. "I know you think you won't be able to make friends, but you'll see . . . everyone will love you!"

*Easy for you to say,* is what I wanted to tell her, but didn't.

I'd told my parents from the beginning that I didn't want to go to a private high school. "But Pathways will help nurture your individuality!" Mom would keep telling me, as if individuality is something I have a problem with. If anything, I'm *too* much of an individual.

"You'll find your passion there," my dad would insist. "You're so creative; you just need a nurturing environment."

My parents think Pathways is better than Palisades or Beverly High, because it's exclusive and a lot of "artists" have come out of there. "Plus," they kept saying, "you get to call your teachers by their first names!" I told them that I'd much rather hang out with Harper than call my teacher "James" instead of "Mr. Franco." (Yes, *that* James Franco. But he was only a visiting teacher so it doesn't really count.)

While I was still sniffling in the parking lot, Mom reached over the seat and handed me my rollerblades. "Mrs. Carina or Rachel will pick you up at four and drive you guys back. You'll have dinner over at Harper's, and I'll pick you up at eight." She kissed me on top of my head and gave me my knapsack. "Now, you go have fun, *jeune fille!*"

I breezed down the boardwalk in my scuffed-up rollerblades, which were covered in sparkly stickers and flaky scribbles from an old Puffy Pen. I took in the life around me: peddlers of all kinds of wares, artisans of chintz and bongs and bongos. Harper and I have our special place outside Pacific Park, not quite underneath the boardwalk, but almost. We found it two summers ago, an empty stretch of beach where you can look to your left and see the Ferris wheel; look to your right and see the ocean. It's where we listened to Lana Del Rey's "Video Games" for the first time, sharing an iPod, dancing around like witches attached at the ears. It's the place where, last summer, those two skateboarding boys followed us, trailing drips of the ice cream they'd bought for us, the sugar sizzling on the boardwalk. Our stomachs stretched tight as drums, we lovingly set down the oversized teddy bears, useless things that Josh and Ben had won for us at the Playland Arcade, and all four of us had run into the water with our clothes on, shrieking. Harper Snapchatted them a picture of us making goofy faces that August, but they never messaged her back. Harper said that was really rude, because you shouldn't buy two pretty girls ice cream and then never reach out again, especially if those two pretty girls didn't even ask for extra toppings and were very chill. I don't know much about this but I believe her. We would have burned the bears in effigy in her yard to cleanse ourselves of their memory, had we not been worried about toxins.

I came to a quick stop at our spot, where I found Harper already waiting for me. She was wearing her go-to beach gear: a blue and white striped Topshop bathing suit underneath a sheer, oversized white cotton shirt that came down to her knees. Her hair was pulled back in a messy bun, highlighting her big brown eyes and the freckles dotting her high cheekbones. Harper's only accessories were her friendship bracelets that both of us wore all the time—we didn't even need to remind each other to put them on, though they sometimes fell off my bony wrists (the only parts of me that are still bony).

Harper is my muse: One time I had her dress up in a big, white gown and this pink wig I found at a thrift store on Melrose, and we shot an entire movie on my cell phone. I wrote and directed and provided the soundtrack, and she was the star. It was about a ghost who doesn't know she's dead, waiting at the shore for her lover to arrive. It had a lot of shots of Harper looking intensely at the sea, and doing romantic stuff like running down the steps of the boardwalk crying "Where are you, Walter? My darling!"

I would say my inspiration for that film was sixty percent Godard and forty percent these cool Vines I saw where everyone looked like they were in *Girls*. Harper posted it online and we got a bunch of comments, including one from one of our favorite TV actors, from that show about the moody cop who always solves impossible crimes. He wrote, "Will be looking for you two next pilot season!" We almost died.

"What took you so long?" asked Harper when I finally took off my skates and skittered onto the sand. She was standing up on her blanket, a vintage copy of *Lemony Snicket* with a cracked spine lying face down next to her coconut water and bag of carrot sticks. "I've been waiting forever!"

"I couldn't leave Mom without one last plea for mercy," I said, slinging my backpack off my arms and unzipping it. "And I had to bring this, too, of course." I smiled. Harper looked inside the bag and pulled out a mangled corpse of wire and fabric.

"Oh no, Lily! I think you bent your wings!"

They were definitely crumpled. The frame had bent completely, and in some parts the wires were sticking out of the purple and blue mesh. It made me sad; they were the last gift my grandmother ever gave me before we left Maryland, and even though I was too old to be wearing a costume, I put them on that very day and promised I wouldn't take it off until the next time I saw her. I'm sure she didn't expect me to keep that promise, but, to be fair, I didn't expect her to pass away before my tenth birthday.

"They look like a mangled Muppet!" I said. Maybe it was the memory of my grandmother, but now I felt completely desolate. Meanwhile, Harper, being Harper, pragmatically got to work trying to smoosh them back into shape. "You know, you *know,* this is a *bad omen!* Something is trying to tell us that going to different high schools is a bad idea." I shivered.

"Don't be silly," said Harper. "It's not a bad omen, it's physics. That's what happens when you crush something into your bag. Plus, they're old, anyway." I must have had a horrified look on my face, because she smiled and gave me a big hug. "Look, I think I can save them. We'll have our superpowers back up and running in no time!"

Harper always knew what to say to distract me from my looping thoughts—including saying nothing at all. "Didn't you bring your towel, Lily? Here, you can share mine." Harper scooted over. "Help me Instagram some final summer memories of the Ferris wheel." She pulled out her phone—which had on a pink rubber case with big bunny ears—and we made funny faces with the park behind us, pretending to be happier than we were. The shrieks of delight from the roller coaster almost overpowered my thoughts, and the heat from the California sun tried to soothe me into drowsiness. My mind was suddenly flooded with the realization that, from now on, Harper and I would be taking selfies in different places, with different people. Before we knew it we were going to become "Like" friends—those kids you see who heart every photo but never even hang out.

After a couple of pics where I must have looked a little too lost in reverie, Harper turned on her side to face me.

"Thinking about Pathways?" she asked.

"Are you a mind reader?"

"Yes. Maybe I should make my own Tarot app," Harper giggled. She stopped when she saw my face.

"Come on, it won't be so bad. I bet you get to take all the macramé and collage classes you want! And you probably won't have to dissect frogs, or do math." Harper's biggest fear in life was cutting into an animal, which was thanks to her older sister, Rachel, who almost got expelled her freshman year after bringing in fifty live toads to biology as part of a protest. The funny thing is, Rachel isn't even the big animal lover in the family. It's Harper who spends all her time taking care of sick dogs at the rescue center.

"I don't care about any of that," I said, picking up a carrot stick and nibbling on it, hoping it would calm my knotted stomach. "I'm not going to have any friends there. Everyone is going to think I'm a weirdo."

"Starting high school is scary for everyone." Harper made a face. "Look, who will *I* know besides Rachel and her friends and Tim?"

"At least you'll have Tim," I said, morosely thinking of my cute ex-boyfriend with his slouchy posture and perfectly hidden tickle spots.

Harper rolled her eyes. "Ugh, Tim." She had never understood my infatuation with her oldest friend. "You're going to find yourself a bohemian boyfriend in ten minutes at school and forget all about him." This was Harper's biggest blind spot. She didn't have any sense for romance. She traded out her guy crushes daily, obsessively checking their stats and info online like she was creating a personal fantasy draft of cute boys. She felt the need to virtually stalk every boy we'd ever meet for weeks, obsessing over his social media history—who he tagged, who he's faved, who he retweeted and whose stuff he "liked"—and determining his crushability entirely on the results of her Internet detective-ing.

I've only liked one boy ever: Tim Slater, who was actually more like our third sidekick and has known Harper since they were both in diapers.

Tim is the perfect kind of guy: sort of geeky in a Wes Anderson-y kind of way, knows the origin story of every super villain from Marvel, and can make any type of nautical knot in under sixty seconds. He's really funny but totally hates the idea of improv groups, can whistle the theme song from every TV show ever made, and—most importantly—has no idea of how attractive he is. He's like a girl in one of those high school movies where you take off her glasses and oversized "Save the Direwolves" T-shirt and brush the hair out of her eyes and *voila!* He's like Clark Kent—dweeby and doesn't look like much—that is, until he turns into Superman. He's even got a really square chin, like a superhero, and very straight, white teeth which, combined with his crooked smile, are totally devastating. His fingernails are never, ever dirty and he has very soft hands, which he used to gently break my heart into a million pieces. *Ugh.*

I shook my head to clear away the spider webs. I had liked Tim and we dated and it didn't work out for a number of reasons, and it was time to stop thinking about him.

"I don't want a boyfriend," I explained for the billionth time. "No boyfriend is going to know that 'Cups' song is from summer camp and not an oversampled Anna Kendrick single. No boyfriend will help me on an intelligence mission to the teachers' lounge to find out if Ms. Bulgari is actually a witch. No boyfriend," I added slyly, "is going to spend a day walking around with me with Skittles in our bras to see if Tim Slater notices that we're candy-padding."

Harper broke out into a big grin. "You don't know that. Pathways is supposed to be full of guys in candy push-up bras who *love* anything campy." We both erupted into giggles that felt relief personified. Laughing with Harper feels like catching my breath after I didn't even know I was holding it in.

Harper scooched over and gave me a big hug. "Lily,

you are going to make TONS of friends!" she whispered, stroking my hair as I began to morph into a cry-baby yet again. "You are the most magical person I know!"

That was such a Harper thing to say. She'd always been super popular. People just wanted her in their circle, and not just because she looks the part of a Californian Dream Girl. Harper's style is pretty understated— her signature look is something like a dove gray tank top paired with jeans and her beach-ready mermaid hair, which sounds super minimalist but she pulls it off, especially thanks to her beautiful dark eyes and her yoga-perfected posture. She's like a Disney Princess in Rag & Bone. She never tried to "express herself" with fashion, always letting herself bring personality to her clothes rather than the other way around, which was such a rarity in LA. People were always stopping her on Melrose, assuming she was an actress. Not in a "Oh, weren't you on that ABC Family tween comedy?" way, either. It was more that you got a sense from Harper, could feel something that radiated off of her telling you that she was someone Special. You could tell just by the way she looked at you, no matter what she was doing, that she was having the best time and wanted to make sure you were, too.

But even if Harper wore a bag over her head, she'd still be picked for captain of the step team and probably class president. The thing is, Harper is classy. She actually *listens* when people talk, and you can tell she isn't just trying to think of what to say next, or worrying if there is spinach in her teeth. She's very "present," which is a term my mom uses a lot to describe people who aren't wracked by social anxiety and neuroses.

"I'm not like you, Harper," I said. "I get nervous

around new people."

"So we'll text each other during every class!" Harper pulled out her cell phone and waved it in front of my face. She was a stealth ninja at not getting caught by teachers with her phone out. "If something's wrong, you text 'GAWKWARD SOS' and I'll tell you what to do! And then at the end of the day, Rachel and I will pick you up. If anyone is giving you trouble . . ." Harper mimed a punch. "KABLAMO!" She picked up my broken wings and studied them. "These actually might be fixable." She began to dig in with her fingers, refashioning the wires and massaging the cloth back over the broken parts. You had to love a friend willing to chip her nails on your wings the day before her freshman year in high school.

I've been gawkward—which is a portmanteau of *gawky* and *awkward*—for as l long as I can remember. But it was only after meeting Harper that I discovered that being different could be a power instead of a curse.

On my first day of school in California all the way back in fourth grade, I discovered my two good luck charms. The first was Harper herself. She was like a human amulet who warded off bad vibes and made me even somewhat accepted . . . or at least, not a totally shunned outcast. The second charm was my iridescent fairy wings, which transformed me from the creepy, weird new girl named Lily into my true persona: the Gawkward Fairy, who could save the world with her social anxiety, making the bad guys so uncomfortable that they would forget about fighting or blowing up the world and just call it a day and go home early for some TV and snacks.

"Hold on one second, I need to get something," Harper said. "You stay right here." She carried my wings with her, but left me on the towel with the rest of her stuff. After a couple of minutes, her phone made a chirping noise, and I picked it up.

It was a text. From Tim. His name on her screen still had the power to make my heart race, which I hated, but the breakup had been mutual, and I knew we were better friends than boyfriend/girlfriend anyway.

Still, I won't pretend it didn't still get under my skin that Harper was the one Tim always ran to first with big news. I guess maybe it made sense though—I wasn't big into my cell phone the way Harper was—for me it was just a tool for texting, not Internet stalking. And even just cellular communications can sometimes get out of control. I found most people's emails and texts to feel very emotionally violating. Like, people send the most intense texts while you are just walking around the world. You could be in a mall casually browsing for crop tops (ew, but never crop tops) and someone you're not even that great friends with will just send you the most insane text, like, "MY PARENTS ARE DIVORCING!??!" And what do you respond? "BRB"? Ugh. Every time you send a text instead of reaching out for real, a little bit of your soul dies. I'm one hundred percent sure that is true.

Still, I couldn't help but wonder why Tim hadn't texted me, too, as I clicked his message on Harper's phone.

"Watch this!" it said, with a link to a video. By the time Harper came back, I wasn't warm anymore. I was cold, cold, cold.

"Ta-da!" She said, holding up my wings. She had gone to buy some scarves on the Pier and was waving them in front of my face. I tried to ask her what they were for, but it was like my throat had swollen shut. "What is it? What are you watching?" she asked. "Is it another ah-mazing cat video?"

Harper delicately pried the phone out of my trembling hands.

"Why are you looking at SchoolGrams?" School-Grams is an app that allows anyone with a student ID number and PIN to upload and access movies and pictures tagged with a school's name. You're only supposed to be able to look at things from your own school, but people share their passwords all the time, and things go viral pretty quickly. The video was tagged #Hollywood-Middle. My stomach sank as I pressed Play. There were very few positive or uplifting videos that got uploaded to SchoolGrams—most of the time they were taken without people's permission and used for humiliation purposes. The school system had tried several times to ban the app after kids complained of bullying, but the developers always made the defense that SchoolGrams was just a platform and it was up to us to determine the kind of content we put on there.

The video was shaky and there was a lot of audio distortion—very amateur. All I could make out were two girls on the park bench having drama. One of them was crying and the other was patting her shoulder and talking very fast and in this really, really high-pitched voice, like she was half-trying to sound reasonable and half-screaming.

"Is that Jessica Samuels and Stephanie Adler?" Harper brought the screen closer to her face and frowned. "No way."

Stephanie and Jessica were girls in our class who were kind of nice, but also kind of NOT nice. We ate lunch with them, but they were mostly Harper's friends from growing up. Until last year, they dressed the same, did their hair the same, they even laughed the same flittering snicker-giggle. Last fall, though, Stephanie's style all of a sudden got all Coachella-street-blogger, while Jessica was still wearing Lacoste Polo shirts and Uggs and doing her hair in tight, Ariana Grande–style ponytails. Then one day, Jessica wasn't even sitting with us at lunch. You could see her blond tresses, finally relaxed from their tight bun, draped over Matt Musher's shoulders as she lovingly fed him French fries dipped in ranch sauce.

"You stole my boyfriend, you slut!" One of the girls—it was hard to tell with all the Shaky-Cam—screamed at the other. "I can't believe you kissed . . . *garbled*. You were my *best friend*!" Here, the angrier of the girls had wrestled her way on top and bent her former bestie's arm back, punctuating her words with a quick, upward yank.

The other girl howled, and the video cut off after some fumbling by the intrepid cameraman.

"Wow, did Steph . . . hook up with Matt?" Harper asked, sounding confused on multiple levels. Matt Musher was a boy in our class who was okay-cute, but kind of a jock.

This was exactly why I hated the Internet: Clicking a link allowed you to peer into someone's personal humiliation file, making you feel dirtier than if you were the one who made out with your best friend's boyfriend. We couldn't think of much to say after that, so I put my head down and closed my eyes, pretending to take a nap. Harper picked up her book and turned over to tan her back.

That afternoon, the minutes flew by between us. I was unable to keep them there, though I wished they'd come back. I wish I could have gathered up those minutes like flowers to hang upside down in my room, until they were dried out: less fresh, but more permanent. So they'd stay with me forever and never die and never hurt.

But instead I could practically hear the countdown clock ticking: eighteen hours, forty-five minutes and thirty seconds till Pathways. Make that twenty-nine seconds. Twenty-eight. Twenty-seven. Twenty-six.

It must have been a little bit later—but not too late, because the sun was still out—that I heard a strange, sad call coming from underneath the boardwalk. A chill coursed through me.

"Whoa," said Harper. "Is that an owl?"

"Yeah, we used to have a lot of them in Maryland."

"What is it doing up so early?"

I sat up, remembering something. Something foreboding. "Harper, have you ever heard of the owl of Minerva?"

Harper sighed and lay down next to me on the blanket, folding her arms above her head and closing her eyes. "I love story time."

I continued.

"Okay, so this owl flew around, crying out warnings for travelers who'd stayed out in the forest past dark, and so were in great danger of getting lost there forever. But the thing is, the owl always flew super close to nighttime, so by the time you saw it, it meant you were already doomed. Harper, what if that's *our* owl of Minerva? What if we're already doomed?"

I knew how intense I sounded, but sometimes intensity is the way to the truth. Or maybe I was just FREAKING OUT.

*Sixteen hours, ten minutes, and eleven seconds. Ten seconds. Nine seconds.*

"Lily, you've got to snap out of it!" Harper was using her annoyed voice. "We are *not* doomed. We're just freshmen! But it *is* getting late, and we still have two items on the agenda."

"You'd be a great events planner," I said, only half-sarcastically, because Harper is actually fantastic at remembering all the details that I'd never remember. Like: Turn off the lights when you leave the house. Don't put on lotion right before you put on jeans and don't fall asleep with your hairband on if you don't want to lose circulation for like ever. Don't leave KIND bars in your backpack for too long or they'll turn into a sticky, backpack-ruining mess.

Like: Oh man, Harper's birthday was coming up. And I knew she was about to ask me about PuppyBash. Every year, on the night before her birthday, Harper arranges for one of the volunteers from PuppyTales, a rescue organization for strays, to drive up to a park or some other public location with about fifteen dogs in mobile cages. We take turns playing with them and giving them exercise, and instead of presents, Harper always asks for donations to PuppyTales. Last year our neighbors, Mr. and Mrs. Beatty, even took home a puppy to adopt: a tiny little Shih Tzu named Maxine. It was brilliant. I guess you could call us activists, kind of.

Actually, please call us activists, it feels very grownup.

"At least you have PuppyBash to look forward to! And whatever else we do . . ." Harper said.

She was always so obstinately vague about her birthdays. She always goes all-out planning Puppy-Bash, but when it comes to her *real* birthday celebration, it's always up to me.

"Yeah, there's always that," I said, trying to cheer myself up, at least for Harper's sake. "That will be fun!"

When I didn't say anything else, Harper dropped the subject, turning her back to me and rustling my wings. "Ta-da! Here! All better!" She had bandaged up the broken parts with the gauzy fabric of the scarves, turning them into something a winged Katniss might wear.

"Oh my god, they're perfect! You made them perfect again!" I tried to hug her but of course I almost smooshed them all over again, so I had to just be okay with spiraling into a sea of *thank you*s, over and over.

"Do you remember the first time we met?" Harper asked softly. I tried not to concentrate on anything else but the sound of my best friend's voice. This seemed important in an all-new way, and for a moment the sound of my mental clock ticking its countdown faded into the gentle roar of the ocean's surf. I buried my feet in the cooling sand, wishing I could grow roots. "How it was true bestie love at first sight?"

"Of course," I said. My skin was pricked with goose bumps. "Everyone remembers the day the weirdo girl in a fairy costume showed up to be eaten alive by the sharks of Beverly Hills."

Harper grinned, digging her feet into the sand next to mine. "I remember it as the last day before I realized life could actually be magical."

"Um, I have told you I don't actually grant wishes, right?" I teased.

"Dummy." Harper gave me a light punch. "The

magical part was that I met my best friend that day."

"Come on, the magical part was where the coolest girl in the Hills decided to talk to me." I tried to say it lightly, like it was a joke, but it was how I really felt.

Harper pulled her feet out of the sand, showering us both in grainy clumps. She turned toward me and pulled her legs up to her chin. "For the billionth time, being cool has nothing to do with how many people say hi to you in the hall. Being cool means saying hi to people and not caring if they say it back."

"I care!" I protested, feeling the well-worn tread of this debate we had at least once a month. "It's not like I try to stick out. I just do. I can't help it."

"Um, exactly." Harper shook her head, exasperated that I wasn't understanding her. When it came to most things, we were on the same page. But this was one topic we could never see eye-to-eye on. Secretly, I knew Harper was giving me too much credit for being "unique" when really I wasn't trying to make a statement or anything. I just liked the way the wings looked. It reminded me of Gram, who had been a dancer in a traveling vaudeville group when she was younger and was the most glamorous person I'd ever seen.

Harper tilted her head, regarding me with a crinkled eye. "Okay," she said, fake-breezily. "I've got an idea. Let's make a pact."

"A pact? You want me to join your cult or something?"

"No! A non-creepy pact."

"Oh, well if it's a non-creepy pact, then sure. But please tell me it involves ritual animal sacrifice."

I tried to laugh it off as a joke, but Harper grabbed my hands and looked at me straight in the eyes. "I know you're nervous about Pathways, but you know that a school can't change you from being yourself, right? Promise me we're not going to fall into this *Pretty Little Liars*-y trap where one moment everyone's best friends and the next everyone changes. We're not going to give in to that basic stereotype, right?"

I shrugged. I didn't have as much faith in me as Harper did, but I guess that's what best friends were for: to believe in you when you didn't even believe in yourself.

"Since we're not going to be around to help one another every second of every day anymore," she continued, "we need to solemnly swear that we're not going to be one of those kids who do this dramatic makeover or have a personality transplant the moment they get to high school. That stuff only works in the movies, anyway. You're the Gawkward Fairy. Don't let anyone convince you otherwise."

I looked off to the water and thought about Harper's words and what they really meant. "Okay," I said slowly. "Then you've got to swear something to me. That you're not going to go to Beverly High and forget all about me. That while I'm 'being me' you're not going to go off to bonfires on the beach and not invite me to come along to document everything. That you won't ever start doing duck-face selfies with girls who all have the same messy-perfect hair as you and you won't start dating some guy named Thad or Chaz or whatever and totally stop texting."

Harper's smile broke open wide, and my heart along with it. "Only if you promise not to read from the Pitchfork comment board in a silly accent without me."

"Promise. Pact made," I said, offering my hand for a

business-deal shake. "But only if you know that you're getting, like, the raw end of the deal. You'll be stuck with me by your side forever!"

"Okay. Promise," said Harper, shaking my hand and immediately enveloping me into a big hug.

We sat like that, eyes half-closed, listening to the waves crashing louder and louder as the light grew dimmer.

"Hey," Harper said gravely, the first to pull back. "I didn't mean to sound like you had to walk around high school in your wings all the time, if you don't want to." Why did she have to say that? Did she know something I didn't? Was Pathways really anti–fairy wings or something? Was there some rule in the dress code I didn't know about?

She must have seen the worried look on my face.

"Stop spiraling!" She admonished. "I can always tell when you are overthinking things! I just mean, wear what makes you feel comfortable, not what makes you look like everyone else. Listen, as long as we are our dope selves we are ALL GOOD. And I'm sure you will find some magical creatures there and I'll have to get my own wings just to fit in with you guys. And maybe our mission in high school is to help people break free of the stereotype that all high schools are just made up of mean girls, jocks, and nerds. Between PuppyGirl's Empathy powers and the Gawkward Fairy, we help those in social distress. We use our powers for good, not evil."

"Oh, darn, and here I was, planning to become a super villain the moment your back was turned." My voice was sarcastic, but I was still spiraling: Why would Harper even say that thing about bullying? Did she think I was a monster? I had never made fun of anyone, ever, but now that she'd mentioned it, I wondered if Harper was secretly scared that without me, she'd become one of the mean girls.

We sat a little longer, but the magical moment had passed. It was getting dark and cold. I could almost hear my own personal Minerva hooting in my ear, and there was nothing more I wanted in that moment than to run off toward the amusement park, away from the Pier, out of California forever, only looking back to cry over my shoulder, "Too late! Too late! Too late!"

Someone should make a reality show about the first day of freshman year. You can get sixteen contestants from all over the country, force them to wake up at six in the morning, get dressed in their most stunning casual outfits, and go face the world sitting down at a desk for the next eight hours. There can be a challenge called "Lunch," where you have to tell yourself "I'm not *not* here to make friends." There can be elimination rounds based on how much chemistry and calculus you can do. And then at two p.m., when that final bell rings, you can stop smiling and pretending that it was "*so* great to *see* you!" to the same group of Traumas—the Murderers and Spirals and Emotional Vampires—that you've known since you were six.

Sorry, let me explain the Traumas to you.

Traumas are basically the people who need to be avoided at all costs, because they will turn your life into a nightmare and never, ever let go. Luckily, Traumas are very easily broken down into the following types, making it very simple to spot one right away:

1. Spirals. A Spiral is a girl who is constantly freaking out over one specific thing, but also everything. If she stains

her shirt with cafeteria food, it will remind her how it was her favorite shirt, which, oh *no*, she can't replace because she bought it on vacation in Morocco with her mom and dad and now her parents are divorced and what's the point of living if she knows she's just going to flunk the SATs? SHE CAN BARELY WEAR A SHIRT, HOW CAN SHE BE EXPECTED TO TAKE A STANDARDIZED TEST TO DETERMINE HER FUTURE??

2. Emotional Vampires. Emotional Vampires are basically people who will bleed you dry of all your love of life in order to feed their love of drama. They will drain you of your heart and soul because they don't have any themselves. You guys will fight and make up and fight and make up and then fight and fight again and then not talk and then you'll hear through someone else that's she's spreading rumors about you, so then you fight some more. Repeat pattern till the end of time.

3. Murderers. Murderers are not actual murderers, but people that show no empathy. They are the closest thing we have to a super-villain, because Murderers have absolutely no capacity to relate to anyone besides themselves. They're not being mean, they're being "honest." And they "wouldn't have to lie to you so much if you didn't get so hysterical all the time." Hanging out with Murderers turns you into a Spiral.

4. Emotional Volcanoes: Oh, Emotional Volcanoes might seem drama-free on the surface, but they're actually dormant. Things are going peachy until you walk by their desk and accidentally knock over their Nalgene bottle. Then it's like, don't bother even running for cover—you're Pompeii, and they're erupting all over you with fiery, irrational anger.

5. Thirsty Animals: Thirsty Animals might be the most confusing and cruel of the bunch. Thirsty Animals don't know why they're driven to make your life a soap opera, but research shows that this drive comes from somewhere deep inside their lizard brains, and they are not going to stop texting you until you answer them about whether you are mad at them. And they won't take "no" for an answer.

So, yeah . . . first day of high school? NOT the best, as you may have guessed.

It started fine enough. I put on my green Ella Moss dress and spent a half hour in the bathroom giving myself a French braid while watching a Michelle Phan tutorial (how did anyone learn anything before those, seriously?) and then slipped on a pair of Toms wedges. They weren't my favorite but at least they matched. I had no idea how I was supposed to dress today. I wasn't nervous, exactly, but I wanted to make a good impression, especially since I'd be meeting so many new people.

I've never lacked friends, even as a baby, which my mom says is because I'm a good listener. Rachel puts it differently. "Sometimes you can be so *desperate*,

Harper," she says. Sometimes when she is being extra mean she calls me "Despi," which I know doesn't sound too bad, but when she says it, it can sound like a swear. But even though I have a lot of friends, Lily and I are *best* friends: yin and yang, vanilla and cherry, Converse and no socks, fro-yo and those mochi toppings they try to hide from you but we all know you can get if you just ask. We balance each other out, and that's why we're not just best friends—we are friends who are the best. Well, also because we have superpowers. But I'll get to that later.

In my opinion, everyone should want to be a best friend. Friendship is the most important relationship in the world, just about. It's so funny to see people get so sensitive about it, like the girls who say they couldn't *possibly* like one friend more than another, or that best friends are for babies. It's like, yeah I want to be the *BEST* friend. SORRY I CARE ABOUT HUMAN HEARTS AND SOULS.

But I couldn't be standing around just giving thought speeches all day: I had to move to go to school! With barely a second to spare, I raced down the stairs and ran out to meet Rachel, who was already in the car and lying on the horn.

"If it isn't the Tween Hobo, ready to hop the rails," said my Twitter-obsessed sister, smirking when I tried to open the passenger door at the curb of our street. "What's the magic word?"

I tugged the handle of Nugget, my sister's gold Prius. "Let me in, Rachel." I hated sounding whiny, which Rachel knew and which is exactly why she provoked me so much.

"Say the magic word!" Rachel had to shout just to

be heard over the engine, which she was revving dramatically with the emergency brake on. Luckily all that car noise brought my dad to the door. He was still fixing his tie for another day "with the suits" at the record company he co-owned with Mr. Slater, my friend Tim's dad.

"Rachel, you are going to burn the brakes doing that!" he yelled from the driveway. My dad always looked a mess, which Rachel says he does on purpose and is just one more sign that he's a corporate hipster *poseur*. She gets a dreamy look whenever she says "poseur," which means she's thinking about her boyfriend, Jacques the Jock Itch (aka Jacques the Jerk, Jacque in the Box, "Jacques-ooze me, have you seen that name of some obscure band around here? I must have dropped it." That last one is Lily™.).

"I'm not burning the brakes, I'm testing them to make sure they work! I'm driving my precious little sister to her first day of high school, after all, and we need to be safe!" Rachel winked at me through the window.

"What?" Dad shouted over the engine's roar.

"Nothing!" Rachel sighed. She popped the lock and I scrambled in, pushing aside an accumulated lifetime's worth of empty organic juice bottles, melted protein bars, and Rite-Aid receipts for sparkly eyeliner. In the backseat, several old bottles of nail polish clanged noisily as Rachel put the car into first gear and a couple tumbled over the seat onto the floor. I picked one up. It was a muddled brown with bright red and blue glitter in it, like bedazzled cow poop. Rachel had the weirdest taste in polish.

Rachel backed out of the driveway, and I waved goodbye to Dad as Katy Perry played on Kiss FM. Rachel claimed to hate Top 40 music, but she didn't change the station, and I caught her singing along under her breath when we stopped at a light.

"So," she said as she adjusted her pout in the rear-view mirror, "Let's talk about your first-day-of-school outfit. What's the vibe you are going for here? TALK ME THROUGH THIS, HARPER!" She patted my leg.

"There's no 'vibe,'" I said, pulling out my iPhone. "I just like this dress."

"Okay, fair enough. So. You pumped yet, Harpo? Freshman year is kind of the worst."

"Sure," I muttered. "Thanks for the pep talk." Even though I knew Rachel was just giving me a hard time, she was still making me sick with nervousness. I need-ed to feel on my A-game, so I texted Lily. "I love you more than all the possible emoji options that exist and will exist."

Two seconds later I got a reply: a Lily-Selfie original of her in the car to Pathways! It was just a shot of her wings, which I guess she'd decided to wear, but under-neath she had texted "Holding my breath until you pick me up. Turning blue. SOS."

Before long we arrived at Beverly Hills High, which from the outside looked like the world's sunniest max-imum security prison. I scanned the crowd of kids as we pulled into the parking lot, but I didn't recognize anyone. They must have all just appeared from another galaxy and landed here. I hoped they came in peace.

"Okay, hop to it little dawg," Rachel smirked. "Woof-woof!"

On the inside, Beverly Hills High didn't seem so bad, but it WAS laid out in the dumbest way possible. I eventually broke down and used Google Maps to figure out how to get to first period, but that didn't help because the GPS lady told me I needed to turn around and get back on the freeway, which seemed maybe not right.

I finally found my locker, which was located directly behind an acne-ridden Goth couple making out. "Um." I cleared my throat. "Excuse me?" I tried to put on my best smile as the boy un-suctioned his face from his girlfriend's lip ring and glared at me. "I'm sorry, but that's my locker. I just need to get in there for a second!" The two slunk off, leaving a trail of black smudged lip liner and angst.

I had managed to shove my backpack into the ridiculously shoebox-sized cubby when the first bell rang. It was my first day, and I was late. I turned to bolt in the direction I hoped would lead me to class, when I felt a hand on my shoulder. I looked up and saw a man with a bushy mustache frowning down at me. "Are you lost, young lady?"

"Actually, I kind of am."

The man's face twitched under his mustache and he blinked his tiny eyes from behind horn-rimmed spectacles.

"I'm Mr. Hamish, sophomore English teacher." He pointed at the classroom full of chattering kids just behind us. "So, you're not where you need to be?" he asked.

I shook my head. "That's just the thing! I have no idea where I'm supposed to be. Well, I know what class I have—freshman history—but I can't find it. This campus is so big. It's going to take me four years to figure out, and I'll probably need a trail of bread crumbs just to find my way out." I expected Mr. Hamish to laugh along with me, but he looked more irritated than anything else, puffing out his cheeks and checking his oversized Swatch.

"Mrs. Miller's room is all the way on the eastern quadrant, second floor," he grumbled. "If you hustle, you'll only be five minutes late." An older, lanky boy with a pile of books under his arm sauntered past us into the classroom. His free hand was up, fiddling with his headphones, which Mr. Hamish clearly misinterpreted as an invitation for the world's most intensely awkward high-five.

"Young sir Travis," Mr. Hamish said with an uncomfortable amount of gusto. "I'm so glad to see that you've decided to take advanced English after all. As Shakespeare said, 'There is nothing either good or bad but thinking makes it so.'"

"Cool," Travis said, backing into the room slowly. "Yeah, that sounds right."

Another bell rang, ominously long this time. A group of older boys ran by, snickering. The shortest one snapped his head back toward me and made an impromptu bullhorn with his hands, yelling "Get to class!" The boys rounded the corner, their laughter echoing in the hallway.

Mr. Hamish frowned, making him look even walrus-ier. "Where was I? Oh, yes: We pride ourselves here on the resourcefulness of our students. If you have trouble finding your room, you should pair up with someone older who can show you the ropes. We call it the Buddy System."

"Oh," I said. "That's . . . cool." Out of the corner of my eye, I noticed Travis blowing spitballs at the blackboard. What *was* this place?

"It *is* cool." Mr. Hamish remained oblivious. "Why don't you flag someone down and ask for directions, maybe make a new friend while you're at it? And remember, as Shakespeare said, 'Better three hours too soon than a minute too late.'"

"Oh yeah, that sounds . . . just like him." I prayed we were done with this excruciating interrogation. If high school was Wonderland, I'd just met that pretentious caterpillar guy.

Luckily, the final bell sufficiently distracted Mr. Hamish, and without another word, he turned around and entered his waiting classroom. "Okay, guys, listen up. Fair warning: You'll be hearing the name 'Holden Caulfield' thrown around a lot in this class, but if I'm using it to refer to you, please don't interpret that as a compliment!"

I finally made my way to history class, no thanks to Mr. Hamish. Usually Lily and I try to get to first period early so we can scope out the good seats and charge our phones, but the teacher, Ms. Miller, was already calling names in the front of the room by the time I arrived, so I grabbed the first available seat . . . directly in front of her.

"Carina . . . Carina, comma, Harper?" she asked, actually saying the "comma" part out loud. What was it with the teachers at this school?

"That's me," I said.

"You're late, Harper," she said. My face turned red-hot-cherry bomb. Lily calls it "flushed" but I call it "pre-acne" because guess what? Tomorrow my skin is going to hate me.

There was a swell of noise from the back of the class, and I pretended to drop a book so I could turn around and see who I'd be dealing with all year. Because staring isn't polite, I've learned some tricks about how to look at people without them noticing, like focusing at one spot in front of you and letting your eyes glaze over so you can pick up motion and colors from the sides of your vision. My mom calls it "assessing the room," and she does it at conferences all the time to get a feel for her audience without seeming judge-y. Mom is a professional public speaker—a self-help coach/ lifestyle blogger ("just like Gwyneth!")—and people pay thousands of dollars to hear advice on how to do every- thing right. Or at least that's what she reminds me of every time we fight about something stupid. "You know, Harper, there are lots of people would pay good money to hear what I have to say about keeping their bedrooms clean, and you get to have all of my wisdom for free." I seriously don't know what is wrong with some people— who would throw away good money just to have another mom tell them what to do? Especially *my* mom, whom I've personally seen peeling off her gel manicure out of sheer anxiety while waiting in line to buy groceries.

Still, sometimes MomTips actually come in handy— though I'd never admit it to Mom. Like "engaging the room," which pretty much just means "how to make people pay attention to you," or "purifying your vibe" which just meant smiling a lot to make people think you're chill no matter what you're really thinking.

So I assessed the room to find a whole lot of un- familiar faces staring blankly back at Ms. Miller. I did recognize a couple people, though. Derek Wheeler, Ka- tie Donahue, and Paul Gilmore. There was Stephanie Adler. It was weird to see Steph without Jessica, but there she was, by herself, in ripped jeans and a faded Rolling Stones tee, her ears studded with crosses and crossbones. One person I was not at all surprised to see was Tim Slater, Lily's ex and the only person outside my family whom I've known for my whole life. He's been an annoying but familiar presence behind me in homeroom since they started putting us in seats, but today I almost didn't recognize him. Tim must have grown at least a foot over the summer while working at his cousin's farm in Sonoma, and with his preppy J. Crew khakis and skin tanned past its usual eggshell-white, he now looked less like a video game nerd and more like he'd be right at home with the sailing team. A huge surprise, since I was so used to thinking of Tim as the little brother I never asked for. The Slaters lived next door to us, and Tim's dad and my dad own a record company together, so we're basically family. I think Rachel always felt a little left out: Tim and I were the same age, and even though he was nerdy and way too into comic books, I was way more open to looking at Superman issues with him than spending time with her. At least Tim wasn't actively wishing for my long and painful demise.

"Ms. Carina," Ms. Miller prompted. I swiveled my head back and she smiled, showing off an uneven row of too-white teeth. "Thank you for joining us. As I was just telling the class before you arrived, I give a grace period for tardiness for the first three days of a new year. After that, I expect all my students to arrive at class on time. Otherwise, detention."

"Oh, okay." My face felt nuclear-hot as I stuffed my backpack under my chair. Detention, the dreaded D word! I don't get rattled that easily, but the idea of spending my first week in school pegged as one of the bad kids was enough to give me a panic attack. Maybe Tim would lend me his inhaler.

After she was done berating me, Ms. Miller dove right into her lecture about early exploitation of Chileans in California mines. I was fighting hard not to pull out my phone and text Lily when I felt something brush against my shoulder and fall into my lap. It was a note, folded up into a little origami swan. I opened it up to find one of Tim Slater's patented Lily-and-Harper superhero comics.

In it, a girl that looked a lot like me was dangling precariously over a cauldron. "Help me, Gawkward Fairy!" read the caption. An evil witch cackled below, looking suspiciously like Ms. Miller in a cape. "Bubble, bubble, toil and trouble!" read the sign above the witch's head.

I turned around to see Tim smiling shyly right behind me.

My biggest issue with Tim was that he was constantly trying to hang out with me during school, which was a definite violation of the Home vs. In Public code of conduct I had drawn up in crayon on our first day of kindergarten together. If I felt any sort of Empathy Power for Tim, I saved it for after classes. I told him he could call and come around as much as he wanted after school if during the day he would promise not to follow me around like a sad-eyed puppy. I know it sounds lame and superficial, but if he hadn't followed that promise to a T, Jessica and Stephanie would have un-friended me faster than I could say "World of Warcraft."

Of course all bets were off when Tim started dating Lily. I never understood what Lily saw in Tim—to me he'd always be an uber-dork, and then there she was, mooning over him for months. I couldn't say I was surprised when they broke up—Tim is about as romantic as an old retainer, and Lily was the type of girl who was saving herself for Mr. Darcy from *Pride and Prejudice.* ("But only the second half of the book, when he's being nicer," she would always add.) The only thing Lily and Tim both had in common was a total disinterest in what the rest of the world thought of them. I could just imagine them being voted "Most Creative Couple" or something, had they made it to high school. And Lily was so head over heels for Tim most of junior high that I was totally taken by surprise when they announced their breakup after barely two months of boyfriend-girlfriend status. "We just wanted different things" was all Lily would ever say on the topic, and I never pressed her further because they never made sense together in my mind anyway. We were all better off going back to everyone being friends, and after an appropriate three-day "cool down" period where the two of them avoided each other in the hall, that's exactly what happened.

Once again, I had to give Tim a double-take. I might not have even recognized the guy behind me as my old, nerdy friend if his *Iron Man* shirt hadn't been a dead giveaway. Even his hair looked better, no longer gelled and spiked like he was trying to be an anime character, but longer and soft-looking. Forgetting the circumstances and the fact that I was pretty sure Lily was still (inexplicably) into him, I grinned gratefully at the familiar face. Then I watched his eyes shift over my shoulder and his smile fade.

I followed his gaze to find Ms. Miller herself reaching right for the note. Did I have time to think *oh, no*? Maybe—I can't really remember because I was internally freaking out so hard. I definitely remember reaching for the comic to try to hide it in time, but Ms. Miller plucked it from my lap while I was still grasping at it.

"I didn't know we had such an accomplished artist in the class." She sneered at me. "Let's see what you were doing while I was talk—" She made a strangled sound in her throat, which I'm sure coincided with her realizing that she was playing the character of "warty witch" in Tim's comic. She looked up at me with a face so red I thought it might actually start melting. Is that what I look like when I'm upset?

"See me after class," she croaked.

"But Ms. Miller—" Tim started. I could tell he felt really bad about getting me into trouble.

"Quiet," Ms. Miller said. "Out-of-turn talking ends now."

"But—" Tim tried to go on, but Ms. Miller shot him a death glare and put up her palm in the STOP position. He looked at me with such an intense guilty-puppy face that I almost felt bad for him, until I remembered he was the whole reason this was happening in the first place.

"I'm sorry!" He mouthed to me once Ms. Miller's back was turned.

I spent the rest of first period with my face buried in my desk so no one could see that it was the color of a Benadryl.

I had never had detention before, not ever, and certainly never at lunch. Who's even heard of lunchtime detention? Did that mean I wouldn't be able to eat? Was that even legal? All these thoughts and more zapped around my brain until noon, when I had to report to the library and serve my mealtime sentence by shelving books.

To make matters worse, Lily was taking forever to answer my freak-out texts. It was a good thing, maybe, that I wasn't able to vent to her how mad I was at Tim, who followed me around for the rest of the day trying to apologize. I swear, sometimes I wish I could go back in time to stop Dad from founding ThrashFocus Productions with Mr. Slater while they were both interning at UCLA's college radio station. Then I'd never have Tim stuck to my back like a giant target that said "Kick me." And I wouldn't have detention on my first day of high school.

I had been the only one to get in trouble during first period—(how humiliating), so I was surprised to see Derek lounging with Matt Musher and three girls from history whom I'd never met before in the same area of the stacks that the creepy Library Gnome whom I'd reported to after Home-Ec had assigned me to.

A crop-topped girl in head-to-toe American Apparel glared at me as I approached. I was about to veer left and sit alone at an empty table, but Derek stood up and intercepted me before I could isolate myself.

"Come to join our little party, Carina?" he asked, cocking his right eyebrow and throwing an arm around my shoulder. "You guys better not mess with Harper here," he said to the girls. "She once turned a hose on me because she thought I smelled bad."

I strangled out a laugh, even though that's not exactly what happened. I've known Derek since elementary school, and we've barely spoken two words to each other. He always ran in a different crowd of really boy-boys, the kind that listened to Lil Wayne Mixtapes. Actually, the only conversation I remember having with him was in sixth grade when he expressed shock over the fact that I knew all of Lil Wayne's verse in "Lollipop." Then he made me perform it for him or I was a dirty liar.

Derek wasn't really mean, but was really lazy and had a sense of humor that really appealed to the lowest common denominator, comprised of the same fart and boob jokes he'd been recycling since first grade. But mostly he was just lazy. He once wore the same D.A.R.E. T-shirt to school for three weeks in a row, and then had the nerve to try to tackle me while I was waiting for my parents to pick me up at the end of the day. Okay, so I might have overreacted . . . and it was not a pretty scene when the janitor, Mr. Kalinski, found Derek shivering on the ground, soaking wet in all his clothes, and me standing over him holding a dripping garden hose left out by the crew team fence. Mr. Kalinski ended up driving Derek home with a bunch of borrowed gym towels on the seat underneath him. I don't know if Mr. and Mrs. Wheeler ever found out why their son had come home drowning in month-old dirty laundry, but the next day he was wearing a new rugby shirt and dorky pressed-pleat pants, and after that he never came in smelly again. We hadn't really discussed the incident—or anything else—since.

Derek's arm was still around my shoulders. He gave them a squeeze. I'd always been a big hugger in my class, so maybe it wasn't that weird. Or was it weird? Wait, did I even care? I had witnessed this kid eat someone else's boogers (not even on a dare), so why was I suddenly admiring the way his high-tops matched his T-shirt or the way his back arched into his jeans?

"You okay, Carina? You looked a little flushed." Derek led me over to a chair by the window and pushed my shoulders down. "Loosen up!" I felt a lot of different things at the moment, but loosened up wasn't one of them. "So, who are you going to torment next period?

You've already got Ms. Miller covered."

"I haven't really given it any thought," I said, trying to own the "bad kid" persona I suddenly felt strapped with. "Maybe I'll just skip the torment and work on my Tweet strat."

Everyone laughed, even Matt, who I am 100 percent positive had never stayed still long enough to read 140 characters of anything. American Apparel girl had a high, fake laugh, like she was a professional game show audience member.

"Hey, you and that girl Lily put up that crazy art video last year, right?" said one of American Apparel's friends. "The one with you as a princess?"

"Actually, I was a ghost," I told her. "It was kind of this ongoing film project we were trying to do."

"Oh, well I don't really get 'films,'" she said. "I'm more into movies."

*Why does that not surprise me?* I thought but didn't say.

"You know where it would be kind of cool to shoot a film?" Derek mused, scraping some flecks of gray paint off the windowsill with his fingers. He reminded me of a cute prisoner trying to bide time till the end of his sentence.

"Where?" I said.

"Murphy's Ranch," he said, turning toward me. "Do you know it?"

I did. It's a straight shot from my house if I rode my mountain bike down Sullivan Fire Road. I'd gone once with Rachel, Lily, and Jacques when my sister was really into her "learning our local heritage" phase. A long time ago, a couple of German Nazi sympathizers living in California built the ranch as a self-sustaining bunker. But the couple was seized right after Pearl

Harbor, and the land was later blessed by a generation of hippies who left a tipped-over VW bug on the
property. It's open to the public now, but you've got to
go through these cast-iron gates in the middle of the
woods and down these forever-steps that lead to sort of
a canyon. There's still a giant house there, and a machine shed, gardens, a massive water tower. The water
tower is the best part, it's got this "urban exploring"
vibe. It's the kind of place you'd imagine Miss Havisham
from *Great Expectations* to live in, if Miss Havisham
was really into punk rock graffiti. The place is covered
in it, like you can't even see an inch of wall space that
hasn't been spray-painted over a billion times.

"Sure. It's near my house," I said, maybe a little bit
too quickly. "I've definitely scouted it for shooting." A lie.
Film crews did shoot a lot of material on the Ranch, but
the place actually creeped me out more than it enticed
me, and I hadn't been back since that first trip. Whenever I ride my bike past it I hold my breath, the way I do
when we drive next to cemeteries.

"Cool. Hey, you could shoot us skating down there,"
Derek said, meaning him and Matt, unless one of these
girls was secretly carrying around a floral-print helmet
and knee guards. "You should come with us. Friday."

Again, he wasn't asking like it was a question,
which I decided to think of as evidence of an attractive,
confident attitude, because otherwise it would be highly
presumptuous and offensive.

"Unless you already have a hot date or something."

"Friday? I don't know, I'll have to check my social
iCal," I said, playing it very cool. In my head, I was already
rushing out to check his relationship status on Facebook.
What if it turned out he was dating one of those crop-top

tweens currently giving me the evil eye? I'd heard rumors of some of the stuff that went down at Murphy's after dark—nothing witchy or culty, just a lot of drinking and kids snorting their ADHD-medication, but it wasn't really my scene. Maybe I'd go, if Lily came with me.

"You do that, Carina." Derek winked. "I'll be seeing you around." Then, as if on cue, as if he'd planned it, the bell rang, and Derek Wheeler picked up his stuff and walked out of the library without looking back. Not even once. Was this a Lifetime movie starring me?

I immediately and impatiently took out my phone. Lily was going to die when she heard about this.

**Harper (8:40 am):** I love you so much I want to make a Lily-suit of your skin and wear it every day but not to bed out of respect.

**Lily (8:41 am):** I love you MOAR!

**Harper (9:28 am):** I am sending you a stealth message from history class to tell you that I love you so much that I am going to start a Kickstarter to support my dream of creating a museum dedicated to the stray hairs I've collected from you.

**Harper (10:55 am):** Look I know you are busy but I just met a guy at the Mexican border who said they can trade me ten mules for all of your organs on the black market. Do you think that is a good deal or should I trade up? LMK ASAP I am having a really hard time negotiating in Spanish!

**Harper (10:57 am):** PS I LOVE YOU SO MUCH!

**Harper (11:50 am):** Hey lady, were you actually kidnapped? I have so many things to tell you! All the things! Are we still hanging out after school?

**Lily (12:30 pm):** !!!! Sorry! Just got this! They have crazy rules about cell phones here and you know how nervous I am about getting caught! You were always better at the stealth cell phone moves.

**Harper (12:31 pm):** OMG! You had me so worried that we were 100% right about Pathways being a front for the Hollywood occult and you were already sacrificed to appease their dark lords.

**Lily (12:33 pm):** Ha! No! And yes OF COURSE we are hanging out after school. I have more hair to donate to your Kickstarter.

**Harper (1:10 pm):** Ha, yes! Dude I got detention and it's ALL TIM SLATER'S FAULT!

**Lily (1:40 pm):** Wait, WHAT? did you say DETENTION?

**Harper (1:50 pm)** Aha, yeah, lunchtime D. Long story. Can't wait to see the Gawkward Fairy and tell her all about it.

**Lily (1:52 pm):** Yes, I need to know how the guy who cried when he got a B+ in Geography last year managed to land you in detention! Has he been re-placed with his evil twin? Is that evil twin cute? We are going to have to catch up on this later, lady . . .

**Harper (2:12 pm):** Okay, but wait. First. Remember Derek? The smelly kid with the DARE t-shirt? He's gotten way cuter and actually knows how to dress now, a little supreme skater but pretty cute.

**Lily (2:30 pm):** Who knew that Derek was just a smelly duckling waiting to transform into a suave swan?

**Harper (2:45 pm)** Right?? He's like the only person here who hasn't looked at me like I was invisible today. Well besides Tim, who doesn't count, and did I mention who got me thrown in DETENTION?

**Lily (3:00 pm):** I need to hear this in full details later in person, text isn't doing this justice. Also I am about to sign up for the craziest thing ever. Artisanal Pickling class! We have a meeting so I have to put my phone away! Cool?

**Harper (3:32 pm):** oh! Sure! Go Gawkwardness!

**Lily (3:34 pm):** See you so soon!

I didn't expect Pathways to be anything like this. There I was that first morning, actually dreading taking the walk down the Lane, the strip of grass that separated the East wing of the school from the West and where all the students seemed to congregate before, in between, and after classes. Despite what Harper had said the night before, I was wearing my wings—took a picture for Harper on my way to school for Gawkward Fairy luck!—and decided to stop for a pre-class acai bowl with berries at my favorite coffee shop. My mind was a million miles away from my body, and I almost didn't hear the group of girls giggling behind me until one actually bumped into me.

"Oops, my bad." I turned around to see a girl with overly plucked eyebrows, wearing a leopard print dress, who could have been anywhere between sixteen and thirty years old. "Sorry, but my friends and I were wondering . . . what are YOU supposed to be?" Behind her, a bevy of girls—all sharp features and synthetically woven fibers—tittered.

"I'm just . . . me," I said, straightening my shoulders and staring Leopard Dress in her overly made-up face. I should be used to people gawking at my style, but without Harper by my side, I felt outnumbered and trapped.

"Yo, fairy girl! Can you grant me a wish?" Another girl shouted at me from behind an increasingly long line of foot-tapping patrons while I stuttered and tried to come up with a witty retort.

Just when I was hoping that a hole would open up in the earth and swallow me up along with all the almond milk and chai flavored lattes in the store, I felt a presence beside me. I was still staring down, so all I could see was a pair of sandals sticking out from a long, flowing hippie skirt.

"Excuse me," said the skirt, as she maneuvered herself between me and the overplucked bully. "Can you back up your fake vintage Chanel purse just a bit? You're standing in my friend's light."

Now it was Leopard Print's turn to be speechless. There was a pop of light and my head snapped up in time to see a photographer standing near the muffin display case. Her dark brown hair was in a halo of tight curls that surrounded her face like a lion's mane, and the yellow of her Peter Pan–collared dress and matching heels contrasted perfectly against her caramel skin. She smiled warmly at me.

"I'm going to put first day pictures on my Tumblr, FancyFashionFeminist," she shouted across the din. "Have you heard of it?"

"Jane is going to be the next Tavi Gevinson!" said the long-skirted girl, waving at the photographer. "You know, from Rookie mag?" She looked back at me and then at Leopard Print, coolly appraising the situation with a cocked eyebrow. "We just saw you in the midst of these knock-offs," she said to me, as if we were alone in the shop, "and I said to Jane, now *that's* a girl who knows who she is." She stuck out her hand, her nails chipped with black nail polish. "I'm Nicole," she said, rolling her eyes like she was being sarcastic. "I know, right? My parents were oh-so conventional when it came to baby names."

I finally managed to make eye contact with my savior. She had short pink hair, a round baby-face, and her frayed-hem peasant shirt hid an impressively large chest. Despite her Earth Mother look, I didn't think she could be much older than me. A Native-American-print Herschel backpack was slung across her perfectly postured yogi shoulders and when she smiled at me I could see the outline of her Invisaligns. Her ears were studded with gold cuffs, and she wore about a million rings with smoke-colored stones in them. She reminded me of an old pin-up model gone rogue, or a Botticelli girl who'd just discovered Amanda Palmer. "Here, let me get a good look at you, Fairy Girl!" she said.

And that's how I met Nicole, the founding member of NAMASTE.

NAMASTE is a group devoted to individuality and tolerance and body-acceptance and a lot of other things I didn't know you could get extracurricular credit for. Nicole is the group's president, except no one calls her that, or even uses the word "leader," though she definitely is that, too! Instead, as Jane explained to me, NAMASTE has a "laterally formed hierarchy" that "eschews the meritocratic and patriarchal values of traditional, tier-based democracies." Or something like that. I'm not sure if I got the words exactly right, but close enough!

Nicole is a junior and a nu-hippie and says she can do my birth chart if I find out what moon sign I was born under. She's got a nose ring and is a vegan and "plus-sized and proud," according to her, though she really isn't all that big. She's a feminist and refuses to listen to music or see movies with actresses who don't acknowledge that feminism means equal rights for everyone, because that kind of stance just shows that they don't actually even know what feminism *is*.

After buying me a kombucha and properly introducing me to Jane and their friend Drew, Nicole told me that she could tell I was a Pathways student even before I turned around in the coffee shop line.

"Pathways attracts the unconventional and you, lady, are definitely not conventional. You could be our new school trendsetter!" She told me my wings were *subversive*. "They totally undermine our society's preconceptions about feminine fragility." I'm not sure how true that is, but anyway, it was way better than what most people called them, which was "silly."

Jane and Drew are also juniors, and Nicole's co-chairs in NAMASTE. Nicole says Drew is a "theater queer," and actually encourages people to use that term because "theater isn't a bad word!" Drew is very tall and gangly and blond, with a baby face and the gentlest eyes I'd ever seen. He was dressed in a doctor's lab coat, which he said wasn't illegal because he never told anyone he was a doctor and plus the big pockets were great for storing things. Then there's Jane the photographer, who runs a fashion Tumblr that's popular with people even outside of school. I didn't want to tell her that, compared to everyone else my age, I was basically Internet-illiterate, so I pretended to know what she was talking about when she listed names like MandyX and Cheshire Chills and KillQueens as a way of describing her aesthetic. (I think one of those is a website and one is a band and the third might be a brand ambassador for a clothing line, but I don't know which one is which.)

As the four of us crossed the street from the café to the imposing arch that signified the entrance to Pathways, I felt a wave of nervousness. What if everyone wasn't as nice as Nicole and Jane and Drew? We'd arrived early—the school had a notoriously lax attendance system, Jane whispered, meaning that most kids sauntered in at whatever time they felt was fair—and there was some time to kill before our first classes— er, *session*, which is what they called classes here, for some reason. Nicole invited me to join her, Drew, Jane, and a couple other NAMASTE members—a group of seven or so older kids who were busy trying to claim some space on a spread of large, rainbow-dyed Mexican wool blankets to practice their lotus position—as Nicole gave a first-day pep talk about holistic messaging and "everybody integration."

"Here, you can sit on my serape with me," Jane giggled, pulling on her hand-knit gold and brown throw.

"Remember," Nicole was saying, "You shouldn't feel bad about being yourself . . . unless you don't like *you* for the right reasons!" Nicole ended her pep talk with that line, which seemed to be her motto, or some Pathways-specific mantra or something. Then she turned to me and said, "Wow, Lily." Everybody turned to look, and I could feel my face getting hot. "I can feel your energy from all the way over here. You are *such* a spiritual person. Here. I want you to have this." She gave me a rose quartz crystal and told me to hold it to my heart whenever I felt I needed to be centered.

"Thank you! I'll keep it right here in my backpack so that way I'll always have it handy."

Nicole smiled and then turned to Jane and Drew.

A look seemed to pass between them, like they were deciding something important through telepathy. I fidgeted, wishing I could text Harper, but knowing that would be rude. Instead, I turned the rose quartz over and over in my hand. I knew this was crazy, but it felt like every time I turned the rough stone over, my stomach did another queasy flip.

"I'm fine, everything is fine, I'm totally safe," I mumbled to myself as I turned the rock over and over. It's my bad habit: I kind of talk under my breath a lot when I'm feeling anxious. Just stuff I'm thinking about, or mantras to make me feel better, or anything, really.

Nicole turned back to face me, and I blushed realizing that everyone had probably been able to hear my stupid word barf.

Instead, Nicole beamed brightly. "Lily, we'd really like you to hang out with us more. You know, as a regular thing," she said, Jane and Drew nodding along with her. "I was just telling Drew the other day that NAMASTE could use a fairy godmother!"

"It's true," Drew said, straightening the lapels of his coat. "And one that can cast spells, to boot!" I didn't know what he was talking about, but I got the sense he was making a little bit of fun at me. Oh man, I'd already blown my chance to meet some actual nice people, who now think I'm the crazy freak who wears wings and talks to herself. ARGH!

"So what do you say?" Nicole interrupted my spiral alert. "Do you think you'd like to come chill with us and learn what NAMASTE is all about?"

I breathed an inward sigh of relief. They weren't planning on ditching me after all!

"That would be great!" I tried not to gush, but I

wasn't really one of those people who had much of a filter. "Thank you so much!" I winced as I heard how high-pitched I sounded.

"Thank *you*," Nicole said magnanimously. "Now let me ask you: do you have different wings for every day of the week? Because that would be cool, if we could coordinate my outfits to your wing colors or something."

"My wings?" I asked, reaching back to feel at the uneven patch that Harper had sewn on the day before. I'd almost forgotten I was even wearing them. Suddenly I felt self-conscious, and remembered Harper's comment that I didn't even have to bring them to school if I didn't want to. "Oh, I only have one pair. These are more of like a good luck charm. You know, my grandmother gave them to me right before she died, and they are really special but I need to take good care of them, so I was really only planning on wearing them the first day . . ." I heard an audible gasp from Jane, and Drew shook his head sadly.

"Nonsense!" said Nicole, trying to maneuver her arm around me, the wings' nylon straps making it difficult. "Those wings are *so* Namaste and *such* a fashion statement. I mean, that's cool, your story about your grandmother, but like, that isn't going to really fit your new vibe as being the 'fashionista with the wings', so maybe just keep that part to yourself? Because believe me, everybody at Pathways is going to be so obsessed with your look. In fact . . . Jane?"

"On it!" Jane chirped, whipping out a bedazzled phone, seemingly from thin air. Her fingers flew around for about a millisecond before she looked up at Nicole. "Found them!" She grinned proudly and handed it over for us to see. "On Etsy, natch," she said, running a finger through her hair. "Am I like a fashion algorithm or what?"

I stared at the screen. "Custom order 'Natural' adult fairy wings, realistic!" claimed the text above a picture of what looked like an exact replica of my grandmother's heirloom appendages. "Free shipping within the US."

I was speechless. I'd assumed my inherited artifact was my own weird quirk, unshared by anyone else. Now it turned out there was a market for it online?

"Good joke, Jane," Nicole said after studying the phone and handing it back. "So let's order, like, five pairs to start and then see if anyone else in NAMASTE wants in." She turned to me. "Look at you, already being such a trendsetter!" I couldn't tell if she was making fun of me or not; "trendsetter" isn't a word anyone's ever used to describe me. Like, ever. But then again, I'd never been in a place like Pathways before, either. I found myself looking around the Lane at my new classmates as they hurried between classes. A girl in a thrift store wedding gown walked past, a parakeet on her shoulder. She waved to a boy who was drawing a fake tattoo of Curious George on his friend's arm, and they both had to jump out of the way when a beautiful dark-skinned girl on a unicycle almost mowed them down. What was this Wonderland hole I had fallen into, where up was down, black was white, and fitting in at school meant wearing giant fake fairy wings every day of the week?

*What would Harper say if she were here right now?* I tried to think. I knew she'd think Nicole's hair was really cool—she loves pink and went through a phase where she really wanted to put lilac streaks or maybe just add it on top for an ombre thing with her natural blond. But she might not be as thrilled about the part where pretty soon I'd look like everyone else . . . but because they were copying my style, not the other way around! Would I be less of a Gawkward Fairy if Nicole and Jane and their friends started wearing wings, too?

I couldn't think. I needed Harper to help me make this decision, but she was miles away in a classroom, probably surrounded by a bunch of new, glamorous friends who got all of her music references. While posing for photos, they would probably all be making that silly open-mouth "excited face" to show their contouring, too. I could even picture the Instagram tag for this imaginary picture before I caught myself and realized: I was spiraling, hard. I shook my head to snap out of it.

Nicole, Jane, and Drew were all still staring at me. How long had I been silent? I needed to say something.

"I guess . . . I could just keep wearing these ones?" Nicole and Jane and Drew squealed and clapped their hands before turning back hungrily to their phones and whipping out their credit cards. I felt an instant twinge of guilt—had I broken my Harper BFF pact about not changing to fit in already? Or did it not count, since I was wearing the wings to school anyway so it wasn't really a change, just . . . more of an adjustment, really. And just what constituted a "change," anyhow? I realized Harper and I had never set out terms and conditions for our pact, but once again my mind had wandered off and it took all my effort to corral it back in.

"Excellent!" said Nicole, as Jane and Drew finished their giddy applause. "So you should definitely come to this year's inaugural NAMASTE meeting. I know you're going to love it. Who knows, you just might be our first new freshman member!"

"Definitely," I promised, almost not believing that finding a new group of friends could be this easy. I mean, it's *me* we're talking about here. The Gawkward Fairy, princess of social faux pas. Not Harper, the Queen of Cool . . . no, that wasn't the way to think about it. I decided that in order for me to not self-destruct entirely from the excitement and confusion of all these new experiences, I had to try to push thoughts of Harper out of my mind—just for now.

The bell rang, and Nicole offered to show me to my first class.

Walking up to the Pathways entrance with Nicole and her friends, I didn't feel any of my former nervousness. The old classroom building that I'd found so threatening in the brochures now looked actually beautiful, in an industrial-Gothic kind of way. Small clusters of kids were sitting out in the Lane, and a couple of them waved to us as we made our way across.

"I love your wings!" called out one boy with blond man-bun knotted on the top of his head, flashing me a patchouli-scented thumbs-up. I grinned back.

"See?" said Nicole, smiling warmly. "When you're here, you're family!"

"Like Olive Garden?" I teased.

Nicole's smile dimmed a couple wattages. "I don't get it."

I blushed. "Never mind, it's a reference to this dumb commercial."

"Oh," Nicole sniffed. "Never seen it." She said it with the sort of casual distaste that most people use to refer to Blu-Rays or Super Nintendos or some other totally worthless piece of junk. I could have strangled myself for bringing up something so lame.

I said goodbye to Nicole and Jane and Drew after they dropped me off at my first cl—oops, *session!* Nicole looked down at my schedule and told me that I would be in good hands with Jamie Godfrey, or "God," as he is better known around Pathways. He teaches my film course "Anxiety of Influence in French New Wave Cinema" and I guess is a big deal around here. I recognized a lot of the other students' names listed on the roster, because their parents are the kind of people who get top billing when their films open internationally. I wondered if we were going to be graded on a curve, or if the fact that I couldn't get someone who'd been on the cover of *Vanity Fair* to star in my final project would be counted against me.

I watched Nicole, Jane, and Drew walk down the hall to their first sessions. Alone and feeling a little panicky for the first time since the coffee shop, I took out my rose quartz crystal and held it to my chest, and tried as hard as I could to center myself. Then I took the deepest breath ever, and headed into God's classroom.

A lot of Pathways sessions involve us students sitting around and sharing our feelings about various topics and theories. There's also a lot of required eye contact with our "learning doulas," which Nicole says is part of a very progressive learning style, but it's definitely a little off-putting at first. During a science session called "Beyond Cosmos: The Exploration of Self and Space" (I know, every session name sounds like a TV show title!) there was one kid, the son of a famous musician, who said that his religion doesn't believe in evolution, but rather teaches that humans first came down here in spaceships from Uranus four hundred years ago. It was really hard to tell if he was just messing with us, but Violet, our learning doula, just smiled and told Uranus Boy he was brave for expressing "such a unique perspective."

Pathways is kind of strange. It's a little like Hogwarts, I guess, in that everyone there is special and kind of an outsider. Plus, a disproportionate amount of students and faculty members seem to believe in magic. Also? There are a *ton* of kids in capes. Like, so many. My wings don't even look that out of place in a school where half the kids seem like they are dressed up for some kind of cosplay event. Even though I was so happy I decided to wear them, I worried they were the only reason Nicole and her NAMASTE crew took any interest in me at all, and that instead of making me stand out, I'd need the wings to *fit in* at school. But maybe I wouldn't *actually* need to wear them every day—maybe I'd be kind of like *Dumbo* with the feather, and it'll turn out I can fly at Pathways even without them!

After my second session, Nicole picked me up outside class and took me during our fifteen minutes of "unstructured social time" to get a chai latte from one of the Vietnamese food trucks parked in the Pathways parking lot during the day. As we mingled amongst the foodies, we ended up actually having a pretty deep talk. One thing I liked about Nicole, or what was *refreshing,* I should say, is that she's really about *empowerment.* I don't know how to describe it, except to say that before Pathways, people would talk to me *despite* my awkwardness. Because they were friends with Harper, they felt like they had to be nice to me. Which was fine . . . I am not complaining *at all.* But Nicole is much more in your face about personal acceptance than Harper is. Like, when I told Nicole that I had recently retired Sir

Zeus, my old imaginary friend.

"Wow, it sounds like your old school was really repressive," she'd said. "Why wouldn't they encourage you to talk more about him and keep him alive, rather than stifle your creativity and tell you to kill him?"

If she'd been there when I was making that decision, she told me, she would have prompted me with "Yes, and?" questions, which promote creativity and out-of-the-box thinking, and improv theater groups too, which Nicole *also* has experience with. She also said I should never think of myself as "gawkward," because even if I came up with that description myself, it's still pejorative, which means bad. Then, when she caught me mumbling to myself when we were washing our hands in the bathroom, instead of calling me a spaz, she started doing it too! And at the end of the day, Jane and Drew caught up to me and asked me to teach them how to chant and do mantras like the ones I'd done with Nicole. Well, that wasn't exactly what I was doing—it's more like whenever I'm embarrassed or nervous, my head starts going in loops and I won't even notice I'm saying stuff out loud. The words wouldn't even make sense if you heard them, they're just sentence fragments, like the end of a thought, or a dream. Word salad. But I guess it's sort of similar to a chant or a charm, which I'd never thought about before, so I just went with it.

Everyone at Pathways seems to like Nicole, even though she says high school is not a contest, and "popularity" is for "normals." Normals are repressive, and keep us from being our best selves, and didn't I agree? So I guess Nicole wouldn't call herself *popular,* but she's definitely well-known and respected, and I could tell no one wanted to let her down.

Like during lunch I maybe let it slip that I've hate-watched that show *Fashion Police* with my friend Harper, and Nicole literally stopped mid-chew. Jane and Drew gasped.

"You. Watch. TV." It was not a question. "You mean you actually willingly *consume* entertainment from corporate conglomerates, whose only vested interest in its production of quote-unquote 'culture' is to exploit idiots for ratings and to reward the ideals of the existing patriarchal power structure with a prime-time lineup of insipid reality housewives and tortured male antiheroes?"

"Sure," I said, immediately realizing that was the wrong thing to say. "Well, I don't really watch it that often," I stammered, trying to figure out the correct response that wouldn't have Nicole giving me the same fierce treatment she had given to Leopard Print.

Nicole pulled a piece of fluff off my wings and frowned at it. "No," she said. "Of course you don't." And then she smiled and kept eating and told the story about how last year Drew staged a monthlong naked protest at PETA headquarters for the way their ads sexualized women, like nothing had even happened!

"Don't worry," Jane whispered as we were walking out of the cafeteria. "We just end up streaming everything on our iPads anyway. Nicole is actually a gigantic *Scandal* junkie."

"Oh," was all I could think of to say.

Then, after lunch we had our Crafternoon session, where Nicole told our learning doula, Sarah Matheson, that she found our syllabus to be "unengaging and pedantic in its overuse of traditionally feminine looming methods." At my old school, that would be enough to get you into real trouble. But not here, where even Sarah seemed worried about not meeting Nicole's high standards. She just nodded and told Nicole that she "appreciated the thoughtful critique."

Another thing I like about Pathways: Everyone really likes being creative, and the energy is for the most part really positive. At lunch, Drew brought out his guitar and asked to name a song, any song. I said "Team" by Lorde, and he just started playing it! (I'm obsessed with Lorde. My mom says it's because she went through a big Kate Bush phase when she was pregnant with me, so I probably internalized a taste for strange, anachronistic songstresses with a penchant for dramatic choreography in utero.)

When Drew got to the line "Call all the ladies out . . ." I started to kind of sing along under my breath, but Nicole yelled "Get it girl!" The next thing I know we were all belting it out. Even kids I hadn't met yet were coming over to join and it was like a big a capella chorus in the Lane, like something out of an old MGM musical where everyone breaks into song. Another freshman—the son of the monster movie director, *The Purge* or *Paranormal Activity* or one of the P-films, I think—pulled up some bongos and Jane filmed the whole thing for her blog and for a moment I felt like what other kids must feel when they score at lacrosse or take a bow after curtains close on their play, or form a formation during halftime at the Super Bowl. Like they were part of something bigger, but that the something bigger had a piece of them in it and you didn't have to feel like such an outcast anymore because here was everyone, singing the same song.

As soon as the song was over, the circle kind of dispersed and it was almost like it never happened in the first place, like it was a magical little moment that I'd just daydreamed up. It was like those flash-mob videos, where everyone coordinates ahead of time what they're going to do, or something out of *Glee* right before a commercial break. I really wished I had asked Jane to send me the video, because Harper would die if she saw it.

Harper. From her texts I knew she wasn't having as awesome a day as I was, and then I felt slightly guilty that I was having such an amazing time at school.

But seriously, how did I get so lucky? Jane and Drew and Nicole are all juniors, but they walked me to each of my classes on the first day and said hi to all of their old teachers. That would be totally unheard of at Beverly High! Even the adults seemed impressed, and not one person asked me why I was wearing wings or hanging out with older kids, or if that was my real voice or why I was mumbling, or any of the things new people normally said to me. I guess these wings are making everyone like me. Even though I'd never really been hurt by the assumptions people usually made about me, it was surprising how nice it felt being able to engage people without feeling on guard, ready for some judgment. It wasn't until the last class was over that I even noticed I had gotten through my first day of high school unscathed.

As I walked out the main door, I thought about the owl of Minerva that visited us on the Pier the night before. Maybe I was wrong after all, because from where I stood it looked like freshman year was going to be *ah*-mazing!

And then I saw the golden glint of Harper's sister's Prius.

The pact! Well, I hadn't broken it yet, had I? Was

it even supposed to be that serious, or was I over-worrying because I am a worrier who needs something to freak out about at all time? The best bet, I figured, was to let Harper take the lead on the divulging of our first-day ordeals, and I'd act like everything was normal until I could figure out exactly where she stood on the BFF Pact issue. Because I was so excited to talk about my new friends and Nicole and NAMASTE, but I was also worried that I'd already messed up. With my mind made up, I started toward the car, but immediately swiveled my head back toward the school. I swear I heard something that sounded a lot like an owl's hoot.

By the time we got to Pathways to pick up Lily after school, I was in such a cloudy, quiet mood that even Rachel got bored of teasing me about detention pretty quickly.

I scanned the kids coming out of the big, Gothic main building to find Lily. Couldn't we just go *home* already? I felt like my brain had just been beaten and fried and served on top of a bed of kale. Not only did I get detention on my first day, but being at school without Lily had been way harder than I thought. All my friends from middle school were gone now, either to different schools or just lost to the cult of posturing high schoolers around the world trying so hard to be way cool. No more hugs in the hallway—now we just have to nod to each other like "'sup?" I don't know, man, nothing's "*sup!*"

Rachel was tapping impatiently on the steering wheel when I caught a flash of fairy wings and rolled down my window. "Hey! Lily!" I shouted, feeling way too relieved to see those fluttery gawkward accessories because that meant that I had finally found my friend.

"Hey!" Lily waved back and did her little jiggle-dance, where she leans back and rolls her shoulders and goes "Woo—wooooot!" I did it as best as I could from the car seat and flashed her a thumbs-up.

But just as I was feeling good for the first time in like eight hours, Lily stopped in her path and stuck out her index finger, telling me to give her a second. She was walking next to this bigger girl with pink hair and a long, flowery skirt. As soon as she saw me, the pink-haired girl slung her arm over Lily and led her away from the car.

"Who is *that*?" Rachel asked, reading my mind.

"I don't know."

"Well, tell Flaky-cake that her ride is here, and that we're not going to wait." I jabbed at the radio to fill the silence.

"*Au revoir*, Nicole!" Lily called behind her when she finally got to the car. She tumbled inside, smooshing her wings beside her in the backseat.

"*Bonne chance*, Lily!" the pink-haired girl responded as she strolled toward the rows of gleaming Mercedes and Priuses that surrounded the school like an invading army. Lily immediately rolled down the window, still without yet having said hello even, and started waving crazily at the girl's back. Rachel rolled her eyes and revved the engine. Unfortunately, the lot was so full that we ended up just idling in traffic.

"How was your day, Lily?" I asked. What I really wanted was for her to ask me how my day was, but Lily is sometimes in her own little world, and in that world there is no such concept as "reading a room."

"It was, um, okay . . ." Lily looked at her feet as she shrugged off her wings and shoved them into her backpack, like she was hiding a dirty secret.

"Just okay?" Rachel and I shared a look. Nothing with Lily was ever just okay. It was either divine, inspired, obsession-worthy, or totally traumatizing.

Either way, she was likely to talk about the scenario for hours. But now she seemed oddly closemouthed and subdued.

"I want to hear about *your* day," she said, staring out the window.

"Look back at our texts," I said, a little annoyed. I could tell my best friend's mind was a million miles away. "Pick a topic."

Rachel nudged me in the rib cage. "Come on, let Lily go first. We regular folks need dispatches from inside the walls of Los Angeles's most expensive institution for creative talent. Give us the scoop! Is anyone already 'the voice of their generation' yet?" I rolled my eyes, but it seemed like Lily took the question seriously, her eyebrows furrowing together in deep thought.

"Well, everyone here is so cultured and sophisticated, you know? Nothing at all like Hollywood Middle. Like my new friend Nicole? She's been to New York Fashion Week and she says the girls from Rodarte asked if they could base their spring collection on her style. And we have the craziest classes, like they are all about self-expression and self-expansion and the only gym we have to do is yoga or guided meditation, and this boy named Drew played guitar for me . . ."

"They should change the name of this school to Parkway," Rachel interrupted as she tried unsuccessfully to both navigate out of the lot and make a joke. Rachel's near-road-rage must have put a damper on Lily's awesome-first-day high, because the rest of the ride out of the parking lot was silent, and awkward in a way I've never felt around Lily before. I pretended to be busy on my phone and sneaked a look at Lily in our rearview mirror. She was moving her mouth in these silent shapes, like she was talking to an invisible friend.

"What are you doing?" I asked, maybe a little angrily.

"What?"

"When did you start talking to yourself again?" Lily used to mumble a lot, just nonsense things you could only half-catch. But sometimes she'd say genuinely sad stuff, like she'd call herself stupid or an idiot. She started to do it less as we got older, but she had a tendency to revert back to it when she was really upset. My mom called it her "verbal coping mechanism."

"Well, I've decided just to go with it if it starts to happen. Nicole—I mean, *someone,* I heard *someone* say—that talking to one's self is crucial to communicating with your identity and your sense of self and maybe even your subconscious. Why, does it bother you?" Lily said all of this in that same under-her-breath voice.

I didn't answer, just turned up the music instead, only to realize after about fifteen seconds that it was a commercial for Worthington Ford. Then I remembered: I had actually made a "First Day of High School" playlist to blast on the way back to the house to surprise Lily and cheer us both up. I had compiled our favorite songs from a bunch of *High School Musical* soundtracks (we were so dorkily obsessed when we were babies), but for some reason I didn't think that Zac Efron's chirpy voice would really fit the mood right now. Looking back in the rearview mirror again, I saw that Lily actually looked totally happy and content to be sitting there quietly by herself.

I guess I was the only one who had failed the freshman first day test.

"So," I said, turning around to face Lily instead of her reflection. "How did you meet Nicole?" Lily wasn't the type to be constantly making new friends, and when she did she was never gushy about them. Usually people would approach her, thinking she was "interesting-looking," and Lily would look right past them or smile for a bit and then walk away. It was hard for her to open up to people, and I wondered how Nicole had managed to get such a fast-track inside.

"Oh, she stood up for me in a coffee shop," Lily said, leaning forward in her seat. "It was hilarious, she totally just told off this leopard-printy woman and her friends who were trying to get in my personal space—"

"I've never known you to have a hard time standing up for yourself," I sniffed.

Lily looked hurt and tugged a little on one of her wings, like it itched. "Nooo . . ." she said. "I don't. Usually. But it was more like . . . the way Nicole did it. She was just really intense and intuitive about the whole thing, and afterward she introduced me to her friend who's a photographer and that guitar boy Drew, who was dressed like a doctor."

"That's cool," I said, turning back around to face the front. I glared out the window at the big red Metro Rapid Line bus in front of us. "It sounds like you had a great first day, Lily." I waited for her to ask me how my day had gone, but it was Rachel who broke the strained silence instead.

"You know," she said, turning on a small side street to avoid the freeway, "one of the best feelings I ever had was on the first day I went to Jacques's class at Beverly Community College." I looked in the rearview mirror again and Lily and I rolled our eyes in sync.

"No, seriously," Rachel went on. "Before I even met my *lover*"—ugh—"I walked through the doors of that new school and into its unfamiliar atmosphere, and I was practically *inhaling* it. It felt so fresh. I felt like life had just granted me a do-over. Whoever I had been before, whatever kids thought of me at school, whatever I'd thought of *myself*—none of these people in my community college class knew about any of it. I could be the girl who was going to Yale next year on a volleyball scholarship, or a Greek heiress who was also a classically trained trombone player, whose parents died in a freak boating accident and had just been taken in by her kindly aunt, who lives in a mansion in Malibu."

"But . . . you don't look Greek," Lily said.

Rachel shook her head. "That's so far from my point that you'd need Siri to navigate your way to it, my little baklava. The POINT is, because of that brand-new-me feeling, I wasted, like, an entire semester ignoring Mia and everyone else from high school, because I was so busy trying to reinvent myself for this whole new group of strangers. Like, I thought it would be so cool to, like, change my whole life and act like I was some new fancy foreign exchange student, only to eventually realize I missed my friends, the ones who knew I was capable of being both a psycho *and* a loving human. People that have been forced to love me forever."

"What does THAT mean?"

"It MEANS," Rachel said as we swung into our driveway, "you shouldn't try to be something that you're not. That's all."

Sometimes I didn't get Rachel at all. Twenty minutes ago, she was making my life miserable and harassing me about detention, and now she was dispensing cryptic life advice. I didn't know if it was her hormones or what, but she was becoming as loony as Mom.

★

As tense as that car ride was, by the time we made it into the house and upstairs, knocking knees while trying to balance our trays of avocado toast and iced tea on my bed, I almost felt that things were returning to back to normal between me and Lily. That's the magic of my bedroom, which is also technically the attic. The walls are sloped like a triangle, so you have to duck to get through the door, but then it widens out to this enormous space, like an optical illusion, or Narnia. It's virtually soundproof, unless you're stomping around or engaged in a two-person dance party, so it's the greatest place to tell secrets and ghost stories. There's even a skylight above the rafters, so I can see the stars on nights when there's not too much pollution. But most important, my room has its own landline, a rare but important thing to me.

I know. You're probably wondering "Who has their own landline anymore?" Well, I earned that phone, in all its tacky glow-in-the-dark glory, fair and square. I ordered it with points from my sixth grade Scholastic book drive and asked my parents to install a separate line as a present for my twelfth birthday. No one ever calls me on it, so I mostly just used it as a nightlight, but it was one of my most treasured possessions.

I wanted to just sit there in this moment of relative normalcy, basking in the harsh light of my clunky phone, and avoid talking about my disaster of a day for as long as I could. Which was actually really easy at first, because it seemed like all Lily wanted to do after we finished our snacks was gush about Pathways. How many stories can one person have after just one day?

Usually Lily is good at making up enough stories for the both of us, but they're never about real things. It's more like she'll come up with an idea like "Lady Pirates," where we are copilots on a flying ship, and she'll have this whole backstory cooked up about our sailing route (NeverNeverLand to Majorca) and whose gold doubloons we are stealing (Jacques's). Stuff like that.

If I hadn't been in the parking lot to witness that pink-haired girl with my own two eyes, I might have thought Lily was making up another story now. She was just so . . . enthusiastic. Like, too enthusiastic, like if I didn't know her any better I'd say she was compensating for something. She couldn't stop talking about "Nicole says this" and "NAMASTE group" that. I admit I was a little jealous, both of Lily for having such a better first day than me, and of Nicole for making such a huge impression on my best friend.

"Wait, what?" I interrupted Lily's continuous stream of conscious storytelling. "What's 'shack-tivisim'?"

"No, it's *Sheganism*," Lily said, sounding a little irritated. "Like *she* plus *vegan* plus *ism*. It's just a way to open up other people's eyes to the repressive nature of both the patriarchy and the inhumane practices of meat consumption and leather-wearing."

"Ah, that sounds intense," I faltered, flailing around for any other material. "Hey, are you going to be wearing your wings again tomorrow? No one gave you a hard time about them today, right?" I must have hit a nerve, because Lily then totally overreacted, turning away from me and mumbling to herself with her shoulders hunched. I could tell she was about to start crying, but before she could say anything the door to my room burst wide open.

"Hello, darlings!" Mom chirped obliviously. She was carrying at least six shopping bags emblazoned with names like Prada, Missoni, and La Brea Bakery. Mom is a shopping fiend and is always splurging on the smallest things that cost the most amount of money. She calls it being "Kiehl's Conscious." One time, she even suggested that Lily and I go to IV Karats and buy some "cheap" friendship bracelets on her credit card. She almost seemed disappointed when we came back empty-handed and told her we wouldn't know what to do with $250 jewelry.

"How was your first day of school?" Mom asked, breezing over and kissing us on both cheeks, the light and musky scent of her Chanel No. 5 wafting behind her like a persistent, fancy ghost.

"It was ah-mazing!" Lily trilled, jumping up from the bed to show my mom pictures of her new friends on her phone.

"Good to hear, my little fairy princess!" My mom loves Lily because she talks to her like an adult. Lily loves her own mom so much and is super close to her, so she can't understand why I don't run home to tell my parents everything the moment it happens to me. But my relationship with them isn't like that. My mom is great and all, and thank god she's not one of those parents whose entire existence is wrapped up in what her daughters are doing. She's got her own thing going on—between the seminars and classes she teaches, she's always being chartered out on private planes to fancy conferences in Hawaii, or Paris, or Dubai, to stand onstage and dish her secrets on living a "productive yet stress-free lifestyle."

Sometimes, I make up fake MomTips based on

the way my mom acts. Like: "Don't have two teenage daughters. Or, at the very least, act like you don't. It's all about aspirations, ladies!"

"And how about you, my little poodle?" My mom gave my outfit a once-over, her eyebrows knitting together. She wouldn't make that face if she knew that it made her forehead bunch and wrinkle into the exact same frown lines that she declared eradicated after her last session with the dermatologist.

Mom was always telling me I should add more "personal expression" to my outfits. "You're so pretty, Harper. But you could be *extra* pretty if you wore something with some color in it!" she'd admonish me while holding up some pink and blue tropical wrap dress that she got at a boutique in Venice Beach. She freaked out every time I got a package delivered from Nasty Gal, and would try to hide my favorite items—the boxy top with the embellished pearls and crocheted flowers, the oversized flannel shirt that I'd belt and wear as a dress, my Charlotte Olympia Kitty Cat flats—because she thought they didn't "enhance my frame." Whatever that means. I know I'm supposed to feel lucky that I'm a sample size, but being a human wire hanger is only good if you're a runway model.

"Gosh, to be your kids' age," my mom sighed, playing with my hair. Then, probably remembering that her website described her as a "*thirtysomething* life coach," she added, "I mean, *not that it was so long ago!*" She clucked her tongue and made some vague noise about getting up early and laying out some clothes for me to wear tomorrow. Luckily, there was little chance of her actually doing that. Mom claimed to have Circadian Rhythm Disorder, which means she can't fall asleep at night and usually goes to bed at four in the morning, and then doesn't wake up until noon the next day. I don't know how Rachel and I ever taught ourselves to rise and shine at six a.m. when our mom had just gone to bed and my dad might have already left the house for a red-eye to Japan to sign the next One Direction (this month it was a boy band that had been featured on the Japanese version of *America's Got Talent*).

"I know how to dress myself, Mom. And I like what I'm wearing," I mumbled, looking down at my wedges. They were so cute in the morning, but now they did look just a little . . . bland.

"Well, you've still got to find your own . . . style," my mom said, for once struggling to find the right words. "I mean, it's not like everyone can have a 'thing' like Lily does, can they?" I rolled my eyes. My mom had a fundamental misapprehension that Lily wore her wings as a fashion statement, as if they were a clutch or something.

"That's right, Karen," Lily said. She nodded seriously and then, catching my eye as my mom turned around, stuck her tongue out a little bit and crossed up her eyes. Good to see my best friend was still in there somewhere after her uncharacteristically perfect day at Pathways. I really was happy Lily was excited about her new friends, but I was already ready for her weird obsession with that place to be over.

"So, I see you girls have already had your snacks." Mom glanced down at our trays. "Lily, your mother texted to say she'll be picking you up at seven." Lily and I both nodded: We'd done the same drill practically every day after school since fourth grade.

"Bye, Karen—I mean, Mrs. Carina!" Lily said as Mom gathered her shopping bags and turned to go. "I can't believe I accidentally called your mom Karen—twice! At Pathways they make us call our teachers—our *learning doulas*—by their first names. Isn't that crazy? I guess I'm getting used to it quicker than I thought."

"That is crazy," I said.

"Hey, can I borrow your laptop?"

I must have gotten some avocado stuck down the wrong windpipe, because I began to choke. Lily had a strict rule for herself about limiting her computer time, and only really liked to use laptops for writing papers and doing research for school. She wasn't a technophobe—she loved her phone and we texted 24/7—but it's not like she has her own Tumblr or has ever subtweeted anything in her life. All in all, Lily lives a pretty vintage lifestyle, and would be happier if all music still came in the form of records or mixtapes, or maybe if it was exclusively performed live, sung aloud by old men in bow ties playing accordions. (Did I just describe Weird Al? Okay, so imagine that, but *not* Weird Al.) It's adorable to watch her try to enter URLs by typing "www" before everything—it's like seeing a monkey dress up and go to the office for a meeting: *Monkey, you do not belong on Wall Street! It's unnatural!*

"I know, I know," said Lily, clearly registering my surprise. "I'm breaking my own rule. It's just that, there's this girl at my school, Jane, and she has a fashion blog with all these photos of kids from Pathways, and she said she'd post some pictures she took of me today. Do you mind?" Lily asked that last part kind of shyly, which made me feel bad. So what if she had a great day at school and some older kids took her under their wing? That's not her fault. Why was I acting like

Lily having a better day than me was the worst thing to happen in the history of humanity? Like, "Oh no! My best friend wasn't treated like a total social reject while I had a level one traumatic day! Quick, *burn everything to the ground!*" But she still hadn't asked me about my day, or even how I got detention because of her ex-annoying-human-of-a-boyfriend.

"Sure," I said after my coughing fit subsided. "I think I left it in the living room. I'll meet you down there in a little bit."

I halfheartedly went to my closet to hunt for something else to wear that might get my mom off my back, settling on a slouchy home-Harper ensemble of black Brandy Melville shorts paired with the best tee ever, the one with a glittery leopard's head that I got on sale at H&M for five dollars. That took all of five minutes, and then I flung myself back down on my bed to wait for Lily to come back so we could work on our Memory Box (a shoebox filled with all kinds of photos and mementos and notes about our friendship) while vegging out to some TV. In my Memory Box, I currently had:

- Stolen matches from my grandparents' 60th anniversary at Mr. Chow

- A stamp card from Yogurt to Be Kidding Me

- Stickers from the farmer's market by the Grove that no one knows is there but is sooo there and so good

- The soundtrack to *Hedwig and the Angry Inch* on Broadway (with Neil Patrick Harris, of course)

I had fun riffling through my Memory Box for all of fifteen minutes while waiting for Lily to join me before I finally broke down and decided to go find her. So I went downstairs, only to find my best friend still glued to the Internet. Maybe Lily was right—maybe the Internet did turn people into zombies.

I took a deep breath. *Don't be basic, Harper.*

"Find your picture yet?" I asked, plopping down next to the Gawkward Fairy. "I guess pretty soon you're going to have to start worrying about the paparazzi." I laughed loud enough for the both of us.

Lily was just staring at the computer screen, with an expression on her face that I knew only too well. She was either at the end of, or about to begin, one of her famous crying spells. Lily cried constantly, at the drop of the hat, about anything, which used to freak me out until I realized she didn't just cry when things were sad but also when things were beautiful: an antique butter yellow teacup with blue daisies, or a pretty butterfly, or how weird the word "orange" was when you thought about it. Even when she was sad she could get distracted by something beautiful—a double rainbow! That video of a dog flipping out when his owner returns from Iraq! Penguins dancing!—and be happy again.

"What is it, Lily?" I said, immediately double-regretting all the bad thoughts I'd been having about her awesome day. "What did those artisanal pickling lady-douches do?"

"No . . . nothing," sniffled Lily. "That's the problem. Jane didn't mention me on her blog *at all*." Her voice cracked and I had to put my arms around her, tight, while she used up all her Lily-feelings. I swear she experienced more feelings in one day than most people do in a month. Being around her can sometimes be kind of an emotional roller coaster that you ride to the peak of an active emotional volcano.

"Maybe they didn't actually like me at all!" Lily wailed into my shoulder. "I knew everyone was staring at me when I sang 'Team.' I'm such an idiot . . . they weren't trying to be my friends, were they? They were making fun of me."

"Wait, you sang 'Team'? In front of people?" Maybe I was focusing on the wrong thing, but that would be another first: Lily's favorite song wasn't something she just performed impromptu in front of strangers.

"Well, yeah," she said, pulling away from my damp, bedazzled tee. "Drew brought out his guitar, and he asked me what my favorite song was, so I told him and he just started playing and I guess I started singing and . . ."

"Lily, you didn't tell me this part!" I looked directly into her china blue eyes, but she was busy wiping them with her own sleeve. "This is very important, so please, try to answer the next question as truthfully as you can . . ."

"Oh . . . kay?" Lily hiccupped, still leaking a bit.

"So." I bit my lip, pretending to weigh my options. "This Drew guy . . . is he cute?"

"Harper!" Lily's hiccups were already turning into little snorts of laughter.

"I'm serious! Is he my type? Does he have a girlfriend? Because if you don't want him, I could totally go for a guy who knows his way around some Lorde."

"Yeah, he's definitely cute, but I'm pretty sure he's not into girls."

"Who doesn't like *Girls*?" I asked with shock. "Everyone loves Lena Dunham!"

We might not have been able to stop giggling had my mom not called us down for dinner at that very moment.

"Harper, I don't know what I would do without you," Lily said when we were both finally able to catch our breath. "You're right. I'm probably just being paranoid."

Except I wish I could have found a way to tell Lily that I did think she should be careful at school, but not because she joined an impromptu jam session during lunch. I don't think she had any idea that transforming from a Gawkward Fairy into a social butterfly in just one day would a) be possible or b) even be fun. But— and this is going to sound terrible, but it's actually the opposite—the truth was, it probably wouldn't last. Not with how Lily really was. She needed to create and live in her own little world, not follow in some pink-haired girl's footsteps. Especially some pink-haired girl who I could just tell was the type to extend one hand in friend-ship while holding a butterfly net behind her back with the other. I might not be as intuitive as Lily was about the changing rhythms of the universe or whatever, but I do know how to read people. And I didn't need a Tarot app to tell me that there was bad news traveling at us, fast.

A month ago, if someone had told me that I'd be looking forward to going to school in the morning, I would have told them to go eat a soggy soy burger. But the truth was, Pathways had turned out to be such a splendorific experience that I wanted to go all "downward facing doggy-style" (a yoga position Drew says is supposed to help you locate your chi *and* access your inner goddess at once. He offered to teach me, but then we both realized how dirty "downward facing doggy-style" sounded and started cracking up).

After my tearful freak-out at Harper's house regarding Jane's photos of me (or lack thereof), I decided to "let go and let goddess" (as Nicole says), but I shouldn't have worried: The next morning, when I woke up and checked the blog, there I was, bewigged and bewildered and smiling for all the Internet to see! There were already a ton of shares and likes and comments, too, and I realized I'd gotten upset over nothing.

The week was speeding by. It was already Tuesday and soon it would be Wednesday, Thursday, and then Friday, and before I knew it high school would be over! Life seemed to be speeding by like a movie montage, where all the boring bits get cut out and all you see is the fun/important stuff. Except the fun/important stuff was happening *all the time*! There were so many clubs and activities to try at Pathways that I wasn't sure I'd ever be able to fit in all the ones I wanted, but here are the ones I'd signed up for so far:

A. Artisanal Pickling

B. Philoso-Fosse (a modern dance/intellectual enlightenment club)

C. Varsity Quidditch

D. Decoupage Club

E. Ren Faire Fare: Cooking 16th-Century Cuisine

F. NAMASTE!

I admit, I'd been getting kind of anxious about NAMASTE orientation all week, especially after I showed up for classes Tuesday morning without my wings. It was like a catch-22, or maybe a catch–bajillion and one. If I wore them, I'd be breaking Harper's pact to never change because of someone else. On the other hand, Nicole had expressly said that the wings were part of what made me "me," and that I was a trendsetter. In the end, I figured Nicole couldn't have been 100 percent serious about having to don wings every day, so I left them at home and went to school with a plan to pretend everything was chill.

Big mistake. HUGE mistake. (I recently watched *Pretty Woman* with my older cousin from Dallas and loved that I found myself rooting for the prostitute.)

I spotted Nicole, Jane, and Drew in the Lane, where they were playing a game of hacky-sack, a popular pastime that passes for a sport in our athletics department. I always thought it was kind of a silly waste of time, until I saw the grace and athleticism the nu-hippies brought to it. In the twelve hours since I'd last seen her, Nicole had dyed her hair from pink to grass-green, which looked awesome, and when she spun around to bounce the ball with her head it was like watching Earth rebuff a squishy meteor.

"Hey, guys!" I said, running over. "Can I play?"

Nicole completed a high kick that sent the ball soaring into the stratosphere before it plummeted down toward her palm, where it landed without her even looking at it first. That was good, because she was *really* busy staring at me like we'd never met before. There was a gawkward silence, and then:

"What. Are. You. *Wearing*?"

I looked down at my outfit: a yellow sundress and super shiny black Doc Martens, the ones that Harper and I had tagged with our names in Puffy Paint earlier in the summer. They were kind of ridiculous, but I knew Pathways was the kind of place that encouraged us to explore the whole DIY spectrum of self-expression. So what had I done wrong?

I must have contemplated that question for too long, though, because Nicole sighed and then asked really slowly, like you would to a child, "More importantly, what *aren't you* wearing?"

I still might not have gotten it had I not looked over at Jane, who had sneakily sidled up behind Nicole and was trying to make eye contact with me while spreading her arms out and flapping them up and down.

"Oh, my wings!" I said, shooting Jane a grateful look. "Yes! The thing is, I thought about it for a while, and they really are more of a 'special occasions' kind of thing. Also, if I wear them too often, they get all worn out and broken, and they also always end up getting caught in stuff, like doors, or lockers, or once, in this girl's hair . . . ?"

Nicole narrowed her eyes and got that weird look again, like the one she had when I mentioned my TV viewing habits. But when she spoke again, her voice was soft.

"Look, Lily, I am not here to tell you what you should and shouldn't wear," she said. "But I feel like maybe you aren't expressing yourself as fully as you possibly can today. I understand that we are all ever-evolving beings, and that no one is the same person they were a day ago. I get it. But I'd be remiss if I didn't tell you that I think that the wings are more 'you' than this . . . *ensemble*. You're not really representing your message well."

"Oh." I nodded, because I wasn't really sure what else to do or say. Nicole nodded back sympathetically, the way a frustrated teacher might. "Sure, no problem," I stuttered. "I totally understand and, um, comprehend where you are coming from? And I will bring the wings in tomorrow?" Suddenly, all my sentences were ending in question marks, but I guess I was saying the right things, because Nicole started smiling. It was as if a dark cloud had passed over the green planet, and now Nicole, the girl who had accepted me for the weirdo I am, was back, like the last five minutes had not been the most tense five minutes ever.

"Fabulous!" she said, swinging her hennaed arm around my shoulder. We began walking toward my first session. "Just think, when I introduce the world of Pathways to wings just like yours, you're going to be a major style icon! And here you were, about to throw all that away for no reason!"

"That does sound silly," I agreed. Wait, was I really

about to become a *style icon*? And what did Nicole mean about getting the rest of Pathways to get wings? Would everyone be dressing exactly like me soon? And what was the "message" that I was supposed to be sending with my wings?

"Just remember, Lily. Here at Pathways we are all about individual expression, as long as you are *expressing the best individual you can be.* You need to think about your personal brand!" Now we were both vigorously shaking our heads up and down like two life-size bobbleheads.

"I totally understand what you mean," I said, even though I really didn't. Wouldn't *not* wearing my wings be a better expression of my feelings, since I was *feeling* like not wearing them? What did branding have to do with anything? I thought that was what they did to mark cattle.

"Also, and this is just a small thing," Nicole said, still smiling. "I would lose those shoes. It's just that, well . . . and I'm only saying this because you're my friend . . . but Docs are totally *not* Shegan. They're made out of leather, and they go against our core philosophy of 'Do No Harm' to animals."

*Oh, no.* I made a mental note to never, ever wear those shoes to school again. The last thing I wanted was to end up on the wrong side of Nicole's philosophical beliefs. With my luck, I'd end up like Leopard Print from the coffee shop, and would be ostracized by the entire school! It was a reminder of how much I missed having Harper by my side. She was always so good at standing up for the both of us.

I took out my phone and texted my best friend.

**Lily (8:56 a.m.):** PuppyGirl! I love you MOAR than a mouse loves brie.

**Harper (8:56 a.m.):** I love you MOAR! like the cat loves the mouse that loves the brie!

As soon as I typed "PuppyGirl," I realized how soon we were going to have to start planning for Harper's PuppyBash birthday celebration. Harper's always been weird about her birthdays. Even though I love her mom, she's not the best at kid-friendly celebrations. Mrs. Carina—Karen—was always planning these elaborate, fancy-schmancy but totally un-fun birthday "events" for Harper and Rachel, and would give them the weirdest gifts—like six-hundred-dollar eyelid cream made out of bee toxin or gift certificates for a Napa Valley Wine tour. So Harper's idea of a great party was going door-to-door and fundraising for PuppyTales. And while that is completely awesome, I grew up in a house where not buying a thoughtful birthday present for someone was grounds for dismissal from the family.

When we first met in fourth grade, Harper had just had her October birthday—she's a Libra, which explains SO MUCH about her—and was so excited because she had raised $120 for her favorite shelter. When I asked her what kind of cake she'd gotten at her party and what the decorations had looked like and what music she played, she looked at me like I was crazy.

"I don't have that kind of stuff at my birthday parties," she'd said, laughing. "Dogs don't care about cake!"

That was such a funny idea that it stuck with me

until the next year, when Harper and I were in fifth grade. The night before her birthday party, I had come over for a sleepover, and brought a giant sleeping bag with me, even though it must have been ninety degrees. I waited up in her attic room until Harper was asleep, and then I crept downstairs to make a little fairy magic.

The next morning we were woken up by Rachel screaming. "Mom, Dad, quick! Someone's defiled the house!" Harper ran downstairs and I trailed behind her, pretending to be concerned. When we got to the foot of the stairs, Harper stopped short and I almost knocked into her and sent us both tumbling down, narrowly avoiding a neck-breaking fall.

"Oh my god!" Harper gasped. "Look, Lily!"

I looked, although I already had the whole scene memorized by heart. The entire first floor of the house was covered in a rainbow of colorful doggie milk bones that I had dyed myself using my mom's Easter egg kit, making sure I left no evidence on my hands. There were also loads of doggie chew toys and little cardboard dog houses with papier-mâché Snoopys and Wishbones and Scooby Doos that my mom had helped me make, like, three months in advance. And in the middle of it all was a giant birthday cake, which Harper's mom had agreed to hide for me: homemade chocolate ganache in the shape of a dog's paw, with giant red frosting spelling out "It's a Pawty!"

"See?" I said innocently. "Seems dogs like cake after all!" Harper turned to look at me with a face of such pure happiness that I knew for sure I'd made the right call.

"Do you like it?" I asked shyly.

"Like it?" Harper was blushing to a bright pink hue, and if I hadn't known any better, I would have thought those were tears in her eyes. "Lily, I RUFF it!"

Ever since then, the surprise party on the Saturday closest to her birthday was my domain, just like the pre-birthday PuppyBash on Friday was hers. I had made it sort of a personal contest to try to best myself every time. There was the year with the scavenger hunt that took us from the Laurel Canyon dog park to Pink's Hot Dogs (because hot *dogs*, get it?) before leading us to The Coop on National, where we had the giant ball pit all to ourselves and all the slides were decked out in a Dalmatian puppy theme. Then there was seventh grade, when I surprised Harper with a personal portrait by my mom's friend, Valerie Leonard, who paints dogs posed like figures in famous pictures and scenes. Now above her bed Harper has an enormous, photo-realistic painting of that famous bow-of-the-ship scene in Titanic, except instead of Kate Winslet, it's a thirteen-year-old Harper, and instead of Leonardo DiCaprio, it's a poofy Pomeranian (Harper's favorite breed that year). And let's see, there was also the year of the dog fashion show, arranged by yours truly, which almost turned into a disaster when a neighbor's cat got out of the house and all the strutting model mutts tried to make kitty-meat on the runway.

Last year I really outdid myself by converting the Carinas' backyard into a doggie obstacle course that let Harper and I see what life was like from a dog's perspective. My mom and Harper's dad made some modifications to their old tree house so it looked like a table with four giant legs, and I hung giant piñatas shaped like burgers and fries from the beams. But, unlike with regular piñata protocol, I wouldn't let us swing at them with bats—we had to just keep running and jumping and trying to "catch" the fake food with our arms flailing in a chomping motion, like dogs do with scraps. Eventually we just started making leaps for the piñatas, which would then come crashing down with us, spilling candy and beads and plastic jewelry all over the yard. I don't think Mrs. Carina ever forgave me for ruining her lawn like that.

The problem was, since Harper didn't like to think about her birthday in the traditional sense, I never had any idea what she might want from year to year. Sure, she would always map out the route for PuppyBash, figuring out which dog parks we'd volunteer and raise awareness at with the PuppyTales owners. But when it came down to the *party*-party part, she always got super demure, like "Oh, it's not a big deal. Let's not even do anything this year." But I knew she'd be heartbroken if she woke up and, instead of a big surprise party, I had just gotten her a card and a gift or something. Of course I didn't mind the planning, I actually really liked it, but it did put an awful lot of pressure on me to keep coming up with ways to outdo my ideas from previous years, and now that we weren't even going to the same school, I wasn't even sure where the inspiration was supposed to come from.

I stressed so much about the party for the entire morning that I was more starving than usual by the time we were let out for lunch.

I found Nicole, Jane, and Drew sitting by their favorite food truck, which sold vegan Mexican food and pressed juice. Today's special was seasonal watermelon—delicious. "Hey, Lily-Fairy!" Drew sing-songed when he saw me, waving at me from inside the small cluster of kids who were orbiting around Nicole.

"Hey, guys!" I said. "I'm just going to grab some food and then I'll join you?"

"Actually, Lily," Nicole piped up, "Can you just meet us after class right here? We're kind of backed up right now with people trying to sign up for NAMASTE."

"Oh," I said. "No problem."

I turned around and headed for the food truck, confused and more than a little bit stunned. I heard rapid footsteps come up from behind me, so I moved to get out of the way, but then I turned around to see Jane and Drew jogging to catch up to me.

"Sorry about that!" said Jane. "Nicole's just busy with club stuff."

"Oh, I can't even imagine," I said, because I really couldn't.

Jane and Drew stood in line with me and then sat with me while we finished our lunches. Drew was even more loud and flamboyant than he'd been on the first day of school, and at one point he had me and Jane laughing so hard I thought I'd choke on my organic juice. I learned that he's in all these super advanced dance classes and I made him promise to show me how to do the Time Warp and (if time permitted before the next big Pathways dance) the Tootsie Roll. Drew was really into learning dances that had names that didn't always translate to what the dance actually was. I also learned that Jane's not the only fashionista in the group—Drew makes all his own clothes!

"Drew's aesthetic is clearly 'hit or missable,'" Jane said, then gestured to Drew's outfit: a suit made entirely out of sewn-together ties. "As you can see, today's ensemble is the latter."

"Pshh, don't listen to her," Drew said. "She's just jealous because I am way more of a fabulous style icon than she'll ever be."

I smiled gratefully. Even if I still felt a little bit dejected by my earlier interactions with Nicole, hanging out with Jane and Drew made me realize that everything was still okay. I hadn't been rejected by NAMASTE yet. It was still only the first week of school, but I cared so much about what my new friends thought of me. Now I just couldn't wait until the club fair at the end of the day, when I'd be able to see what Nicole's group was actually about.

♥

When jazz session ended at 2:30, I carefully packed up my piccolo (I also play ukulele, but strings session isn't until Thursday), and with a faint sense of anxiety, headed back out to the Lane for the club fair. The moment I opened the heavy wooden doors, I was practically blinded by what I at first thought was a mirage: a twinkling, shining metallic "lake" made out of long swaths of tinfoil where the Lane used to be, in the middle of which was a plywood stage and a podium spray-painted bright gold. Though I couldn't really see anything because of the harsh glare, I could hear the roar of what sounded like about half of the K-12 student body of Pathways as they pushed and shoved their way into the narrow real estate that separated the two campus buildings.

"Mic check!" yelled a familiar voice, reverberating through my skull as feedback from a powerful sound system keened on behind me. I could feel myself start to sweat. There was a reason I didn't like live concerts, and it mainly had to do with my fear of things like loud noises and confined spaces packed with a lot of people, both of which I was now experiencing in the extreme. I shut my eyes to try to block everything out.

"Confined, confined, confined," I could hear someone echo beside me. I pried open my eyes and whipped my head to the left before realizing that I had been talking to myself again.

And then, in a span of mere moments, this metallic version of the Lane had now been transformed into a mosh pit, with Nicole in the center, elevated on the makeshift stage.

"Friends, colleagues, and esteemed Pathway students!" Nicole said, her eyes fervent with passion, obvious even from way back where I stood. "Welcome to . . . NAMASTE!"

A large cheer rose from the crowd, the kind that sounded more like a reaction to a rock solo than the *ohm*s of the peaceful yoga class I'd imagined the NAMASTE meeting would be like. Come to think of it, I really had had no idea what the NAMASTE group actually *was*, or even what it stood for, but had been under the impression it was something vaguely spiritual in a nonthreatening way. Nicole raised her arms in the universal gesture of *Saturday Night Live* hosts that need their fans to settle down so they can continue their monologue. She had changed into a piece of gauzy red fabric wrapped around her body as a dress, which amplified her curvaceous figure. It stood in stunning contrast to her bright hair and pale, freckly skin. Her outfit almost looked like a sari, if saris were supposed to be halfway transparent and worn without a bra. I wondered, not for the first time, what Nicole's natural hair color was.

"Many of you already know me, but for those who don't, my name is Nicole Schumer, and I'm a junior here at our fine institution," Nicole began when the crowd had settled. "I'm here to tell you about my personal journey through this institution, as well as my struggle to find an individual identity in a school full of unique personalities. That struggle led me to founding the NAMASTE Club. Hopefully, some of what I say this afternoon will resonate with you, and you can sign up for one of our 'Humane-ity' meta-curricular programs." She nodded offstage, and I saw Drew and Jane come forth from behind her, holding aloft a bunch of colorful fliers. Holding the papers above the fray, they made their way back past the first couple of rows as Nicole continued.

"When I first arrived at Pathways, do you know what I wanted more than anything in the world? It wasn't good grades, or a group of friends who encouraged me, or a path to carve out that would distinguish me from others. What I wanted was to go *backward.* I wanted to go back to my old life, where I had been comfortable. But my mom and dad, goddess bless them, they paid all this money to send me to this amazing school, to provide me with this . . . this . . . *once in a lifetime opportunity.* And you know how I repaid their kindness? Was it by saying, 'Thank you mom, thank you pops, gee, I hope I do you guys proud?' No. I thanked them by coming home after my very first day, locking myself in my room, and crying for about two months straight because '*no one at school likes me!*' Because 'everyone thinks I'm weird' and 'I don't have the right accent!' I must have spent half my first semester begging them to take me out of Pathways and re-enroll me in public school, where all my so-called 'friends' went."

Here, Nicole stopped pacing and scanned the crowd. Maybe it was just the reflections in the foil lake playing tricks on me, but I could have sworn her eyes stopped right on me. I realized I had been holding my breath, and reminded myself to consume oxygen like a normal person. But still, how did Nicole know I'd had some of those same exact thoughts? It was like she'd been reading from my pre-Pathways mind.

Suddenly, the crowd was quiet enough to hear a safety pin drop. Looks like I wasn't the only one affected by Nicole's magnetism.

"But screw 'being normal!'" Nicole shouted, piercing through the silence and rousing everyone to start cheering again. "There is nothing worse in life than normalcy! It's the opiate of the complacent, bourgeois masses, who tell us not to deviate from the boring standard, lest we be considered freaks, social outcasts, rebels. *Screw* the normies and screw the besties, with their cliquish identities that make them dependent on other people. The only person you should depend upon for your identity is you.

"And that's what NAMASTE Club is about. It's about being different no matter what, at all costs. It's about having the balls to break away from what society tells you to do—like staying 'true' to who you *used* to be, or keeping ties to a community that is actually just tying you down. In NAMASTE, you'll learn about the true, core message of Pathways: That there is no 'us' in Individual, but there is an 'I'. In fact, there are three of them."

Watching Nicole speak was like being hypnotized.

I was there, but I was also watching myself from above, hovering just a few feet away, and looking down at me looking at Nicole. The funny thing was, the more Nicole talked about being herself, the more I wanted to be like her, too. She was so different from anyone else I knew, so aggressive in her beliefs and so confident in her identity. This wasn't at all like the first time I met Harper, whom I immediately recognized as a friend, but who was ultimately on the same plane of existence as myself, like an extension of the preexisting me. And, sure, Harper could be a little . . . passive sometimes, though it's not really fair to compare friends. Especially when they were so different! My feelings toward Nicole were much more aspirational in nature, like being around her felt a little like being able to sit in the presence of Queen Bey. She made me want to be a better *me*. Just like she was saying!

"So, fellow Pathways-goers," she continued. "What I am asking of you today is that you become *Is* instead of *Us*es. Stop being scared of being different and start being scared of being the *same*. Join NAMASTE, and learn about our core tenets: N for Nature, A for Art, M for Magic, A for Alienation, S for Sheganism, T for Thought and E for Energy. That's what NAMASTE stands for."

*Oh!* I thought, equal parts relieved that someone had finally explained it, and more confused than ever about what that acronym actually meant.

"Do yourselves a favor and join our club so you can start being the truest version of you today. And remember: NAMASTE is all about letting you transform from the caterpillar of conformity into the butterfly of creativity! That's why I'm pleased to announce that our new official club symbol is now *fairy wings*, which we'll be rolling out over the next couple of weeks. The message to remember here is that NAMASTE gives you wings! Thank you."

Nicole's closing lines reminded me of the end of an infomercial, but when she said them, the crowd began to roar again. I was stunned, not sure if I should clap or cry. Did Nicole just base her club's logo off my outré accessory? I felt flattered beyond belief . . . no one had ever liked my style enough to start a whole trend off of it! I found my voice cheering harder than anyone else's, and I couldn't decide if Harper would be weirded out or obsessed with what was happening. Maybe, I thought, if the Gawkward Fairy clapped her hands loud enough, she could actually start believing in the magic of transformation herself.

NAMASTE!

I wish I could say the rest of the week went better than Monday, that I spent the rest of freshman year making a name for myself as the chill girl whom everyone loved because she had the superhuman ability to befriend everyone in our class.

But yeah, *no*.

Tuesday was even worse. I spent all day texting Lily and getting frustrated when she wouldn't respond fast enough, and I kept wishing we still went to school together so we could skip the texting and just talk in person. I knew I was being needy but I WAS IN NEED. What I didn't need was Tim, who was getting on my last nerve, apologizing over and over for me for getting me in trouble with Ms. Miller. The way he was trailing me around like a broken apology robot, I almost wished I were back in detention so I could get some peace and quiet.

"Seriously, I was just trying to make you laugh," he said, trailing me in the hall before fourth period. "I thought it would cheer you up to see a new installment of the fan fiction I used to write about you and Lily!"

I picked up my step, hoping to shake off Tim, forgetting all the nice things I thought about him when I first saw him in class yesterday after a summer away. Even then I couldn't help but think that his too-new preppy clothes, paired with his Batman backpack and unstylish crew cut were burning a bull's eye into my back. If Derek and his crew didn't think I was a spaz before, just wait till they met my new BFF, the Boy Wonder. Unfortunately, Tim and I took all the same AP classes, which were spaced approximately ten yards apart from one another, giving everyone in school ample time to check us out and peg us as Beverly's nerdiest non-couple.

"Look, Tim, it's fine," I stressed as we arrived at our calculus classroom. "I told you not to worry about it. Just, maybe next time? Cool it on the comics, and saying stuff like 'fan fiction' in public."

Tim grinned. "Why?"

"Because," I said, searching for the right words. "It's like you're *trying* to be a stereotype. And you don't have to be! You're not even that dorky-looking anymore. You could be totally passable . . ." I stopped before I said something more unfortunate.

"Passable for what?" Tim said, but he was still smiling. Oh god! Did he think I was hitting on him? I blushed just thinking of how upset Lily would be if she found out that Tim Slater thought I was calling him cute. The right thing to do would be to cut it off at the pass.

"Passable for not a loser," I added, doing my best Rachel impression before turning on my heels, walking into the classroom, and choosing a seat in the back corner, far away from Tim.

I cracked open my textbook and pretended to go over my homework as I texted Lily yet again.

> **Harper (1:34 p.m.):** I think ur ex is determined to land me in detention again.

> **Lily (1:34 p.m.):** Curse him! Just ditch school and come here and hang out with me. We're making time capsules in Philosophy of You class today and Nicole gave me a gemstone with healing properties that she and Jane found when they were freshman to put in it. How sweet is that?

How many updates about how much FUN she was having at Pathways with Nicole was she going to send me? I was proud of Lily for thriving at her new school, but part of me couldn't help but feel totally abandoned. Had my little fairy flown the nest?

See, I knew from the first moment I met Lily that I had to emotionally adopt her. I've always had a soft spot for strays and misfit toys; for baby birds without their moms and the Barbies that my sister Rachel would use to practice her (terrible) hair stylist skills. Basically I'm a sucker for people and things whose actual dopeness goes unnoticed. I'm kind of an Empathy Addict (it's my kryptonite), and my spirit animal is the Statue of Liberty. Just give me your hand-me-downs, your shelter strays, your hopeless fashion messes, and I will see the best in them.

So what else could I do but save the day when an adorably lost girl in fairy wings wandered into my fourth grade gym class like a mouse wandering into a cat party? Lily looked like something I'd dreamt up one night, maybe after having too many diet sodas and gummy worms at a sleepover with a bunch of gossipy girls who, had you asked me at the time, I would have called my besties. Sometimes you don't really think about what certain words actually mean until you meet someone special, and then everything shifts inside and you take a big red marker to the dictionary in your head and under "best friend" you write in an entirely new definition.

That's what it was like when Lily entered the lemon-cleaner-scented gym that day, almost two months after the school year had started. I remember it was right before Halloween because the gym was decorated with big pumpkins and those weird little misshaped squashes and fake, synthetic straw. I also remember the squeaking of sneakers on the buffed floorboards, the *thwump* of dozens of dribbling basketballs, and then the harsh echo of Mr. DeJulio's whistle as he alerted us to the presence of this odd, rare species. A new student? We hadn't had a new kid in our class since two Januaries ago when Matt Musher's dad moved the family from Pittsburgh, so this was *big*. Did something tragic happen to her family? WAS SHE FAMOUS? Is she from one of those Disney or Nickelodeon shows and now we'll get to go to premiers where they give out gift bags with fancy nail polish in them?

She shuffled up behind Jessica and Stephanie, who were doing their best to maintain an authoritative distance, so as not to infect themselves with a case of the Weirds.

Back then, Jessica and Stephanie were the epitome of my old definition of "best friends." They dressed the same and talked the same and sometimes would even tell people they were twins, which was funny (in the way creepy clowns are kind of funny) because they actually looked nothing alike. Jessica was short with brown hair and a narrow, oval face while Stephanie was tall with surfer-girl blond hair and a perfectly round face. In fourth grade they would both wear their hair in tight ponytails and big bouffant-y top knots, and when they put their heads together to whisper—which was all the time—it would look like two scoops of ice cream, like a hair sundae. Of course, there was no way I'd ever tell them that observation. Jessica and Stephanie had supersensitive radar detection for anything that was gross or weird, like Tim Slater's Batman obsession (weird) or the matzo PB&J sandwiches my mom packed in my lunch during Passover (gross). Talking about hair-cream-sundaes would have been both.

Anyway, back to Lily. She moved to say hello to Jessica and Stephanie, but before she could get the word out, they crossed the gym really fast and refused to look behind them, as if they were being chased by a zombie and were afraid to see how close it was. In their (small) defense, Lily did look like something from another world: In a sea of sneakers, shorts and ponytails, in walks this tiny girl with long, blunt bangs, wearing a robin's egg blue leotard, white cowboy boots, and a too-big tutu. And that was what you noticed before you got to the fact that she was wearing giant purple butterfly wings and a crown made of flowers and sticks in her hair. She would have looked more at home in Narnia than a California elementary school.

Mr. DeJulio must have felt bad about the hair twins blowing off the new girl, because the next thing he did was order Jessica to give Lily a tour of the gymnasium. Stephanie attempted to give Jessica a look that said "I'm sorry!" but that mostly just came off as "Thank god he didn't pick me!"

"And here's the gymnastics station, and over there are the pull-up bars. . . ." Jessica was rushing through her tour so fast she didn't even bother to introduce Lily to anyone, nor did she even stop once to look behind her to see if her charge was still following her. "You do have gyms back . . . where you're from, right?" Jessica called over her shoulder without breaking her stride. When she walked past me, she gave an exaggerated grimace and rolled her eyes. Stephanie must have felt bad, because for once she wasn't walking right in step with Jessica, but instead kept pace with the strange little fairy girl who wandered the gym with her lips slightly parted. Stephanie gave the new girl a wide berth, as if she were an exotic animal you don't necessarily want to touch.

She was small, like short, swamped by her too-big clothes, with giant, bright blue eyes and pale skin, which was a novelty in sunny California, where sunbathing counted as an unofficial after-school sport. You would think someone who dressed like that would be used to getting tons of stares, but this girl seemed to pulse with a nervous energy, fidgeting and mumbling to herself, taking out a be-doodled binder and scribbling something in it as she grew more and more oblivious to everyone's eyes. She seemed lost in her own world, and I suddenly had a fierce to desire to know what she was thinking. That is, until Mr. DeJulio broke the spell of silence by blowing on the whistle and calling out, "Okay, now that our new student has had a chance to get the lay of the land, let's all say hello to her. Honey, come up and tell us a little about yourself! Kids, this is Lily Farson."

Jessica muttered something I couldn't quite catch, but the next remark was loud enough to ring through the room.

"More like Lily FART-son," Matt shouted from beside the equipment basket, cupping his hands and imitating the grossest noise imaginable. Derek Wheeler, Paul Gilmore, and a bunch of other boys who all wore oversized T-shirts all laughed like donkeys, too dumb to know that if you were going to be a jerk to someone, you better bring something better to the table than poop jokes.

"Musher! Principal's office—now!" Mr. DeJulio shouted. Matt threw a peace sign to his buddies and jogged out of the gym as if he were going shopping for more giant T-shirts instead of to go get punished. "Sorry about that, Lily," Mr. DeJulio said once Matt had gone. "You can go ahead and introduce yourself whenever you're ready."

No one moved a muscle. Behind me, I could hear one of the guys cough, and a couple girls started to giggle and whisper nearby. One of the whispers sounded a lot like it belonged to Jessica, actually, and then I heard a violent "shush!" that seemed to come from Stephanie. Lily kept her eyes down and Stephanie kept her eyes on Lily. I tried to beam Steph a psychic MomTip about subtlety, but her shiny bun must have been blocking transmission. My entire inner being shut down with empathy and secondhand embarrassment for this new creature. But Lily didn't seem to feel any embarrassment. In fact, she didn't seem to register that this so clearly humiliating experience was even happening to her at all. I knew, all of a sudden, that this girl was *special*.

After a few too-long beats, Lily finally seemed to recognize that she was supposed to start talking. With a tiny sigh, she trudged her way back to the front double-wide doors of the gymnasium, with Stephanie now trailing behind her like a sleepwalker.

Lily didn't walk like a fairy. Dragging her feet, she made her way to the front of the room, her shoulders sinking as if each step she took made her wings heavier and heavier. When she got to Mr. DeJulio, she turned around, slowly, and faced the rest of us. Her jet black hair looked too big for her head, and it was hard to see her eyes with that big mess of bangs in front of them, which were being pushed down even more by that bizarre flower crown. Her lips were moving, but if she was talking, no one in the gym could hear her. Stephanie, who had clearly softened toward her ever since the Fart-son incident, cautiously approached Lily and asked her a short question, which warranted a violent shake of her black waves. Stephanie shrugged and slowly walked back toward the rest of us, eschewing her usual spot next to Jessica to stand, hip cocked and lips pursed, next to me.

"Uh," said Mr. DeJulio, looking nervously from Lily to a wrinkled piece of paper in his hand. He must have been as confused as we all were. "Lily has just moved here from Ellicott City in Maryland," he said, reading from the paper. "Those are some cool wings, Lily. Do you want to tell us about them?" I could tell that, like me, Mr. DeJulio was a sympathetic person. He was nodding his head up and down like he was trying to give Lily a clue as what she should say.

The fairy girl shrugged and kept mumbling—or maybe she was humming? She didn't seem upset, just . . . busy. Like she couldn't really be bothered to introduce herself because she was much more interested in perfecting whatever song she was mumble-humming. For a second I thought maybe Mr. DeJulio had gotten it wrong and Lily was from someplace where they didn't speak English, like Spain or the French part of Canada. My shin received a little kick from Jessica's floral print Keds as she came up and stood behind me.

"Maybe she's like . . . special," Jessica whispered, but loud enough for the whole class to hear. Derek and a bunch of other kids started laughing. If I were Lily, I would have died of embarrassment. Instead, she suddenly smiled and gave a dramatic bow, as if everyone were applauding her. I felt my cheeks go warm, and I squirmed uncomfortably. My mom says my blush is my "tell," the thing that alerts a room to your nervousness. Mom also says she doesn't have a tell, but I've definitely noticed that whenever she's upset she hums like a maniac. (Also see: the peeling off of gel manicures thing I mentioned earlier. Or her overflossing habit, which she does before, after and sometimes DURING meals.)

"I'm Lily, and I'll be performing an interpretive dance to a song I wrote called 'Oh Mighty Sir Zeus'! It's to the tune of Beyoncé's 'Single Ladies.'" She had a small-loud voice, like the kind you'd hear in a cartoon or in an old movie. "The song is about me and my best friend, Sir Zeus, who is part Chesterfield pony and part narwhal. Most of the time Sir Zeus and I just go on adventures and fight bad guys in high-crime neighborhoods. But we're taking a sabbatical this year because my mom is doing an installation project for a gallery in Hollywood. So now we're focusing on broadening our art portfolio."

I didn't know what the word "sabbatical" meant, but I knew the word "Sabbath" from Hebrew school. It means "day of rest." I thought maybe Lily's parents were resting for a year?

"Oh," said Mr. DeJulio, clearly out of his depth

on this one. "We don't actually need you to perform anything today."

The fairy didn't miss a beat. "That's okay," she said. "I'll do it anyway."

I don't remember much about the ensuing spectacle, only the looks on my classmates' faces, which ranged from stunned to amused to horrified. Lily must have realized she wasn't quite moving her audience, but to her credit, she kept singing and dancing to her weirdo song about Greek gods and how *if they liked it they should have put a ring on it.* I had no idea what she was talking about, but it was definitely memorable.

When she finished, I was at once relieved and sad that it was over. I looked at Lily up there, expecting her to burst into tears any moment. Instead, she was totally beaming. She brushed her hair out of her eyes to give her captive audience another giant bow, despite the total lack of applause her performance was greeted with.

I knew that if it were me up there, I would have been mortified. I would have literally crawled into a hole and died. It would feel so nice, I thought, to jump up and just act silly like that, without worrying about Jess and Steph calling me weird and gross, or living in fear that Matt was going to make a fart noise after a teacher said my name. It'd be nice to just say "WHO CARES!" because, actually, who *really* did care? I wanted to believe in my own kind of magic, too, even though I was scared about what it would mean to be that bold.

No, scratch being scared. I desperately wanted to believe in Lily's world. And sometimes wanting to believe in something is enough to make it real.

"Harper, what do you think you are doing?" It must have really freaked Mr. DeJulio out to see one of his best, most quiet students getting up without permission and joining the new girl up front. In fact, I didn't really know what I was doing, either. I just knew I wanted to feel as brave as Lily.

"Um, I just wanted to say . . ." I looked across the room full of my classmates, my mind a total blank. Had I really been wondering what it was like to be this girl? Because I had already known: there was Derek and Phil snickering, there was Tim Slater looking over his glasses, something between amusement and concern flashing in his eyes. There was Stephanie, chewing on her lower lip, her eyebrows creased with worry. And there was Jessica, quickly scooching her way to the front row and trying to get my attention.

"*Ohmygod* . . . Harper, get down!" hissed Jessica. "Are you having an episode?"

"I just wanted to say," I ignored Jessica and started again, my heart beating out of my chest, desperately darting my eyes around to find a friendly face and finally landing on the girl right next to me, who inspired this insanity in the first place. Lily was looking at me— really looking at me, with her bangs finally out of her face—and for once her mind didn't seem so far away. It was as if she saw me, and that she was interested in what I had to say, and that that was enough.

"I just wanted to say that I really liked your performance, Lily." I took a deep breath. "And I just wanted to know, um, where did you get those really cool wings?"

Lily smiled. "They were a gift from my grandmother, thank you for asking," she said. "I like them because they remind me of her . . . and of those sour blue lollipops that make your mouth look like a Smurf's."

"Oh, I love those!" I said, surprised that Lily actually ate regular human food. "Have you ever tried to eat one while wearing root beer flavored lip gloss?"

Lily giggled. "No! Is it good?"

"Um . . . not really." All of a sudden, it was like Lily and I were the only two people in the room. I didn't care what anyone else thought of us, and it was like I had been waiting my whole life to meet someone who could take away that constant anxiety of being judged.

"I like your shoes, too," Lily said. "Did you make them?"

I looked down at my feet in confusion. I was wearing my crocheted low tops that I'd somehow convinced my mom buy for me after telling her that no, I didn't think Kate Spade sneakers would be appropriate to wear when we were running laps. Did Lily think I had sat there with a needle and a ball of yarn and just, like . . . made a pair of shoes? Was that even a thing you could do? Suddenly the world seemed full of formerly implausible, now totally possible, DIY projects, and I wanted to try every one.

The bell rang, saving Mr. DeJulio from having to deal with the two crazy girls who had taken over his classroom. It was like a spell had been broken: Immediately it was mayhem as usual as everyone scrambled to the locker rooms to change back into their regular clothes and go to lunch. The show was over, nothing to see here, folks. Lily followed behind me as I made my way to my cubby.

"Do you want to maybe . . . tell me where I could get a pair of shoes like that?" Lily, looking down and scuffing her feet on the shiny floor, seemed shy again.

"Sure," I said brightly. "Actually, do you want to come over to my house this weekend? My mom can take us to

Bloomingdale's and we can get you a pair just like mine."

Lily's smile was neon-bright. "That would be really splendid, thank you. Are you sure you won't mind?"

"Not at all," I said, though I was mentally cringing at the idea of Rachel teasing my new, odd friend. I'd have to bribe her with ten Pixie Sticks just to get her to keep her mouth shut. "I'm Harper, by the way," I said.

"Lily. But you already knew that, I guess."

On our way to lunch, Stephanie caught up with us and asked if Lily wanted to sit at our table. She said yes, and the rest was history. Now that Lily was around, I'd thought, life would never be boring again.

Which is exactly why I felt so alone now, back in my boring life without a gawkward fairy to guide me.

On Friday I rushed home after school and got ready to go to Murphy's Ranch. At six p.m., I left a note for my parents saying that I was going to ride my bike over to Lily's house for dinner and a movie, knowing that they would never suspect that I wasn't going to be exactly where I said I was going to be. Plus, I was pretty sure Mom was out of town for the weekend on some Clear Your Clutter, Free Your Mind conference in Belize, and Rachel was with Jacques.

I didn't know what to expect when I got to the wrought-iron gates that led into the compound. I could hear music below, where the graffiti-covered bunkers were, but the giant outdoor staircase looked too daunting to maneuver with my bike, so I ended up leaving it hidden in some bushes near the entrance.

For a moment I felt like Cinderella as I descended

those epic steps. Like, maybe I should leave a shoe or something? The whole scene was very cinematic, the way the wild courtyard opened below me into this giant ravine, the music blaring like a thousand trumpets (if trumpets sounded like Eminem). I wondered for the umpteenth time if I had dressed up too much. I must have tried on a billion outfits before settling on something I hoped said "funky-casual-sexy": a red and white striped Madewell dress and my brown Anthropologie moccasins. I'd completed the look with one of those stupid, floppy wide-brimmed hats, which at the last second I decided to ditch with my bike in the bushes near the gates.

"Hey, Carina!" a voice shouted from below, near the giant barn that served as the ranch's headquarters. "Come on back here and let's start rolling!" Both my pace and my heartbeat quickened, and I nearly tripped down the rest of the stairs in my rush to meet Derek.

As my eyes adjusted to the dusky light inside the ranch, I saw that Derek wasn't alone. Of course he wasn't, I chided myself. What did I think, that he'd invited me out to the middle of nowhere to make out with me or something? Well, of course that would have been the ideal scenario, but . . . no. In fact, everyone from our Monday detention was there—including Matt and the snotty American Apparel crop-top girl, whose name (obviously) was Kendall. She was draped on top of Derek like a slutty poncho.

There were a bunch of kids—guys mostly—who I didn't know, and who looked older. Possibly even in college, or at least college-*aged*. They were hovering over a cooler full of beer, which they would reach into every time they'd finished crushing their last can under their feet and then threw it like a Frisbee out the barn door. I doubted that they'd be picking them up later as part of the ranch's "Leave No Trace" policy.

"Hey, Harper, want to come over here for a second?" I turned around and was more than pleasantly surprised to see my old friend Stephanie Adler, who I guess was playing the part of my guardian angel tonight. I gratefully plopped down next to her. Out of all the kids hanging out, she was the only one who was actually dressed for skating. In a baggy sweatshirt and faded boy jeans, with her blond hair shoved underneath a beanie, she could almost pass for one of the guys.

She kicked one of her black Vans against my leg affectionately, like she used to do when we were little. "Hey, don't worry about Kendall," she said, nodding toward Derek, who was trying to untangle himself from American Apparel's embrace. "She's been panting over him ever since we all met in summer camp."

"I didn't know you and Derek went to camp together."

"Oh, well, yeah. It wasn't anything exciting," Stephanie laughed. "Basically just a place for parents to dump their kids while they're vacationing in St. Barths, or whatever."

"I didn't see you and Jessica together in class . . ." I began, stopping when Stephanie made a face. I had forgotten about their SchoolGrams fight video. "So . . . you and Jessica . . ." I trailed off, not really sure how to bring up the topic tactfully.

"Yeah. Me and Jessica. Ancient history, I guess." Stephanie laughed ruefully.

"I guess what I'm asking is, did you and Jess have . . . are you guys still . . ." Apparently it was impossible for me to talk about BFFs without sounding like a befuddled Elmer Fudd.

Stephanie turned to me and looked out from underneath her beanie. "Let me guess. You saw the video."

"What video?" I played innocent.

"Ha, you were always a terrible liar, Harper, even when we were kids. Everyone saw that video, even my parents somehow got a link to it." Stephanie shook her head and a strand of blond hair came loose. "Do you know how humiliating it is, when there are multiple Vine accounts looping of the worst moment of your life to everyone in school over and over again?"

"I guess not," I conceded. "The version I saw was pretty grainy. I couldn't even tell what it was about. Did you guys have a fight?"

"We were always fighting," she muttered darkly. "By the end we didn't even like hanging out with each other." She shrugged, stood up, and dusted off her legs: a signal that the conversation was over. She picked up her longboard—I was no expert, but this one wasn't cheap—and turned to give me a hand up.

"You know, I remember when you first started hanging out with Lily. Jessica and I used to think you guys looked as attached as the Olsen Twins allegedly were before the surgery." Stephanie broke out in a grin, and for a second she didn't look like a model who was slumming it, but like the nine-year-old girl with gap teeth and a too-tight hair bun I remembered from that day in gym class.

"Gross!" I laughed.

"But seriously." Stephanie looked at Matt, who seemed to be at least three beers ahead of everyone else, shouting about how wasted he was, as if it were his crowning achievement. "It's hard to find people who let you in so easily."

I could tell Steph was getting upset about Jessica, so I changed the subject to Matt. "Are you guys hooking up?" I was actually genuinely curious. Sometimes it seemed like Stephanie and Matt were a couple, and sometimes it looked like they just happened to run in the same group. They spent a lot of time with each other, but I'd never see them make out or even hold hands. Then again, what did I know about dating? Currently I was one half of a Dorky Duo with a guy I didn't even like. Well, not *like*-like, anyway. And I spent the rest of my time obsessively Internet-stalking Derek. (Things I've found out so far: He didn't list his relationship status, all his photos are of either Kurt Cobain or skateboards sans filters, and he has more Twitter followers than I do.)

"Hey, Carina, do you want to start filming?" Derek called out, having found his way out of Kendall's clutches. "I was thinking we'd set up the first shot near the water tower."

"Great," I said, standing up a little too quickly. "Can you walk me through the story here? It might, um, help with my set up?"

We left the barn together, alone, and I caught Kendall giving me the evil eye as Derek threw his arm around me. God, maybe this would turn into my Cinderella night after all.

The water tower was huge, a towering, dented, rusting giant with a giant Super Mario mushroom tagged on the side. I pulled my camera from my handbag and made sure we had enough light for a video. Then I did a test run of the audio, where I asked Derek to stand in front of the water tower and say a bunch of silly words.

He made a face. "Okay, are we ready now, Scorsese?"

Thank god the light was dimming because I could feel even my hair turning red when he said that.

I guess I can get really obsessive about projects. Even though Lily is usually the one who dreams up the ideas, I'm the one who usually puts them in motion. Like with our Memory Box, which has been sitting in the back of my closet since August, despite the promise we'd made over the summer to add to it at least once a week during the school year.

"You know, I don't know anything about this stuff," Derek said, scuffing his dirty shoes on the ground. "But I've always wanted to be a filmmaker. You know, like a revolutionary badass. Like the dude who made *Spring Breakers*."

"Harmony Korine," I said.

"Well, not 'harmony,' per se," Derek said thoughtfully, his broody brow wrinkling in thought. "I'd go more for, like, *disruption*. You know, damn the man! *Spring Breakers* forever!"

"No," I said. "I meant the guy who made *Spring Breakers*. His name is Harmony."

"For real?" Derek smiled, and shook his head. "Damn, Carina. You know a lot about cinema!"

"Oh, not really. I mean, just the basics," I said, trying to resist the urge to show off. "I've seen like, all of Sofia Coppola's early work." I did a cool shrug, like it didn't really matter.

Derek looked suitably impressed, though it was hard to tell because suddenly he was standing so close to me that our arm hairs touched.

"All the Coppolas, though, are good." Oh god, now I was babbling. Some remote part of my brain was telling me this was a good thing to say, that as long as I kept talking, he'd keep moving closer. "Um, did you know Nicolas Cage is actually a Coppola?"

"Okay, Wikipedia," Derek said. "Hey. Don't worry too much about getting the video set up just right. You know, I only wanted an excuse to get you out here, anyway."

My brain was going "Say something sexy! No, make a joke! Say a sexy joke!"

"Yeah?" said my mouth, smartly not listening to my brain.

"Yeah," Derek smiled. Up close, I could see that one of his bottom front teeth was chipped, and he smelled good, like fresh sweat and burnt leaves. Funny, in fourth grade I would have put "smelling Derek" on the top of my list of "Most Effective Torture Techniques." I guess I still would have put it there now, but for different reasons.

"Hey, remember how you always wore that same T-shirt every day? And when Mr. Kalinski had to drive you home because you were so smelly?" I said, before I could to stop myself. Derek gave me a crooked grin.

"Yeah? What made you think of that?" He asked, picking up his arm and waving his pit dangerously close to my face. "Are you trying to give me a hint?"

"Dude, gross!" I said giggling as he waggled his arm, thinking with horror that I'd transformed into one of those tweeny-boppers who burst into laughter every time a cute boy burped. What was happening to me?

Suddenly Derek lowered his arm around my shoulder and he was pulling me closer. Everything was moving in slow-mo. I had time to think about how doleful his eyes looked, like they belonged to a heartthrob on the cover of *Tiger Beat*, with some headline like, "Harry Styles Talks About His Secret Love . . . !" only for the article to reveal that the "secret love" is chocolate ice cream. And then time sped up all at once again, and then his mouth was on mine and we were kissing.

My first real kiss was happening . . . and with Derek Wheeler! The most random person I could have possible chosen from the yearbook!

I sent a secret mental message to Lily ("SOS!"). But like all things lately re: Lily, I knew she probably wouldn't respond with any real emotional depth. Plus it was kind of hard to concentrate on Lily, what with me focusing all my energy on making sure I was a good kisser.

After an eternity—okay, five minutes, tops—Derek broke away and stared at me, as if he were looking for some kind of change in my features, or maybe memorizing them.

"We should get back," he murmured, and I, not trusting my mouth, mutually agreed and followed him as obediently as a puppy.

We walked back to the barn in silence, almost-but-not-quite holding hands. Back with the group, I tried not to notice Kendall staring daggers or Stephanie's look of concern, and instead focused on counting the number of empty beer cans that had been strewn around the room. Derek must have misunderstood why I was staring at that particular scene, because he sauntered over and handed me his half-drunk can. "I wasn't sure if you wanted any," he said with a shrug. "But you can have the rest of mine."

"Oh, actually, I don't. . . ." I stammered, trying to find the right way to tell Derek's blue-flecked eyes that the only reason I'd put that can near my mouth was to get another taste of his lips.

But I never had a chance.

"What did I tell you?" Kendall sneered, wobbling over to us in too-tall heels like a demented stork. Outfitted in yet another belly shirt and a shellacked-looking skirt that was short enough to expose a stunningly impressive thigh-gap, Kendall snaked her arm into Derek's and narrowed her eyes at me. "I said, Harper is going to go call her best friend the Super Dork and have him save her from all us bad lil troublemakers!"

"Really?" I replied coolly. "Super Dork, that's the best you could come up with? Did you buy your sense of humor at American Apparel, too? Is that why it's so low quality?" Stephanie made a sound like a strangled laugh, but when Kendall turned around to look at her she pretended to be coughing.

Kendall snapped her attention back to me, which seemed to take more effort for her than it should. Her eyes kept floating upward and I wondered if she was going to faint and save us all some trouble. Her breath smelled like soggy, moldy bread. "Oh, and you have a sense of humor? Obvioush . . . obviously I had you pegged all wrong! Here, let me make it up to you. Want some?" Kendall produced a hot pink flask as if it were a magic trick.

I grabbed the flask from Kendall before she could see my hands shaking. *It's no big deal, it's only alcohol, you baby*, I chided myself as I unscrewed the lid. The wafting, overpowering stench hit my nose like a slap. I wondered if everyone could tell that I'd never taken so much as a sip of wine in my entire life. In fact, Lily and I had absolutely no interest in drinking or drugs. It wasn't about being cool or uncool, it was just who we were, and the concept of "peer pressure" seemed so ludicrous when it was just the two of us that I'd never even imagined how it would be when I was all alone, holding a flask in hostile territory.

"Come on, Dorkgirl." Kendall was listing so hard she should have fallen over already. "If you're going to wuss out, I'm going to need to ask for my flask back." I knew I shouldn't have let such a lame insult get under my skin. I had always counseled Lily to ignore the haters if they couldn't even bother to be original. But this was different: I had just had my first kiss, and Lily might as well have been a million miles away. This wasn't peer pressure, I reasoned, as long as I was only doing it to get Kendall to shut up and make Derek like me.

All eyes were on me as I brought the hot pink container of liquid death to my mouth.

**Harper (4:45 p.m.):** SOS! EMERGENCY!

**Lily (5:45 p.m.):** ?????

**Harper (5:47 p.m..):** Things have gotten 😭 😭 😭 and double plus insane. Can we meet up? Ferris wheel your house my house I don't care. I NEED YOU ASAP.

**Lily (5:47 p.m.):** PuppyGirl! What's going on??

**Harper (5:48 p.m.):** Ugh I can't even over text. Can we meet in 15? Near the pier? My sister can drive us if you want to get picked up.

**Lily (5:49 p.m.):** Oof! Whatever it is sounds awful. I really really want to meet but I can't bc band practice.

**Harper (5:51 p.m.):** . . . Band practice?

**Lily (5:52 p.m.):** Yeah! Well, we're not like a band, band–yet. I play the ukulele and sing, Jane is on harp and Drew plays the water jug. Guess what we call ourselves?

**Harper (5:53 p.m.):** Lily can you call me for a second? I really, really messed up, and I could really do with some Gawkward Fairy love right now.

**Lily (5:53 p.m.):** We're the Jug Judies!

**Lily (5:53 p.m.):** Oh Harper I'm so sorry I wish I could.

**Harper (5:54 p.m.):** Maybe I could come over and hang out afterwards so we can have a ♡2♡?

**Lily (6:01 p.m.):** Awwww I can't! I am already so so so late to finish my pre-midterm project for Lit Sesh. They're letting me decoupage a conch shell for my project on Lord of the Flies instead of writing a paper!

**Harper (6:05 p.m.):** Okay.

**Lily (6:10 p.m.):** We will see each other soon I promise. I love you so much im going to sell your organs on the black market and use the profits for the next puppybash.

**Harper (6:15 p.m.):** Can you just call me ASAP?

**Lily (6:16 p.m.):** I will I promise. I'll call you tomorrow after our NAMASTE meeting.

**Harper (6:16 p.m.):** NAMASTE?

**Lily (6:18 p.m.):** I have so many things to catch you up on! And I love you MOAR than metaphysical cops love donut wormholes. Let's hang out soon! How about a Walgreens lip gloss run next week?

**Harper (6:20 p.m.):** I love you and I love that but are you INSANE. by next week I could be put in cedars sinai hospital for being in a full spiral. just call me soon, ok? I need your advice.

**Lily (6:31 p.m.):** Yes, totally, hugging you SO HARD through the phone right now!

"Okay, that one sounded like 'Greensleeves' meets Haim, for sure," Drew huffed happily after Jug Judies rehearsal in the Pathways music room. It always took him awhile to catch his breath after thirty straight minutes of "tooting" (as he called it). "Lady Lily, why didn't you tell us you had such an amazing set of lungs?"

I grinned. "Is that your nice way of saying you don't like the way I strum my uke?" I gave my instrument a loud twang for good measure.

"Shush your face, just shush it!" Drew said, pushing his blond mop-top out of his eyes and grinning at me. "If I had your talent I would have sold it to Disney already so I could be the next Miley."

"Oh, please, if there was anyone off today, it was me!" Jane said, pushing her chair away from her oversized harp, swooning over toward me, and laying her gigantic fluff of ebony hair into my lap. "Lileeee! Please sprinkle some of your magic dust on me, that I might play as fair a sound as you, m'lady!"

I threw my hair in front of my face and scratched at it furiously, sending a cloud of dandruff down on Jane's head. "Here ya gooo!"

"Settle down, you two!" mock-scolded Drew. "Remember, here at Pathways we're all about NAMASTE!"

We all giggled furtively. In the last week or so since we founded the Jug Judies, Jane, Drew, and I have become much closer friends. Nicole would probably be offended if she heard the way we sometimes laughed about NAMASTE, but that was only because she was so dedicated to her club that she didn't really have a sense of humor about it. We all agreed that it was really inspirational, the way Nicole was able to get up in front of a group and give a big talk like she did the first week of school, and that none of us would even be friends if it wasn't for her. We really owed her everything, but the truth was, I was still really shaken by the whole fairy wing thing, and I felt more relaxed when I didn't have to put one-on-one time in with anyone. But I felt bad for even thinking like that because Nicole was the kind of person who could definitely read your thoughts.

The fact was, Drew and Jane were a lot more laid-back than Nicole was, and easier to be around. I hadn't known this when we first met, but Jane's father was one of the first African American television network heads, which is how Jane became so media-and Internet-obsessed, having spent most of her life defending her dad against racist trolls in the comment section of *Deadline, Variety,* and *The Hollywood Reporter.*

Jane's blog, FancyFashionFeminist, gets thousands of hits and she's even been written about by *Teen Vogue* and Refinery29 and a bunch of other publications who keep putting her on lists about young tastemakers. Not that I know much about that world, but I think Jane sells herself a little short. She really does have amazing taste and a fantastic eye for fashion, and unlike most of the Internet, Jane's posts are always funny and well-written. She writes from a platform of body-acceptance and reaches such a large and diverse audience that she was once even mentioned by the ladies on *Good Morning America*.

I didn't realize how late it'd gotten until I glanced at the clock above a row of music stands. We had to go to a quick catch-up meeting for the NAMASTE officers, and then I had to hustle out to meet Harper, who I really, really owed. She was having a rough time at school, and I'd been so worried that I was maybe betraying her and our pact every single day I wore my wings at Pathways that I didn't even know how to talk to her like a real person anymore. Could she tell how shady I was being over text? I hoped not, but Harper is so socially intuitive that I was sure that was just wishful thinking. For the first time ever, I felt nervous about meeting up with my bestie.

"Guys, maybe we should pack up," I said. "Nicole is supposed to meet us in five minutes and you know how pissed she gets if our 'extras' make us late." Nicole considered anything outside of sessions and NAMASTE to be an "extra," i.e., "a nonessential part of the core growth opportunities offered by Pathways." The Jug Judies seemed to particularly rub her the wrong way.

As we left the music room, Drew goosed me from behind, I screeched, and we all ended up running and laughing down the hall. There were small pockets of kids still roaming around, going to and from various activity groups, and you could tell one from the other based on the way each student-cluster was dressed and styled. But the one thing they all had in common is that when we flashed by one another, almost everyone waved and smiled at me. Someone even shouted, "Hey, it's Fairy Girl! Fairy Girl!" I turned back and give a dramatic bow. The hallway, I'm not exaggerating, *cheered* for me. I didn't even know a lot of these kids; a lot of them looked older, but they all knew who I was. It felt amazing. If I didn't know better, I'd think I was popular.

Not that it matters, or anything. But it's *nice.* Especially to have people like you for the right reasons, like how creative and unique you are. Is this what it's been like for Harper her entire life?

Nicole was walking toward us in the Lane. She was kind of hard to spot, as she was rocking a shoulder-length blond wig over her real hair, which she'd recently changed from bright green to a beautiful shade of blue.

"*Namaste,* friends," she said as we all hugged hello.

"Oh! I almost forgot," I said. "My friend Harper? I've told you about her, she's my best friend? She goes to Beverly High? Well, her birthday is coming up and I haven't been able to see her in a while, so I'm going to make a Walgreens run with her today after school."

"A . . . Walgreens run?" Nicole said, wrinkling her nose. She had on metallic eye shadow and a black romper with a red vinyl belt and white stilettos. It was *trés* punk rock.

"Yeah, it's just this silly thing we do," I said, looking to Jane and Drew, but they were both suddenly busy on their phones. "But it's kind of Zen-like, you know? Walking through all those aisles and finding the nail polishes with the craziest names and trying on Burt's Bees samples, or buying a giant container of Cheez Doodles for a dollar and then pigging out on them in the parking lot. We could spend hours in there, and definitely have. It's actually very relaxing. It's like . . . *flow.*"

Nicole made a snorting noise, but didn't say anything. Neither did Drew or Jane. Sometimes when I talked about Harper, or about anything from middle school, really, they would all just get really quiet, and I didn't know why. I thought maybe it was because they thought I was bragging. Like, "Ooh, have I told you yet about this popular blond cheerleader-type girl who's chosen me to be her best friend?!" Seeing that Pathways was so alternative, I could understand why Nicole and the rest of them might not have ever fit in with Harper and her friends. Maybe they felt left out when I brought her up or told them stories about her, even though that was silly—Nicole was unlike any other person I'd ever met. That was kind of the point Nicole was trying to make: There was no one else like her, so don't even try.

"Maybe you guys want to come with us? Harper is so great, and she's always asking about all three of you!" *Shoot,* I thought, of course not thinking to think until *after* I'd invited them. What was I doing? If Nicole came along with me to Walgreens, then I'd have to wear my wings and then Nicole would mention how she'd bought a pair too, and then Harper will know I'm only wearing them because Nicole told me to. Even though the wings were my "thing" before I'd ever even met Nicole. And then Harper would meet my new NAMASTE friends and then we'd all become best friends and then Nicole, Jane, Drew, and I would make care packages to send over to Beverly High and—

I was broken out of my daydream by Nicole. "No, that's okay Lily, I think we'll pass," she said, dismissing the idea with a wave of her hand. "Though you should totally have fun at your . . . Walgreens spree."

"It's a *run*," I said, still smiling like an idiot. "Not like a fashion spree or anything. More like a 'Oh, let's crank up the radio and play Adele, get some frozen yogurt and do a Walgreens run!' run. You have to see some of these names they give their off-brand nail polish. One time, Harper and I found one that was called 'Thanks a Latte' and we couldn't stop saying the name to ourselves over and over again in this really sassy Valley Girl accent, like *'uh, thanks a latte for this super tacky manicure!'*"

Drew cracked first and I smiled at him gratefully.

"Jane, I bet you could do a whole blog post just on the sheer ridonk of some of the stuff you'll find in their beauty section. Seriously, Wet'n'Wild has a whole line named after TV shows . . . 'How I Met Your Magenta', 'Gray's Anatomy', 'Sa-green-a the Teenage Witch' . . ."

"Are you telling me that this mega-chain is actually stocking some meta-commentary on a Melissa Joan Hart show in the beauty aisle?" Jane was almost bouncing from excitement. "I've got to see this for myself."

Jane looked to Nicole, as if asking for permission. Nicole picked up her book bag and started heading for the exit, and for a second I thought that she'd been persuaded, so I gathered my things and started following her out. But then she stopped and motioned for me to stay behind with her while ordering Jane and Drew to meet her at her car.

I loved Nicole's Tesla Roadster. It was hot pink, and everyone was jealous because apparently they hadn't even released the electric cars in novelty colors to the general public yet, but Nicole's parents had one special-ordered to arrive right before school started. Nicole had been giving me rides home every day, practically, except for my first day, when Harper and Rachel came to pick me up. Once I'd started up with all my extracurricular stuff, it didn't make sense for Harper and I to carpool anymore, which actually felt like a blessing in disguise since I wasn't sure what my new Pathways friends would think of my BFF. As much as I loved and was obsessed with Harper, I had to admit that her laid-back style didn't at all fit Pathways' intensely creative vibe. And when I saw Harper, I wanted to be able to fill her in from the beginning about NAMASTE and the fact that the Gawkward Fairy had started a fashion trend. In fact, I'd already started seeing a couple of pairs of wings pop up here and there around the Lane: DIY dragonfly blades made out of luminous cellophane on a girl dressed in a steampunk corset, feathery angel wings on a willowy boy who looked like a Bollywood star, and even a couple of kids who had taken to wearing backpacks shaped like monarch butterflies. Jane dutifully took photos of each new example of "NAMASTE-solidarity"—as Nicole called it— and even though Jane and Drew and Nicole were still waiting for their custom-made wings to arrive, the last thing I wanted was for Harper to think that I was wearing mine just because they had gotten trendy. I still couldn't believe that being trendy was even a thing in my atmosphere.

When Jane and Drew had walked out of sight, Nicole grabbed my arm and turned to me. "Look," she said sweetly, but she was squeezing a little too hard. "I don't care what your friend Harper thinks about falling to the false idols of consumer packaging and corporate megastore commercialism. But I *do* care about what my friend Lily thinks of a store that exploits their employees."

"Hey, they do not!" I said, because for once Nicole was really wrong. I'd done a paper in middle school about businesses with good labor practices. Walgreens was really not as bad as a lot of other places, which is why Harper and I chose it as our fun-day treat emporium.

Nicole sighed at me, as if I were some puppy she was training and she was just totally exasperated with me. "Lily, if you need to run to meet your friend, by all means," Nicole said, stepping aside and loosening her grip and guiding me the rest of the way out of the building. She didn't say anything again until we'd caught up with Jane and Drew, who were standing by the Tesla in the parking lot. "I'm just so sorry that *we* will have to decline." Jane and Drew looked down to the pavement and mumbled apologies.

"Hey look, it's the NAMASTE girls!" A senior boy in a derby hat and suspenders shouted as he drove by in a vintage blue Mustang. A couple girls giggled in the backseat and waved. "Love what you ladies are into!"

"NAMASTE!" The four of us yelled back, as peacefully as we could.

"Is that David Copperfield's son?" I asked, my eyes glued to the crystals hanging from the rearview mirror of the receding car. "The magician prodigy who froze himself in ice and then was dropped out of an airplane?"

None of my friends answered me, as they had all been busy getting into Nicole's Roadster. I still had no idea what her parents did for a living, because at Pathways it was considered gauche to ask (though usually people ended up telling you within the first twenty seconds of meeting them, so I didn't really understand that rule).

I tried to open the door to the roadster, assuming Nicole was at least going to give me a ride, but there was only a metallic *clink* noise telling me it was locked, and my stomach began to sink. Maybe she'd just forgotten to unlock the door? In the passenger and back seats, Jane and Drew were once again wincing into their electronics. Were they texting each other about me? No, that was an insanely paranoid thought. Though . . . why won't Nicole let me in?

I walked around to the driver's side door and knocked at the window.

"Oh, hello," Nicole said, with a mischievous grin. I let out a long breath. Maybe it had been a prank after all? "Look, I would love love *love* to have you come over to help pick this year's NAMASTE delegates—you know we need a rep from the freshman class—" Wait a second . . . I thought I had already been named the freshman delegate . . . "—but I totally understand that you had your heart set on that Walgreens game. Sorry! Tell Harper I said *hi,* though!" And with that, Nicole squeezed her little car out of the parking lot, peeling off with barely a final "NAMASTE!" out the window.

I was left in a cloud of dust, my mouth still hanging open. Nicole was going to take away my freshman delegate title? I was such an idiot! Why did I have to mention Walgreens?

But the worst feeling was yet to come. As I watched my new friends drive off, I realized I no longer had a ride. My parents were at work, and I didn't know anyone else who could drive. Feeling like the actual worst friend on the planet, I took out my phone and texted Harper the bad news in the most cheerful way I could think of.

"So this is your fortress of solitude, huh?" Tim Slater stood next to me in the beauty aisle, shrugging his backpack up onto his shoulder over and over, only to have it immediately begin sliding down his arm again. "It's awful . . . bright in here."

He had a point. The fluorescent lighting in Walgreens, which I usually found to be delightfully crisp and no-nonsense, like in a library or supermarket, was today giving me a headache and making everyone around me look sickly-pale and pasty. I knew I probably looked super washed-out too in my white, fringed-hem minidress, and regretted not adding any colorful accessories, and then I freaked out a little bit because when did I start thinking like my mother?

Still, I really wished I had put on at least some lip gloss, but didn't know why I even cared. It wasn't like anyone who mattered was going to see me. Just Tim. Irked because I didn't know why I was irked, I tugged at my loose braid and shook out my hair, glaring at my split ends and willing them to smooth out.

"You can leave if you don't like it here," I huffed, scooping up brushes, makeup remover, nail trimmers, a bag of gourmet sea salt caramels, body lotion, an eyelash curler, face primer, and a vampy Maybelline nail lacquer called "Green with Envy." And then, because Tim still wasn't getting the hint that I just wanted to be left alone to wait for Lily, I threw in a box of tampons for good measure.

"No way. I'm having a great time," Tim said.

My phone buzzed with a text, and when I checked it, my heart sank.

Lily was bailing. Nicole needed her for something NAMASTE-related. Of course. Why was I surprised? *Was* I even surprised?

"What's up?" Tim asked.

"That was Lily. She's not coming."

"Oh. Hey, I'm really sorry Harper. . . ."

"I'm done shopping," I announced, putting my phone back in my bag. Now I was stuck with Tim yet *again*. At first I was happy that he caught me on my way out the door—I was *that* desperate for company—but now he was just getting on my nerves. Rachel wouldn't be here to pick us up until after her community college class, but all I really wanted to do at this point was go home immediately and hide under the covers for the rest of my godforsaken life.

I can't believe I still hadn't been able to talk about Friday night at Murphy's Ranch with Lily. I shuddered as I remembered the whole scene again now. The worst part of that whole nightmarish scene? I didn't even drink. I wasn't drunk at all. I realized that wanting to get wasted just to show up Kendall would be just as silly as paying money to join a social media site. (Uh, it's been known to happen. That's why I stick with Facebook. And Instagram, and Twitter, but you get the point.) It's so predictable and stupid, and as soon as I saw what was really going on I was like *nope.*

And it would have been great if I had actually *said* "nope," and then just walked away, got on my bike, and went home. But what I did was way, way worse. Instead, I'd just put Kendall's flask up to my lips and pretended to take a sip. Like when they gave me wine at my bat mitzvah. And then it all went downhill from there. . . .

"Hey, have you ever checked out the As Seen on TV section here?" Tim asked, pulling at my arm. "Come on, I've got to show you something." The bright white ceiling tiles glared down at me and the narrow aisles suddenly made me feel claustrophobic. Maybe this was what a panic attack felt like? It was either that, or I was dying.

"It's a Clapper!" Tim exclaimed, pressing a heavy hunk of beige plastic into my hands. "But for your re-mote control!" I knew he was just trying to distract me. At this point he knew more than Lily did about the night at Murphy's Ranch—I'd already told him the whole humiliating story because I thought I was going to go crazy if I didn't talk about it with *someone*—but there are just some things that boys aren't able to un-derstand. If Lily were here, she would have hugged me and told me that she was proud of me for not drinking, and that it didn't matter that I had completely embar-rassed myself, *on camera*, for the whole school to see.

"That's pointless," I told Tim. "Every time someone on TV claps, it'll change the channel. How will you get through even five minutes of *The Voice*?"

"I don't watch those kinds of shows," Tim sniffed. "Still, I see your point."

I turned away from him and closed my eyes. Stu-pid, stupid me: I've never actually *been* drunk, so I had zero real point of reference. But I'd figured it was like it was in movies, where college kids or high schoolers at house parties are jumping up and down with beers and going "Woo! Spring break!" I should have known something was wrong when Kendall kept shouting that someone should be Vining me. But I ignored her because I was in the zone. I was totally method acting, something I learned from when Lily and I made that movie, when I actually spent all this time researching ghosts and spirits and stuff, and I actually started to believe that I was this lost soul looking for her dead husband. I was so far inside the head of the character of "Wasted Chick" that I told Derek Wheeler I *couldn't feel my legs*. Remembering that genius move, I groaned and buried my head in my hands.

Tim pulled a blue box from the bottom shelf, featuring a photo of a grown man with a creepy smile and a bushy mustache, dressed in pajamas and an old-timey sleeping cap, holding a gigantic pillow.

"'Magic Pillow'?" I said, distractedly. "Is this, like . . . a sex thing?"

Tim read off the back of the box. "It's a body pillow that has a 'patented medical fill that stays cool and conforms to your *exact individual needs*.'" He waggled his eyebrows. "But I'm pretty sure its most common use is as a sex doll substitute."

I laughed. "Oh, well in that case, give it here."

Tim turned around and put on the same creepster smile as the guy in the photo. "This one is *mine, dearie*," he falsettoed while grinning lasciviously.

That was too much, and I laughed so hard that people began to look over to see what was wrong with us. Which made me immediately think of Lily again. Being here with Tim, her ex-boyfriend, felt wrong. But I'd known Tim all my life and it was still kind of weird and new for me to think of him as "Lily's ex." Or even as a guy, really. He'd always just been, like, this . . . creature. But now I couldn't help but see that he was also a boy.

Tim was the one who called me up Saturday and told me that there was a new video on SchoolGrams, and that I was in it, and I could tell by the tone in his voice that this wasn't good news. I'd seen girls get burned by these things before—the video of Jessica and Stephanie's fight came to mind first—but I'd never thought that I'd be dumb enough to end up right there with them on the public embarrassment express after only the first week of classes. I wouldn't have even gone to school that following Monday if Rachel hadn't dragged me there, kicking and screaming all the way to the gates of hell. That whole first day back I felt like I was surrounded by emotional bullies shoving cell phones into my face, forcing me to watch my humiliation over and over again. And when they weren't making me relive the *American Horror Story* of my faux pas, they were totally ignoring me.

How had I made such a mess of things in such a short time?

*You're only as vulnerable as your game face lets on,* I'd kept telling myself at school as I tried to put together my features into something resembling a cool girl's. Good posture is more intimidating than any threat. Ridiculous: Even at my most dejected, I was still giving myself MomTips.

"Harper, you shouldn't worry about the School-Grams thing," Tim said now in Walgreens, still holding the creepy body pillow box.

He'd told me the same thing on Monday morning

after he saw me walk through a punishing gauntlet of kids staring and laughing behind my back. "It's like a badge of honor. And you actually seem like you're having a good time in it! You look awesome!" I'd just groaned and buried my head in my hands, trying to ignore the pointed comments Kendall was throwing from the other end of the hallway about "some people not being able to handle their *liquor*."

I had been *such* an idiot on Friday night, stumbling around, pretending to be drunk and slurring like an old-timey hobo. I could feel my face getting red just thinking about it. Like when I kept trying to pick a fight with one guy's skateboard, and the skateboard won. At one point Stephanie came over to help pick me up after one of my many falls, and I told her that she looked like Elsa from *Frozen*, and that she should just "Let it goooo!" I also gave a lovely impromptu monologue about how people are always insisting they have really unique spirit animals—like tamarinds or snow leopards or axolotls—but deep down most of us know we'd really be dogs. Because dogs are the best, and everyone always forgets about dogs, and everyone takes dogs for granted and leaves them at home all day or stops wanting to play with them as soon as they grow up and stop being puppies. . . .

All of that is embarrassing enough, but how was I to know that the night was going to take a turn when some good Samaritans overheard our little party and called the police? (Right? Like, *who does that*?) Suddenly the dark night was pierced by a bunch of flashing lights and screaming teenagers scattering in a million directions. I hadn't done anything wrong (well, except for lying to a bunch of jerks and Derek about being drunk), but still I went right along with everyone else, ducking and weaving through the shrubs and tall grass, and then all of a sudden there's this bright light on me, and I freeze. Like, complete deer-in-headlights freeze. But the cop's flashlight wasn't pointed at me—it was pointed at Derek, who was standing on the trail with his bike. He was kind of leaning into the frame like he was about to fall over, and another cop swooped in on the other side to hold his bike up and force a Breathalyzer in his face.

Who knew that riding a bike while intoxicated in California was illegal? I thought it was just douchey.

Obviously I needed to use some of my Empathy Superpowers on Derek. I knew that I needed to help him, the way I help everyone in peril, but that doing so was going to get me into a whole heap more trouble than I was already in. What I didn't expect was that helping Derek would also result in the ruination of the rest of my life. Like, of course it had to be smelly Derek Wheeler—that walking, talking "Before" in a commercial for ADHD medication—who would go down as not only my first kiss, but the jerk who had videotaped my most humiliating experience to make me the laughing stock of the whole school. And he had to team up with *Kendall* to do it. *After* I tried to help him get out of trouble with the police. That's what you get for trying to be the good guy, I guess. . . .

Before I could inwardly reminisce about the last and worst part of Friday night, I was startled out of my regretful reverie by an unfortunately familiar voice screeching down the beauty aisle.

"*Hello?* Don't you carry MAC at this location? I'm out of Microfine Refinisher and I need more pronto!" It was Kendall, berating a hapless, patient-looking woman, who had the misfortune of being the closest person in her vicinity wearing a Walgreens employee smock.

The woman blinked back, unimpressed. "I'm sorry, but we've never carried that line of cosmetics."

Kendall groaned as the woman turned her back and continued stocking mascara. "Are you *sure*?"

"You must be thinking of Sephora," the woman replied, not even bothering to turn around. "That's usually where whiny girls buy overpriced bronzer, right?"

The look on Kendall's face was priceless, but I could only see half of it because I was still trying to chameleon myself into the aisle to savor the moment. *Too late.* Looking for a new victim to terrorize, Kendall's eyes met mine, and her face lit up with something akin to savage glee.

"Well, if it isn't good old Super Drunk Girl! And what do you know? She has Boy Wonder by her side! Why, this is a huge surprise . . . to absolutely no one."

Tim shrugged with his usual good nature and offered out a hand, which Kendall completely ignored as she zeroed in on me. I felt myself start to sweat under the hot bulbs.

"Gee, things got kind of . . . sloppy the other night, wouldn't you say? Looks like you're doing a lot better today, though." Kendall gestured at Tim. She kept advancing forward and I kept backing away until she bumped me up against a shelf in the Pets and Home section. My leg bit uncomfortably into a box of doggie pee pads, the kind you use to train anxious little terriers, and she had me cornered in there so forcefully that I accidentally kicked some off the shelf. Before I could catch them, a column of pee pad boxes tumbled down and skidded across the floor. Reflexively, I bent down and began picking them up, putting myself at direct eye level with the silver straps of Kendall's high-heel sandals, the same ones she was wearing Friday night.

And to think, none of this would have happened if I hadn't been trying so hard to help Derek. The cops didn't hide their surprise when they saw the crazy girl in the kitten shoes stomping out of the shadows, screaming "Hey! It's cool! That's my bike! I'm not drunk! I'm completely sober! Breathalyze me! Breathalyze me!" And oh, god. The look on my face. A robust mix of sheer panic, desperation, and terror. I'm sure it was the same face I made the next morning, when Tim called to alert me to the video of my "drunken" ramblings all over SchoolGrams. It was posted anonymously, but it was pretty clear who the cinematographer was. Apparently, Derek's film project was more of an unscripted reality series kind of thing than a stand-alone feature. Starring me.

"Hey. You down there," Kendall snickered. "Um, Earth to BasicWear." Great, a new nickname. I guess she was confusing the true meaning of the term "basic" with the fact that I usually only wore "basics," as opposed to her current ensemble: a hot pink mesh onesie and an oversized gold-plated shark she wore on a tiny choker chain. I'm pretty sure I knew who would win in a "being basic" contest.

"I *said*, I'm so glad to see you're doing better after such a sloppy night."

I wanted to respond with something vicious, like "Have you caught any fish in all that mesh you're wearing?" Or something else that I could imagine easily coming out of Kendall's mouth. But who was I to cast stones, when I could so easily see myself hiding behind those bushes with Kendall and her friends, shivering and feeling bad for Derek. *Derek*, who formerly held the title of Dirtiest Kid in Class, but who now seemed kind of sweet and maybe also a little bit sad in a way that I somehow found endearing.

Just then, a familiar voice sounded out behind me. "Hey, what the hell, Kendall?" For a second I thought it was Tim, but then I realized that he was bending down right there next to me, busy helping me clean up the aisle. I shoved one last box back on the shelf and stood up, turned to meet my savior . . . and grimaced in embarrassment the moment I saw who it was.

*Derek*. The same Derek who had studiously avoided acknowledging me in any way at school ever since he posted the video of my "performance."

"Hey Derek," Kendall cooed, immediately adopting a less sociopathic tone. "I was just saying hi to our friend here. We haven't had a chance to catch up with Harper since . . . well, since after the police dropped by the ranch for a little visit!" She shot me the coldest warm smile ever. "God, I mean we were seriously wasted, weren't we? Derek could barely work the video function on his phone. Luckily, he got some great footage anyway."

I was such an idiot . . . hadn't he told me his dreams of being a revolutionary filmmaker? And now the whole school was seeing me in *Spring Breakers 2: Sober and Stupid*. Except, you know, I wasn't as cute as Selena Gomez.

"Hey," Derek mumbled in my direction, practically an admission of guilt. I wanted him to look at me, but he kept his eyes on the ground. Clearly he was too

ashamed . . . was it because he was sorry about releasing the video? Or because he was embarrassed to
have kissed the girl who freaked? It was probably the
second—I hadn't turned out to be the cool girl he believed me to be, and he felt like he had been tricked into
putting his lips on a phony, lying loser like me.

I didn't need to be judged by Derek or Kendall; I
knew that I was better than that. I was still trying to
think of something cutting to say when I realized where
I was: out of breath and in the parking lot. I guess I had
unconsciously followed one of those patented MomTips
that I thought would never come in handy: If you can't
change the room, change the location.

I didn't even know I was running until Tim grabbed
me in the parking lot, saying "Sorry, sorry, I'm so sorry,
Harper." Right then I needed my Lily more than anyone
in the whole world, but she wasn't here. I also needed
human contact from anyone with an actual heart and
soul who didn't see me as a total joke. I collapsed into
Tim and let him wrap his arms around me and I closed
my eyes and felt nothing but the relief of not falling.

"Hello, Pathways!" I sang-yelled into the old-fashioned microphone to a small test audience of a select group of NAMASTE members. It was our first public performance, and I was kind of freaking out—but in a good way! We were stuck in the music room, where the acoustics were pretty awful, but we'd been booted out of the auditorium, this time by the Pathways Improv Dance Troupe, who were practicing some sort of gyrating adaptation of *Pippin*. "We are your entertainers this evening! Allow me introduce you to the one, the only . . . the Jug Judies!"

Our first couple songs were a little shaky—our version of Haim's "My Song 5" wasn't quite as subtly haunting as we would have hoped because my soft vocals were totally overpowered by Drew's enthusiastic tooting. Our "Anything Could Happen" by Ellie Goulding was actually coming together, though, and Jane was killing it on Miley's cover of "Team," now re-covered by us, with just me on the ukulele and some very enthusiastic jug playing—but we didn't really hit our stride until everyone had finished the tempeh stir-fry from our favorite food truck, which Drew had hired to cater the event.

"This next one is also a cover of one of my favorite

artists, Katy Perry," I said cheerfully, announcing my lead-vocals debut. I was getting friendly with the small crowd, marveling over the fact that I, Lily Farson, was *actually* telling an audience information about our music! That I was playing live for real people! And they were listening to me! Sing one of my favorite songs! AH! Yikes. Maybe this was actually a mistake? But before I could lose my nerve I saw Nicole flash a thumbs-up sign from the back of the room—her new purple hair unmissable even in a sea of totally unique faces and a few fluttering wings. Nothing to do now but perform.

"This one I want to dedicate to Nicole and NAMASTE," I said. "For helping me realize my best self is me!" Drew counted off—"One-Two-Three!"— and then suddenly, I was singing.

> *I used to bite my tongue and hold my breath*
> *Scared to rock the boat and make a mess*
> *So I sat quietly, agreed politely*
> *I guess that I forgot I had a choice*
> *I let you push me past the breaking point*
> *I stood for nothing, so I fell for everything*

When filtered through our homegrown sound, the music was like a playground rhyme set to a lullaby.

> *I got the eye of the tiger, a fighter,*
> *dancing through the fire*
> *'Cause I am a champion and you're*
> *gonna hear me roar*
> *Louder, louder than a lion*
> *Cause I am a champion and you're*
> *gonna hear me roar*

As soon as it had begun, the song was over. Everyone cheered and the applause was deafening, thanks to the room's weird acoustics.

"Fairy girl! Fairy girl!" Started a chant from the back of the crowd, and pretty soon everyone was calling out "Fairy Girl! Fairy Girl!"

Jane, Drew, and I took our bows, and I squeezed their hands as tight as I could. I couldn't believe how different everything was. How different being popular . . . or, not popular . . . but being *liked* was! Even though we had yet to play a real show that was open to the whole school, it seemed that everyone was interested in us and wanted the chance to talk to the Jug Judies. For instance, everyone knew about the party Jane was throwing to celebrate the re-launch of her FancyFashionFeminist blog, and at least twenty people had already asked if I was going, and if the Jug Judies were going to play. Even now, as we packed up and walked down the hall toward the Lane, a couple of junior girls who spent all their time in Cinema sessions asked where they could get wings like mine. Two freshman girls I hadn't met before approached shyly and asked if I would pose for their drawing session. It was the same day as an environmental nature walk I was taking with NAMASTE, so I told them that I'd have to think about it. A boy in a plaid shirt and adorable Harry Potter glasses asked if he could get my autograph.

"Seriously?" I laughed.

Even when I wasn't hanging out with Nicole or Jane or Drew, kids in the Lane would call me over and ask if I wanted to eat lunch with them. ("Can't, going to band practice!" "Next time, then? *Ciao*, Lily!" "NAMASTE!")

"Great job, Lily!" Jane said, putting her arm around

me. "You really are this beaming ball of good energy." I blushed . . . no one had called me a beaming ball before!

The other good thing about being part of NAMASTE is that even the teachers treat you like you're special. Earlier that week Jamie Godfrey asked me to bring in the film I made with Harper, and we spent a whole session analyzing its themes and our artistic vision. Apparently my movie was a lot deeper than I'd thought: Godfrey said it was "a cinematic interpretation of female colonialism."

The only part of my Pathways schedule that kind of sucks is the hour I have after lunch, in a session called Life Lessons. It's supposed to teach us about the real world and giving back to the community, but so far it's just like giant group therapy. Our instructor, Bill, always wears wool sweaters, even when it's like eighty degrees out (which is literally always because we're in LA) and is constantly eating beets from plastic Whole Foods containers with his fingers, which in turn are perpetually red. We met in the gymnasium, where everyone sat in a giant circle, about thirty of us of all different grades, and went around the room "sharing" our feelings.

Most of the time kids would just say normal stuff. Like, "My dad decided making an appearance at Cannes was more important than coming to my one-man show" or "I used to be inspired by Bret Easton Ellis but then he decided to remodel the place next to ours and the noise is driving me insane and maybe *Less Than Zero* wasn't even that good?" Once in a while though, someone would say something really crazy. The day of our practice concert, a really tall boy with a voice like a girl's stood up and told Bill he had something to say.

"So I just found this out," the boy began, his eyes focusing on the ground. "And I don't really know what to think about it yet . . ."

"Go on." Bill motioned with a beet-stained hand.

"Well, so, I went to the doctor because I was getting all these stomachaches, and I guess they saw something in there, and I was really scared it was going to be cancer." The room held its collective breath . . . cancer was the kind of serious topic that wasn't joked about in the land of SPF 100. "But when they removed the . . . mass, well . . . I guess what happened was that, before I was even born, I had a twin. And I ate him. Or her. Like, in the *womb*."

I know it wasn't supposed to be funny, but the combination of his sweet voice and the morbid story it was telling, and then watching everybody's grossed-out reaction, well, I couldn't keep a straight face. I could feel my mouth twitching, and then I caught the eye of that cute senior in suspenders who drove the blue Mustang, and he had his hand over his mouth but I could tell he was smiling. The next thing I knew, I was snorting back laughter with tears streaming down my face. It was the kind of laughter I hadn't busted out since middle school, when Harper and I would come down with daily laugh attacks.

As if on cue, the rest of the class started giggling, too. Quietly at first, but then louder and louder. The tall boy looked surprised for a moment, and then struggled to talk over everyone with his soft voice. "I mean, it was before I was born! When I was in my mom's uterus!" He looked totally mortified, which made me feel bad for a second, and for some reason I was struck by a quick flashback to that day in fourth grade gym class, when I first met Harper. Because I realized that, if Harper were there, I probably wouldn't have started laughing at all. Harper is supersensitive to other people's feelings and never likes to laugh at someone for saying something weird—*especially* when it was something that person didn't have any control over. Neither did I, as a general rule, but . . . "in my mom's uterus" was just too much. Even Bill, trying to get everyone to settle down, was not doing a very good job of hiding a bewildered grin at the absurdity of it all.

After class, though, I felt terrible for being the one responsible for starting a class-wide laughing fit after some poor kid was just trying to get something off his chest. I told Nicole about what happened, hoping she'd say something to make me feel better or give me some pointers on how to make amends, but instead she just started cracking up, too.

"Lily, it's totally fine to laugh when someone says something ridiculous like that in front of a group of strangers," she told me. "Laughter was your natural reaction, and by acting on it, you were being true to yourself."

"I guess that makes sense . . ." I said. Maybe, without Harper there to influence me, this was just what I was like. I was a girl who laughed when something was funny, rather than one who analyzed scenarios to death to figure out whether it was okay to laugh.

"Oh my gosh!" a somewhat familiar voice called out from behind me, and I turned around. "Lily? Lily Farson, is that you?"

It took me a minute to recognize Beth-Lynne Jacoby, the daughter of the couple who ran PuppyTales. She was a year older, used to volunteer a ton at the shelter, and had made it to a couple of Harper's PuppyBashes, and although Harper and I weren't that close to her, she was always super nice and bubbly. Even though she was roughly our age, she reminded me of someone's aunt, with large, frizzy hair that was always held in place with the same tortoiseshell clip, and penchant for extra-large flannel shirts and unflattering Levi's. She had a wide, broad nose and a loud, horsey laugh that stopped just short of being startling. But all that could have been excused (and since when did I critique people's sartorial choices like this??), but the worst was yet to come. Beth-Lynne had horrible taste in shoes, as was evidenced by the bright pink Ugg boots she was sporting today.

I had heard from Harper that Beth-Lynne had cut down on her volunteer work last year when she started feeling the strain of high school AP-level courses, but I had no idea she was at Pathways. Don't get me wrong—I liked her a lot—but standing there in the hallway in her signature oversized shirt, workman boots and jeans, she looked about as creative as a Denny's value meal.

"Beth-Lynne? Hey! I had no idea you went here!"

"Yup," she said. "Since seventh grade. I'm in the Science Tech wing though . . . we pretty much keep to ourselves. We call ourselves Pathways 2.0." Beth-Lynne cracked herself up, braying with laughter at her own joke. I tried to match her enthusiasm, but my chuckle caught in the back of my throat.

"How are you?" Beth-Lynne asked. "And how's Harper? Still hanging with the bad dogs?"

"Well, you know Harper," I said weakly. I heard a sound behind me, and turned to see Nicole tapping her toe impatiently and scrutinizing my old acquaintance's get-up. Beth-Lynne, totally oblivious, plowed forward.

"Man, Lily! It's so good to see you! But I've got to ask, girl, are you really still wearing those wings? I remember when you first showed up at PuppyTales when you were eleven in those things! My mom thought you had just come from a rehearsal of a school play!"

"Ahem," Nicole said, making that throat-clearing noise but not actually clearing her throat. She pushed her way in front of me and looked Beth-Lynne up and down. "Bethel, is it?"

"Uh, it's actually Beth-L—"

"Whatever. How dare you make fun of Lily's iconoclasm while you stand there, encouraging conformity of fashion trends in corporate America with your mall jeans and that hideous Australian footwear. Made in Taiwan, no doubt. Double Ugg."

Oh my god, what was Nicole doing? Beth-Lynne just stood there, looking totally stunned. A small group had gathered around our little circle, nudging each other and taking out their cell phones to record Nicole's takedown of this hapless girl.

"Lily," Nicole said, startling me out of the imaginary shell I'd retreated into. "Tell Bathilda here that you refuse to let her shame you into not wearing the wings that are literally the most important symbol of your individuality!"

Beth-Lynne's eyes bulged like she had been slapped. I wanted to tell her to close her mouth, which was gaping open: She wasn't doing herself any favors by just standing there. Even though she hadn't done anything offensive, not really, I felt myself getting unusually irritated at Beth-Lynne. Maybe she didn't mean anything by it, but Nicole was right: She was sort of putting down my look. Ever since I moved to Los

Angeles, people have felt like they have the right to just stop and stare at my wings or make comments—"Hey, Tink, got me some magic fairy dust?" "What's with the costume?" "Can you grant me wishes?"—without stopping to think that maybe me wearing my grandmother's outfit wasn't an invitation to question my entire identity.

I honestly had no idea what to do. On the one hand, Nicole was right: Beth-Lynne, whether she meant it or not (and in my heart I knew she hadn't) had been *rude*. On the other hand, I knew Beth-Lynne, and knew that she, like Harper, cared about saving animals' lives and was generally a good person, if a little clueless. But there was Nicole, staring daggers at me, and I could tell by her look that my future membership in NAMASTE would be determined in how I answered. I had to make a decision.

So I made one.

"Beth-Lynne, instead of being so obsessed with my style, maybe you should find one of your own," I said icily. "You notice how I never ask you why you're supporting animal cruelty every time you put on a pair of those *fugly* pink Uggs? Why do you assume I have all day to answer your questions about what *I* wear?"

"You tell her, Fairy Girl!" someone shouted from the hallway crowd. Nicole smiled triumphantly and for a second I felt vindicated and righteous: Damn the man! But that lasted as long as it took to take in the look of Beth-Lynne's reaction.

"I'm sorry, Lily," Beth-Lynne mumbled. "I . . . I didn't mean it like that." Beth-Lynne had never been that gifted with words, but I knew that she was truly sorry . . . for ever talking to me in the first place. Her shoulders slumped and her usually milk-pale cheeks flamed bright red. She could barely look me in the eye, and I realized that I had totally, utterly humiliated her. The way she looked at me . . . well, I never want to be looked at that way ever again. Her eyes spilled over with tears, and she hurried away without saying another word.

"See?" said Nicole. "If we hadn't said those things, we would have been lying to both her *and* to ourselves. There's nothing wrong with being honest."

"Right," I said. All I could think about was Harper, and that I was thankful she wasn't there to see this. Because if she had been, I don't think she would have ever spoken to me again. At least Pathways had banned students using SchoolGrams, because if there had been video footage of my dressing down of Beth-Lynne, I wasn't sure I'd ever be able to look in the mirror again.

On Wednesday, Rachel offered to take me to my PuppyTales volunteer session. When she dropped me off at the Beverly Gardens Park, she said to text her whenever I need to be picked up. Lately I've noticed that Rachel's been being eerily nice to me, which meant even my snarky older sister felt bad for me. At least I didn't have to deal with her and her friends teasing me on top of everything else—that's one thing going my way. Well, that and my awesome grades: the combination of Lily-withdrawal-weirdness and a fear of running into Kendall anywhere outside of school meant that I wasn't really leaving the house much, and with nothing to do there but study and absorb some new MomTips, I've been pulling straight As.

In the summer the park tends to get overrun by tourists, but now that fall was arriving and everyone was back in school, there were fewer people than usual sitting on the perfectly manicured lawns, alternating between lattes, spring waters, and bottles of cold-press green juice. (Los Angelenos can micromanage their beverages like nobody's business.) I was running late: By the time we pulled up, there was already a line of kids and exasperated parents snaking back behind a tan-and-white RV that read "PuppyTales Mobile Center." One of the panels of the RV was open, like a food truck whose window extended all the way to the floor. In fact, when the Jacobys originally bought the Mobile Center, it was a recently retired vegan taco truck, but they renovated the kitchen and bathroom area so that now the entire space is used to transport their rescues.

As part of our organization's outreach program, the Jacobys invite kids and families into the center once a month, and let them play with some of the dogs. They also give out literature for the kids to hand to their parents when they (obviously) run back and beg their moms to please please *please* let them get that Jack Russell terrier puppy with the crooked tail and the wonky ear. We also go to schools, low-income areas, and occasionally rehab centers and correctional facilities (though I'm not old enough to volunteer at those places yet). I also help out as the PuppyTales social media manager, which means I put the word out about where the Mobile Center is going next, and let our followers know what dogs we have up for fostering and adopting. My goal is to eventually become an "angel parent," which means I would get to host some of the puppies in my home to help them adjust to family life. But I can't right now because a) You have to be at least eighteen to be an angel and b) my mom is allergic.

I don't want to be a vet or anything. I just really love dogs. Lily and I used to joke that the reason I get along so well with people is because I'm able to love unconditionally, the way dogs do. I know it's silly, but there's something magical about the way dogs look at the world. They're loyal and devoted, and they don't judge you the way that you *know* cats do. Dogs don't run or fly or swim away like other animals do when people try to pet them.

They are just love, manifested as bundles of fur and paws.

Of course, some dogs need a little more love than others. The rescues at PuppyTales have had hard lives. Many of them have been beaten and trained to view other dogs and animals as enemies. Not to be overly dramatic, but after my first week at Beverly High, I could kind of see their point of view. We're only as nice as we're allowed to be, we're only as good as our conditioning. Some might find that worldview cynical, but there you have it. At least if I decided to bite Kendall, I wouldn't get put down. Probably.

PuppyTales is a total labor of love for the Jacobys, who are good friends with my parents. Mr. Jacoby is a mad inventor type, but he's never invented anything real before. He made a fortune back in the 80s after he bought a patent for some weird, super specific car part that no one had ever heard of, and that all of a sudden became standard issue in every single GM vehicle ever made. Their daughter, Beth-Lynne, used to volunteer at PuppyTales all the time and was a regular PuppyBash attendee, but eventually she got so busy with all her honors classes that she had to cut way back and I hardly ever see her anymore. Now I spent even more time volunteering for the Jacobys, picking up some of the extra duties Beth-Lynne left behind, like coordinating cage clean-up, scheduling vet appointments, and organizing awareness benefits, like PuppyBash, which I've done with Lily every year on the night before my birthday. Well, every year until this one, I guess. My birthday was in less than two weeks, and Lily still hadn't brought up our plans for Friday *or* Saturday.

This was especially weird. Lily knew how important

her birthday parties were to me. Growing up, my mom would always use our birthdays as test labs for any new product or service she was promoting on her site. On my eighth birthday, I received a gift certificate for a laser hair removal treatment, which Mom promised to keep in a security box for me until I turned sixteen. Another year, Rachel woke up to discover three men from *Ambush Makeover* in her room tearing everything apart: Mom's "present" to her was an on-camera makeover and redecorating session with some second-rate Bravo-lebrity wannabes. For two years afterward, both Rachel's bedroom and outfits were dominated by ruffles, undertones of seafoam green, and a general air of being overpriced and basic.

It wasn't that Mom didn't love us. It's just that, despite all her MomTips about how to hack motherhood, she needed a lot of help planning and managing her own life. She was much less independent than Rachel or me; for instance, she always needed someone to remind her when to pack for her next conference, and then she needed another someone to tell her what to pack. Even our lame birthdays required all of Mom's staff on deck—drivers, assistants, publicists, nutritionists, trainers, data analysts, interns, documentary film crews—just to support her supporting us. By the time I was ten, I had already figured out that not bringing up birthdays to my mother was the best way to ensure a drama-free house in which I celebrate quietly—Rachel and I learned pretty early that the more we'd talk about our upcoming birthdays, the more cameras and nonessential staffers would be involved in the "celebration."

Of course, all that changed the moment I first walked downstairs in fifth grade to discover the giant puppy surprise party Lily had planned for me. I don't think I ever told her how much it actually meant to me, to have a friend who made the day about me, and not about herself.

"Why, hello there, Harper!" Mrs. Jacoby waved as I slumped out of the car, lost in thought.

"Sorry I'm late, Mrs. Jacoby!" I gave her a big smile as I climbed up the Center's retractable staircase.

"Oh, don't even think about it. You're always so dependable, Harper."

Secretly I felt a little bad. I hadn't been spending as much time with PuppyTales since high school had started, telling my mom that I was too busy with work. The truth was, I hadn't felt like leaving the house since Canyon Park and then the Walgreens incident.

Today the Mobile Center was full of noise and smells and shedding fur—all things that are as familiar to me as the cast of canine regulars inside. There was Humps, the sweet, blind pit-bull the Jacobys rescued five years ago, now so arthritic that she walked with her hind legs hunched up. Cocoa, a brown Labrador retriever mix with white patches on his chest and a bandana around his neck, making him look like he belonged on the cover of a Boxcar Children book. Dottie and Bandit were both part Maltese and part mutt, and they looked so similar that we were almost positive that they were siblings. Maxine, a yappy terror of a terrier who only calmed down when she was gnawing at a squeak toy, but was so loyal to the Jacobys that she once tried to attack a coyote prowling in their backyard to protect them. Buffy, the Great Dane with the gold eyes. Bruschetta the poopy poodle. Manny the Chihuahua. Georgie the beagle. Tonto the Welsh Corgi, who was so beautiful that he'd been adopted by at least three families, despite our warning all of them that he refused to be housebroken. Poor Tonto never lasted a week in any home before he was back at PuppyTales.

"Oh Mommy, can I hold the puppy?" A blond post-toddler waddled over in a fitted cardigan and suspenders, wearing a porkpie hat and the type of chunky, plastic rimmed glasses you usually see on aging indie rockers. Without waiting for an answer, the child put his hand near Maxine's cage which caused his mom, who up until that point had been engrossed with her cell phone, to snatch her son's hand in midair like a magic trick.

"Wolfgang! You don't know what kinds of diseases these animals have!" She scolded, vacantly, still scrolling through BabyFashionastas.com with one hand while admonishing her son with the other. I've got a cozy space in my heart for moms who can multitask like that, since they're the ones signing up for sessions with my mom, and thus essentially paying for my home and meals.

"Oh, don't worry, ma'am," I said with a bright smile. "All of our dogs have had their shots and are up to date with their medical records. It's the *people* around here you have to be careful of!" It was a joke I'd been telling for so long now, I didn't even feel that weird about throwing in a wink.

"See, Mom?" Wolfgang whined in a petulant voice. "He's not going to hurt me! Can I play with him? Please?"

The mom, blond and coiffed, looked at me doubtfully. Obviously she hadn't come here with the intention of adopting a dog; she probably hadn't even realized where her son had been dragging her until it was too late. This kind of prospective foster parent was what my mom would call a "tough sell," but I could use the distraction of a challenge.

"I was such a handful at his age," I said, nodding my chin toward Wolfgang. "I drove my parents nuts asking for a dog all the time."

"Yes, well, we don't really have the time to take care of another family member," Mama Wolfgang said, starting to move away. I could see the tears spring preemptively to Junior's eyes. Man, sometimes these kids made it so easy.

"Of course, we're not trying to sell you on these dogs," I said, as sweetly as possible. I opened up Maxine's cage and let her scramble into my arms, where she promptly began her ascension upward to frantically lick my face. "They pretty much do that themselves, anyway." I laughed as Maxine's wet snout snuffled at my neck. "Aw, who's a good girl?"

Wolfgang looked up at his mom, his face as red as mine must have been, in anticipation of an oncoming tantrum. Mama Wolfgang looked beaten.

"Okay darling, if they have an area where you can play with it . . . her . . . I could use ten minutes of me-time, anyway."

Wolfgang and I beamed. "Of course, right this way, ma'am," I said, leading them to our outdoor playpen. As soon as I put Maxine down in the pen, the puppy ricocheted at the highest velocity possible into Wolfgang's torso, thumping him down and sending his ridiculous hat sprawling across the grass. There was a stunned silence, and then the kid began to giggle.

"Again, again!" He demanded, and Maxine, whose energy never subsided, was only too happy to comply.

Later, when Wolfgang's mom was talking to Mrs. Jacoby about Maxine's possible reaction to a gluten-free diet, I slipped out of the Mobile Center and headed toward the park to clear my head.

Though people think of Californians as being ultra-laid-back, the truth is that Los Angeles can be just as stressful as anywhere else in the world. I think we—and by "we" I mean the people who have grown up here, not the ones who come here chasing dreams of stardom or whatever—are better at pretending to be easygoing and relaxed, because we've spent so much time practicing how to give off the "not sweating it" vibe. It's as if we're always auditioning for something, and whoever's the most chill will win the part, but then we don't even *care* if we don't get the part. We're just happy to be here. Sometimes we keep up the mirage of coolheadedness so well that we almost buy into it ourselves. It's kind of tempting to present this image of yourself to the world, where you're all like, "Oh, I love surfing and donuts and Boba tea and macrobiotics and Soul Cycle, la-la! Let's all go to Coachella and jam out and eat fro-yo while doing yoga!"

But inside our heads—well, inside mine at least—it's more like "Oh my god, how badly did I wreck my life before the world even had a chance to wreck it for me?"

In Beverly Gardens, there is a smaller-scale model of the Hollywood Sign. But instead of being gigantic and up in the mountains, it's in the middle of a park, surrounded by gorgeous cypress and ficus trees. I don't know why—it's kind of like my Walgreens obsession—but I always felt more drawn to that smaller version of our famous beacon of hope.

I used to think it was normal to like things that everyone else in the world liked: convenience stores, the Hollywood sign, dogs. Now I was starting to think that, in this town, my attraction to normality was what made me a secret weirdo.

As I approached the walled entrance to the sign, I recognized a pair of fairy wings sitting on the lip. *It couldn't possibly be* . . . was all I had time to think before I saw the wings flutter and the figure they were attached to turn around, stand up, and come running toward me. All of a sudden the be-winged creature knocked me to the ground harder than Maxine had with Wolfgang.

"HARPER!" Lily screeched, gracelessly tripping into me with a giant bear hug. "Puppyyyyyy!"

I smiled and mumbled out a greeting that got lost in our mad scramble to untangle from each other.

"Namaste, my sister!" Lily giggled and nudged my shoulder, as if she was about to start a fight with me. "How are you? I can't believe it's been so long since I've seen your face! I know I said it before, but I'm still really sorry about missing Walgreens the other day."

I delicately brushed myself off, waiting for my best friend to explain why her text messages had been eerily cheery and placating and emoji-filled these past two weeks. A smiley here and an XO there: THAT does not a Bestie convo make. I'd really needed her after the Murphy's Ranch disaster, and all she could do was tell me to cheer up and try to distract me with stories about how cool her new friends are.

But I couldn't afford to be mad at Lily right now. Just seeing her again made me want to bask in the warmth of our BFF vibes and finally press Pause on the full shame spiral I'd been tragically circling since the first day of school. But I willed myself to stay steely. Something was up with Lily, and I needed to know what. And I couldn't let her get away with being a zombie-bestie any longer.

"I know, I've been the worst friend lately. I'm sorry.

But I promise I'll make it up to you." Lily always erred on the side of melodrama. Now, with a fake wail, she threw herself onto me and started tickling that spot right under my arm that drives me crazy with laughter. It was hard not to soften into a big pile of warm BFF goo, especially when I was literally collapsing into a pile of giggles, but I had to stay strong. Or at least aloof, until I got the answers I wanted.

"So what's been going on," I asked, disentangling myself from Lily. "I've been trying to talk with you—like, really talk with you—for forever. You've barely sent me any updates!"

"I've sent you updates!" I could see the tears start to tremble in her eyes.

"I mean *real* updates, Lily. Not just smiley faces and exclamation points."

"That's not all I've been sending you." Lily gave a dramatic sigh and wiped away the last of her tears, which had ended as abruptly as they'd started. She pulled out her cell phone. At first I thought she was going to show me something—I had the weird hope that maybe there was something in that tiny hunk of metal that would explain her abrupt absence from my life— but she just looked at it, squinted, and then put it back in her pocket.

"Is that a Samsung Galaxy?" I asked. You can't just change your phone and not tell your BFF. That was like coming to school and announcing that you were changing your name to "Robot Monster."

"Oh yeah." Lily looked sheepish. "Nicole says iPhones are made by exploited Chinese laborers."

"Whatever. Can you please just explain where you've *been* since school started? I mean, I know where you've been, physically. But where have *you* been," I said, pointing to her heart. "I've been texting you my heart and soul and I feel like all I'm getting back are auto-responses from a robot programmed to always be happy. I feel like I'm going crazy. But now I'm more concerned that maybe my *bestie* is going crazy. Who answers BFF emergency texts with rows and rows of flowers and sad faces and then tips on how to relieve stress through the practice of yoga? That is straight-up ILLEGAL behavior!"

"Well when you put it like that. . . ." Lily said, looking frazzled. "Things are just . . . really . . . different right now. This band is taking up so much of my time, like more than I realized it would, and Jane just named me the new creative director of her blog and we're in the middle of a big re-launch and I know how upset you are about stuff at Beverly High and it breaks my *heart* that you have to deal with all those terrible people there every day, and anyway I guess it just got to this point where I've been feeling so bad about all that that I didn't even know how to tell you. . . ."

"Tell me what?"

"Um, well. That I can't go to your PuppyBash this year," Lily said it slowly, her eyes squinting and her hands up at her chest, as if she were bracing herself for an attack. But even if I'd wanted to attack her (I kind of did), I couldn't. Her announcement stunned me so much that I felt frozen, rock solid, in place. She went on. "It's just that, like I said, Jane is re-launching her blog, and as creative director there's so much that I'm responsible for. Jane and I have to work all day and night on this party she's throwing for the re-launch, and the only free time she has for prep is on the same day as PuppyBash. I know this is awful and I tried everything I could to avoid it, but I promise I'll make it up to you. I'm really, really sorry Harper. I'm sorry in a million different ways."

I narrowed my eyes. This was so typical Lily. She's always been in her own universe, but at least before it was a universe I have always been a part of. I was always there for Lily through her drama. Like when I rescued her from the clutches of an Emotional Vampire at her summer arts camp two years ago. Or that time that Quebecois exchange student claimed to be Lily's third cousin and accused Lily of stealing her "look," because one time she had worn angel wings in a school pageant. In Quebec. Or the time when Lily didn't take my advice and dated Tim Slater, only to break up two months later. I was always there for Lily when her wings needed mending, and what does she do? Act totally emotionally vacant over texts and then tell me she can't come to our annual pre-birthday tradition. It was really hard not to be annoyed at her lack of thoughtfulness.

Lily's phone had magically popped back into her hand. She was pretending not to look at it, but the screen was so gigantic that it was impossible for her *not* to see it without even trying. This was the girl who had once asked me if Twitter was a "web forum for bird calls." Catching me glaring, she put away her phone again.

"I was just checking the time," she said. *Yeah, right.* "Look, I said I was sorry. And I *will* make it up to you. And I'm here now. Tell me everything. Tell me about that awful girl—what's her name? Kendra?"

"Kendall. Stephanie and Derek met her at summer camp." I tried not to be annoyed at her late-in-the-game catch-up. "She's actually the worst person I've ever met. *She* showed up, when we were supposed to meet at Walgreens the other day. She backed me into a corner and

kicked a bunch of pee pads in my face!" I saw Lily's confused look, but just decided to press forward. "Anyway,
she is this sociopathic, domineering crazy person. It
feels like it could turn into a total *Black Swan* scenario.
I think she's going to murder me in my sleep."

"She sounds awful," said Lily. "Where does this
Murderer live? I'll get rid of her before she has a chance
to kill you in your sleep."

"Ha. I don't know. Maybe I'm just becoming a Spiral."

"Naw. Impossible. Of the two of us, I'm the queen of
Spiral Mountain. Hey, so what *happened* last weekend?
What did this girl do to you?"

I took a deep breath. I'd been dying to tell Lily about
the video and what happened at the ranch, but now that
she was right in front of me, I didn't know where to begin. As I was trying to come up with the words, a loud
chirping noise interrupted my thoughts. Lily frowned
and sneaked a look down at her phone.

"Agh, hold on, I have to answer this . . ." Lily trailed
off and turned her back to me, but I could see the corner
of her mouth curl up in a smile as she whispered excit-
edly on the phone. The worst part was hearing her corny
little gasps and giggles, like she was trying to contain
herself but *absolutely couldn't* because whatever was going on in her phone was *just that fascinating*. Finally she
hung up.

"Okay," Lily said as she turned back around. "My
friend Jane is in the park, taking photos for her website
and says I should go over to the Kusama Gardens ASAP.
I'm sure it's fine if you come too!"

The Kusama sculptures were really cool: giant fi-
berglass flowers in trippy *Alice in Wonderland* colors (the
original Disney, not the scary Johnny Depp one). But

right then I didn't feel much like meeting any of Lily's new friends.

"I'm going to pass," I said. "But you should totally go, if that's what you want to do." I was making it pretty clear, I thought, that it would be totally unacceptable for Lily to leave the conversation as-is. But Lily, being the Spiral Queen, wasn't very good at reading body language for social cues (or *words* for social cues, actually. Any cues at all: not Lily's strong suit).

For a moment, Lily looked torn. "Okay," she said, "but . . . I really do want to hear what's going on with you, Harper!" She seemed to consider me then, scrunching up the side of her mouth and giving me a long look. "Are you sure you don't want to come? We should really talk about . . . you know, your actual birthday plans at some point. I'm really sorry about the PuppyBash. Maybe you could do it with Stephanie? Or even . . . Tim?"

"No, that's okay. I think I'll skip it this year," I said. I wasn't even planning on really skipping it, I just couldn't give this one to her. I couldn't let her get away with thinking this was at all okay. The Lily I used to know would have never ignored me, would never have canceled our annual pre-birthday ritual, and would never spend more time looking at her phone than at the beautiful world around her. This person in front of me was becoming a total stranger. I didn't know what her deal was anymore.

And then, with no bestie to confide in and nowhere to direct my anxiety, I really started to spiral—about everything. My feelings about Derek were just totally jumbled up. Before school started, Derek barely existed in my world. And now not only was he my first kiss, but the entire reason my life had become such hell. I had let a rando upset me!

But on the other hand, I had *liked* kissing him. And I still couldn't help but think of him as just like one of these rescued puppies that needs a good home. A really cute puppy that I could take home and bathe and teach some manners to and . . . no! This was the type of obsessive thinking that, combined with my Internet stalking tendencies, would get me in big trouble. I stopped myself from spiraling and turned an icy glare back to Lily.

"Aw, Harper. Don't do that. I'll help you figure out another solution. PuppyBash *will* happen this year! But . . . you promise you're not mad at me?"

I was weighing my response when a familiar voice called my name.

Lily and I turned around to see a lanky figure jogging toward us.

"Hey, Stephanie."

"Hey, Harper," she said as she trotted up to join us. I backed up a step without thinking about it, until I was standing between her and Lily. Though Stephanie hadn't been avoiding me like the rest of the kids from Murphy's Ranch were, she also hadn't gone out of her way to sit next to me in the cafeteria or anything. And I didn't want her bring it up in front of Lily, who still didn't know what I pariah I am.

"I thought I saw you with . . . with . . ." Stephanie was out of breath, craning her neck to get a look at Lily's fairy costume. "Oh, it IS you. Hi Lily."

"*Namaste*, Stephanie," Lily said, grabbing my hand and guiding me back to face her and turn away from Steph. "We were just catching up," she said to Steph. Was it just my imagination, or was Lily giving one of the most popular girls in the 90210 zip code a brush-off? Another sign that this was zombie-Lily: the real version always got along with Steph, the nicer half of the hair-scream twins, and though we'd never been close-close, the three of us definitely had a pretty rich history of sleepovers and day trips between us. But apparently Lily had forgotten all about Steph, as well.

"Sure, oh sure." Stephanie bit her bottom lip, still staring at Lily as if she were an exotic, slightly deranged animal—just like she had in gym class on Lily's first day of school. Lily glared right back with a level of snooti-ness that seemed totally foreign on a girl in gossamer wings and a poodle skirt. Unlike the costumed Lily, Stephanie's faded denim shorts and mint green peasant blouse made her look like the spokesmodel for Casual Normality. The fact that she had on pink knee pads and was carrying her longboard just contributed to her effortless-chic vibe. She was even wearing a helmet—black and chrome and sleek. Leave it to Stephanie Adler to make safety gear look cool.

Stephanie looked at us and smiled, but didn't leave. Surprisingly, the Gawkward Fairy's powers of social awk-wardness didn't seem to be working, because Stephanie refused to take the hint. She kept staring at the two of us . . . well, mainly at Lily, who had dropped my hand and retreated even farther behind me.

"Um?" Lily said, and I felt a surge of embarrassment.

"Yeah," Stephanie said, "it's just that . . . I hadn't seen you guys in a while. Both of you, together, I mean." Stephanie's eyes seemed to laser right through me and cut straight into Lily. "Do you want to hang out? I'll just be sitting with Matt. . . . Lily, you remember Matt Musher from school, right? Anyway, we're sitting by the fountain, if you wanted to, like, come by. Okay." Stephanie turned and started walking away, stopping after a couple feet to set her longboard on the ground. But instead of leaving, she just rolled it back and forth with one of her shoes, as if she were deliberating. Finally, she made up her mind and called over her shoulder: "Harper? Me and Matt are just friends, if that's what you're wondering."

Lily looked at me and shrugged. "Okay," I called back, confused by so many things. "That's good to know."

"Bye, Harper. Bye, Lily." Stephanie pushed off without turning around again.

"What was *that* about?" Lily was already deep into the world of her phone again, probably texting Jane, but at least she looked up to direct her question at me. And though I was still mad at her, and I still didn't have answers—about where she'd been both emotionally and physically, about what was going on with her, about the status of my birthday plans—in that moment I knew the perfect thing to say.

"Stephanie has actually been a really great friend to me lately. I'm probably going to go over there in a minute."

I expected Lily to look hurt, but instead she just smiled, oblivious. "That's great, Harper! Things have been moving so fast, haven't they? Let's GChat soon, okay? And I promise, I'm going to plan something extra special for your birthday to make up for the PuppyBash."

"Sure," I said. "Whatever."

The trick about cell phones, I thought while waiting for Jane in the flower garden, is to constantly be doing something with them, even if it's something like typing a list that you'd usually write longhand. People will just assume you're talking to your friends, and while it's still rude, it doesn't generate the weird looks that, say, reading a book at the dinner table will.

I sat there typing nonsense into my phone, not really knowing how I came up with that tactic, and similarly not knowing why I had walked away from seeing Harper feeling so upset. It's like, here is the thing that Harper really doesn't get about me right now: It's not all good vibes and sprinkles and rainbows in my world. People constantly expected things from me now, needed me to live up to their ideas of what wacky, peculiar girls should act like at all times. It's actually *exhausting*.

I felt like I was going to pass out and had to buy myself one of those butter-smeared sticks of roasted corn from Golden Maize, a nearby food cart.

I'd spent my entire life not fitting in, which was just fine with me. I'd never needed a lot of friends or a group of kids to sit at a lunch table with me. All of that looked kind of boring, frankly, and I had always told myself that I would never change who I was just to lose my self-identity to a group mentality. The irony was that now I'm at a new school, where I made all these friends pretty much on accident, all because of the exact same things that made people look at me sideways before: mumble-talking, my obsession with folklore and old-timey stuff, being an over-achieving creative type in general.

So now I'm finally in a place where I can say with some authority that I was wrong. Having a bunch of friends isn't boring. It's *exhausting*. All these demands: "Lily, show us your wings!" "Lily, play us some music!" "Lily, be the freshman face of NAMASTE!" "Lily, be the Gawkward Fairy at all times, and don't for one second relax or wear an outfit from this decade or say anything less than totally precious!" "Lily, be our toy!" "Lily, be our pet!" "Lily, be our mascot!" "Lily!" Why couldn't anyone just let me "do me," like that emo rapper Drake who Harper is always quoting says. But I guess everyone else "doing" me was the problem here.

Still shaky from the Harper run-in, and wiping greasy crumbs of salt and cayenne pepper off my fingers, I fished out Nicole's quartz from my bag and held it to my chest. I needed to think.

I did feel really bad for bailing on PuppyBash this year. And, okay, I felt bad about a lot of other things I'd done lately that I'm pretty sure Harper would hate me for. But I had to focus. I was in a band now that people actually wanted to hear play, and the blog party was really important to Jane, and these were all responsibilities I couldn't shirk—no matter what the reason.

"Lily?" It was Jane, making me jump at the sound of a voice outside my head. She waved her polka dot manicure in front of my face. "Hello in there, anybody home?'

"Sure." I forced myself to laugh. "Just zoned out."

"What would our LilyFairy be if she didn't have her head in the clouds?" Jane playfully pinched my side. "Well, wake up girl! We've got a photo shoot to do! The FancyFashionFeminist waits for no woman, even the ones with wings."

The pictures of me that Jane had taken on the first day of school had started to get some major buzz, not just on her website, but on other fashion blogs around the Internet. Readers were submitting their own interpretations of my style—as well as their own version of the "Fairy Look"—so many that Jane had to hire a "curatorial intern" from the freshman class to go through all the pictures people sent in and pick the best ones. A new set of photos ran each week on the recently dubbed FancyFashionFeminist's Fairy Fridays. The whole thing was kind of weird, but I can't pretend I wasn't psyched when *Lucky* ran my photo online to go along with a feature in a style section called "Be DIY Fairy Chic (for fairly cheap)."

What was less awesome was when people posted their own pictures of me on other random websites or social networks; candid photos of me walking around school while I obliviously went about my day. One time I saw one of me exiting a Godard retrospective at an indie theater, and I have no idea who even took the photo—so creepy! On Twitter and Instagram and SchoolGrams, #LilyFairy was actually a trending topic, and there were entire ask.fm threads about #lilyfairy—and people weren't even being totally awful in the comments section.

As Jane walked me around the park ordering me into different poses for her fashion shoot, I thought about how all of this was kind of overwhelming in a scary way, the feeling that someone might be watching me at any moment. Especially since Nicole demanded such high standards of excellence from members of NAMASTE. Not only were we supposed to be vegan and not wear leather or any other animal products, but we routinely had to "patrol" other kids in our class for non-NAMASTE behavior. Since I was the freshman delegate, I was in charge of kids in my own year. If I saw another freshman wearing leather sandals or eating an almond butter (Pathways has been peanut-free since 1998) and honey sandwich, my job was to call them out in front of everyone, Beth-Lynne style, because bees are apparently the original repressed workers, slaving away in their artificial hives and apiaries just so we can feel good about using a natural sweetener instead of refined sugar or chemicals. Who knew? Nicole had recently suggested using even more "guerilla" techniques for enlightening students, like throwing red paint on anyone we see wearing faux fur, or replacing someone's animal-tested lip liner with a blue ink pen.

Most of the time, things only got as bad as they did that day with Beth-Lynne. (I still have to compartmentalize that whole thing happening. I have idiot shivers just thinking of that moment and myself.) But I was worried that soon Nicole would ask me to take a really revolutionary step to prove myself to NAMASTE, and to someone as nonconfrontational as me, the idea was really cringe-worthy.

"Good!" said Jane, finishing up a round of photos of me sitting down and smiling on a bench. "Now go pick some of those flowers over there."

I couldn't talk about these things with other kids at school, especially Jane and Drew, and I was so tempted to just break down and tell Harper everything when I'd run into her in the park. But when it really came down to it, I couldn't. I wanted to tell her everything and anything, like always, but today it felt like we were two BFF's on two total different time zones . . . and we were in full jetlag mode!

All I could do was tell her that I couldn't make it to PuppyBash (at least I'd been honest about something) and watch her walk away from me, super disappointed. But she had to know I was acting weird and totally unlike myself—so why didn't she ask what was going on with me? If anyone had the power to pry secrets out of me, it was Harper, but she hadn't even tried. Thinking about our failed catch-up session now, I realized I was even more upset than I'd thought. Upset because I needed her, and sad and confused because she made me feel like I had let her down, without trying to understand what I was going through.

"Huh? What did you say?" Jane put down her camera and gave me a weird look.

"Oh, nothing. Sorry," I said, not realizing that I'd been muttering my spiraling thoughts aloud.

I guess my mind was really wandering while going through the various poses Jane was having me try (blowing kisses to people on the street! Swinging from one of the big flower sculptures! Being generally boho-chic!), because after about twenty minutes she was shaking her head and angrily punching buttons as she scrolled through our takes.

"I can't use any of the ones where you're just frowning and muttering to yourself," she sighed. I shuddered inwardly; my conversation with Harper was affecting my real-life work.

Jane looked up from her camera and cocked her head at something behind me. "Hey, Lily, I think someone's waving at you." I turned and squinted between the man-made petals of a sculpture, and for a second was sure that it was Harper, having changed her mind about not wanting to meet Jane. But, no, it wasn't Harper, it was Mrs. Carina, swooping her arms at me like those people at airports who direct planes with light sticks. She must have been there to pick up Harper from PuppyTales, though in her Prada dress and Louboutins, she looked like Victoria Beckham at one of her son's soccer games

I jogged over. "Hey, Karen," I said, putting on a smile that didn't feel quite right. "Sorry, I don't know where Harper is. I saw her earlier though, with Stephanie."

"Oh?" Mrs. Carina's dazzlingly serene facade drooped for a second, and she looked almost confused. If that level of emotion was manifesting on Mrs. Carina's immobile face . . . well, who knows how worried she really was. "Well, it's just as well," she said, matching my forced smile with an overly cheerful one of her own. "I've actually been hoping to get a chance to talk to you alone, anyway."

Now it was my turn to look confused. Despite what Harper always said, I never thought Karen had really shown much of an interest in me, other than in what she called my "unique" sense of fashion. Don't get me wrong, I liked Harper's mom and we got along, but while I couldn't imagine not telling my mother everything about my life, Harper's mom seemed more like a distracted, bubbly aunt than someone to give you advice about life.

"Darling, I know you like your little surprises," Mrs.

Carina simpered, putting one red fingernail against my cheek. "But I simply have to know what you plan on doing for Harper's big Saturday birthday event! Last year I ended up having to distract her with a Cold Stone run so you could put the finishing touches on your little funhouse, remember?"

"How could I forget?" I said, trying to keep my voice at a normal tone. Creating a human-sized doghouse, complete with tunnels to neighboring "kennels" had taken the good part of three months. With a sudden jolt of anxiety I realized that I had less than a week to plan something new.

"So, Lily," said Mrs. Carina, scratching at her thumbnail, "what can I expect from you this year? Please tell me you haven't booked that horrible singer from those rescue commercials I keep seeing on TV." Harper's mom had a bad habit of peeling off her gel manicures in public, like a nervous tic, which was something I could relate to.

"Ha," I said, trying to force a laugh. "Not quite." Translation: I've been so busy figuring out how to cope with being popular and with the fact that I was maybe a terrible friend and I hadn't even begun to think about what I was going to do for Harper's birthday.

Brushing little scraps of nail polish to the ground, Karen went in for an "aw, you!" hug. She must have noticed something in my expression though, because when she stepped back she kept her hands on my shoulders, studying me from an arm's length away. Her gaze softened.

"Lily, you know, if you're feeling overwhelmed this year, I'd be more than happy to help with the party." It was like she had read my mind! I should have been paying attention to more of those MomTips Harper was always spouting off sarcastically . . . maybe they actually helped! "Of course I won't actually be able to *be* there," she continued. "I'll be traveling—the life of a life-coach is never restful!—but I would still love to give you a hand."

I was about to gratefully accept her offer, but Karen immediately snapped her four-fingered manicure. "In fact, I know this amazing botanical healer . . . she's worked with Gwyneth . . . and I bet she'd be more than happy to come up with some feng-shui designs for the garden if you wanted to have a little tea party!"

"Drat, that sounds great, but I've already got this really special event planned for this year," I lied. "Thank you so much for the offer!" I couldn't bear to hurt Karen's feelings by bringing up her daughter's severe pollen allergies . . . and the fact that she hated tea parties.

"Well, whatever you do," said Mrs. Carina, "I'm sure it's going to blow us all away. You're just *so creative*, Lily! I'm sure you'll come up with something magical!" Then, like a woman without a care in the world beyond the topic of her next TEDxMom Talk, Karen Carina clacked back down the sidewalk and hit the *beep beep* noise on her car lock.

I hoped Mrs. Carina was right about me being magical. Because it would take something extraordinary just to get me through the next week.

**Harper (7:08 pm):** Hey, sorry if I seemed out of it at the park today. But I heard my mom got a drop-in from the Gawkward Fairy this afternoon . . .

**Lily (7:09 pm):** Oh, no big deal, we were just talking about your super-exciting birthday plans. Heheh.

**Harper (7:09 pm):** Ha, good. Did she mention she wasn't even going to be here this year?

**Lily (7:10 pm):** Whaaa?

**Harper (7:10 pm)** Conference in Qatar, OF COURSE.

**Lily (7:10 pm):** 😱

**Harper (7:20 pm):** Don't cry for me, Argentina! At least I have you!

**Jane (7:20 pm):** Hey Gawkward Fairy! The relaunch party is coming together great! I'm setting a date today. Can you be there early to help?

**Lily (7:21 pm):** I wouldn't miss it for all the worlds and stars and moons! *Happy Dance*

**Jane (7:23 pm):** Actually, I was hoping you could help talk to Nicole for me. She thinks that I told everyone that she was being gender normative the other day but that is definitely not something I would say. Do not know how the rumor got started . . .

**Lily (7:24 pm):** Lay it on me!

**Jane (7:25 pm):** Actually this is something we need to go off-web for. Your phone has FaceTime, right? Or we can Skype. Want to have a Skype session?

**Lily (7:26 pm):** Hold on, call me and walk me through this Face Time thing you speak of.

**Harper (7:30 pm):** Herro?

**Harper (8:00 pm):** Did our friendship just run out of minutes?

"Ew!"

"That's the grossest thing you've ever heard, right?"

"I don't know," I said. "I guess it depends on whether you actually ate that spider. You absolutely did not, right?"

Tim shrugged, which I only noticed as a tremor from inside the giant red egg he was sitting in. Our cafeteria has an outdoor lounge, which was basically just created for kids whose parents only felt comfortable sending them out into the world if VIP seating was available. One of Beverly High's most prized pieces of real estate was in one of the lounge's "womb chairs," which looked like the Death Star cut in half and resting on a swivel base. You could climb in and spin around or curl up with a book or make out (although they were technically supposed to be used by only one person at a time). But today, during our free period, I was content just to listen to Tim talk about his most traumatizing coming-of-age experiences from inside what was essentially a padded bubble.

I was midlaugh when the last bell of the day rang, which meant that the campus—which normally divided itself up into social cliques better than a red velvet rope ever could—was about to turn into the Wild

West. Scruffy outlaws would collide with rich, dashing cowboys, and primped-up debutantes would walk past unkempt ragamuffins and sneer. All bets were off, and it was like Tim and I were sheriffs around these here parts. (Unless Kendall was close by, in which case, I would try to hold very, very still and hope that she had the sensory perception of a T-Rex.)

"Did you really think they would give you super-powers?" I said, trying not to make it obvious that I was checking my phone. Nope, no texts. From anyone.

"It's how Spider-Man got his!" Tim protested.

"No, I believe Spider-Man got his from a *radioactive* spider bite." Like I *wasn't* the girl who had paid to see Andrew Garfield shirtless three times when that movie came out? "And you were how old then? Seven?"

"No, this was in eighth grade English." Tim popped his head out from the walls of the womb chair and grinned. Once again I was struck by how much older he looked compared to last spring. No offense to the guy who had spent all of middle school dorkily bent over a sketch pad, drawing Lily and me into his comics, but he'd always given off this baby brother vibe. Now, with his longer hair and striped Uniqlo polo shirt, Tim looked . . . well, I don't know what he looked like. An *older* brother? A cousin? A really, really distant cousin with semi-acceptable taste and surprisingly broad shoulders?

"*Touché*, Harper, *touché*. Okay, so what's the most embarrassing thing *you've* ever done?"

Instead of answering, I stretched out on the cool metal bench that attached to the mod white lounge table, soaking up the last of the day's sun. Tim already knew all the embarrassing things I'd done at this point.

In fact, there was an argument to be made that Tim knew me better than anyone else, since Lily still didn't know about my historic Beverly High crash and burn.

"You know, people don't think palm trees have a smell," I said, changing the subject. "But they really do. You ever notice it? They smell like salad that's been out of the fridge too long. But not like, too-too long. Just a little bit long. Like you'd be on the fence about eating it, but then you'd just say 'whatever' and eat it anyway." I was babbling. "The salad, not the palm tree."

"You're stalling," Tim said, one of his blindingly white Nikes popping out to nudge me on the leg.

I sat up and took a deep breath. "I don't have any secrets," I said. "That's my big secret. You know everything about me, which is fine, but just kind of depressing. My secret is that I'm depressed you know all my secrets." I paused. "Or, no, scratch that. My secret is that my best friend is abandoning me the day of our pre-birthday volunteering ritual."

"Oh." I could hear Tim rustling to scoot closer to my prone form on the bench. "I don't want to make you depressed, Harper. And the dog thing—"

"Oh, that's not what I mean, Tim!" I rolled my eyes. Why did he have to take emotional stuff so seriously? "Don't worry about it. We're young, our feelings aren't supposed to last more than fifteen seconds anyway, right? They just die and regenerate, like, really quickly. Like starfish."

"Sea cucumbers. They do that whole limb regeneration thing, too." Tim, ever the nerd, had to one-up my WikiFact. I gave a lying-down shrug. "Sponges do, too."

"Sponge Feelings, now you might be onto something."

"Anyway . . ." Tim trailed off, thinking about whatever it is he thought about, and I shielded my eyes from the sun with the back of my arm and basked in my lazy lizard feeling. One nice thing about Tim is that, unlike some nerds, he doesn't feel the need to be in front of a screen all the time. He's pretty good at listening, and easy to talk to and, ugh, yeah, a really good friend. I should stop being so mean and selfish and ask him about his problems, I told myself. So . . . what were Tim's problems, again? I realized I had no idea.

"So, young man!" I kicked myself up and swung out my legs. "What were you about to say earlier?"

"About what?"

"I don't know. . . . Lily stuff, maybe? Are you still into her?"

Tim coughed. I wasn't sure if that was one of his tells, or if he legit had something caught in his throat. "No, I like someone new," he said after a pause.

"Oh!" This I could work with. "Tell me more, tell me more! What's she look like? Show me on Facebook! Can I check her out right now?" I pulled out my phone, barely noticing my lack of texts from Lily.

"No!" Tim shouted, startling me into dropping my iPhone on the ground. I scowled as he picked it up for me, and noticed that his hair was getting a little too long in the back. He needed to have it cut. I resisted the urge to flip over his shirt tag, which was sticking out from the collar, as always.

"You're such a spaz, Tim. What's the issue? OMG, is she too cool for social media?"

Tim scrunched up his nose and didn't even look at me as he handed my phone back. "I don't want to talk about it," he muttered. It was very unlike him, I thought, to give me such a cold response. Maybe I was getting on everyone's bad side these days. Now, the silence between us didn't feel as comfortable as it did earlier, and I quickly flipped through my mental list of things to talk about.

"So," he said before I could ask him to explain continuity in the Marvel films, "do you need someone to go with you to do that dog volunteer thing? The . . . Puppy-Bash?" He sneaked me a look. "That is, if Lily can't go or whatever."

"It's not like I need someone to go with," I stressed, even though, emotionally, I really did. "But . . . I guess it would be nice to have company. Why, are you free to spend your Friday night with me and a bunch of mutts?"

Tim grinned, and it was a relief to feel him warm up to me again. God, how desperate was I to be around someone who didn't actively think I was worthless? Who thought I was worth making plans with?

"I can't think of better Friday night company," he said, and kicked my shoe with his. It connected with a comforting thud.

The day after the photo shoot in the park, I told myself I was going to start a vision board to help me figure out what to do for Harper's birthday party. Inspiration hadn't struck yet, but there was no reason to think it wouldn't. After all, Harper was my best friend in the entire world, and I knew her better than anyone else. So why was I having such a hard time remembering what she *liked*?

My nonproductive reverie was broken when I heard a knock at the front door. Relieved to have an excuse to take a break from brainstorming, I shot up to answer it.

"Lily Farson?" said the large man who definitely looked like he might have a penchant for bear fighting in his spare time. Or *murder*. I started backing away when he brought out a clipboard and requested that I "Sign here, please."

"Why?" I said. Which was a legitimate question, but then the delivery guy gave me a look that I hadn't seen in a while, that "Are you an alien?" kind of a squinty stare. Then he scribbled something on his sheet.

"Uh, because otherwise I can't give you your package."

"Oh," I said. Well, that made sense. "What's in it?"

Another alien stare. It was like we were in an old Western movie and were having a standoff at high noon.

"I don't know what's in the package," he said slowly. "I'm just here to deliver it."

"Oh," I said. "Right. Sure, sure." After I scrawled my name onto the waiting form, the man handed me a large brown box, complete with one of those bright red FRAGILE stickers. It was big enough to hold a large television, or a small person.

I tentatively signed and waited as the man put the package down. "Have a nice day!" I called after him as he trudged back toward his truck. Then, for good measure, I shouted after him, "I hope this isn't a body part because my dad has guns and I know what you look like!"

The bewildered man drove off, leaving me alone with the mystery box. I stared at the package, expecting it to explode at any second, but when it didn't, I started to get excited. I had never had an unexpected delivery before! I almost didn't want to open it, because as soon as I did, this feeling of anticipation would be gone forever. While it was still wrapped, anything could be inside: gold bars, balloons, a musty old manuscript harboring clues that would lead me to unlock the mysteries of the Egyptian tombs, Schrödinger's cat . . . anything! To open it would be a sadness, in a way, removing all the possibilities of what it could be and replacing it with what actually was.

I held out for maybe three minutes, tops, until fantasy gave way to practicality. There was a reason people sent overnight packages, and it wasn't so that the recipients could sit around for days without opening them. I went and got the scissors lying next to the now-forgotten vision board, slit the top open, and peeked down at what was inside.

It was a shopping bag. A glossy, white shopping bag, like the ones Mrs. Carina is always carrying around, or like an oversized version of the kind you get when you buy expensive jewelry wrapped in tissue paper. I pulled the bag out, surprised by its heft. Something inside the bag shifted with a hollow *thwack*. Great, my first surprise gift and I had probably already broken it.

A cream-colored envelope was taped to the top of the bag. Inside was a laminated badge and an invitation printed on thick cardstock. It was hard not to notice the giant fairy wings illustrated on both the badge and the invitation . . . both bore a stunning similarity to my own pair. I read the card.

What in great Zeus was F³? I knew about Art Rebel through my mom. It was an awesome space in Sherman Oaks that hosted things like graffiti parties and supper clubs and theater classes. But what did that have to do with me? I tore through the bag for more clues. Inside I found the following:

1. A gift certificate for a free blowout and makeover at Andy Lecompte's salon.

2. A Birch Box filled with a fancy line's entire new fall collection, including bronzer, foundation, concealer, shimmer, lip liner, lipstick, lip shimmer, topcoats, bottom coats, mascara, eyeliner, eye shadow, eyebrow pencils and something called "eyelid base."

3. A gold Uber gift card pre-loaded with $150.

4. Two different flavors of coconut water.

5. A tub's worth of something called Juice Beauty's Stem Cellular Repair CC Cream.

6. An *iPad mini.* (Seriously? I couldn't believe it myself.)

7. A CABOODLE! (Possibly more exciting than the iPad.)

8. A Polaroid Instant camera with the "F³" logo stamped on the side.

9. A handbag (well, technically, it was a "Mini Polka Dot Satchel from Z Spoke by Zac Posen" according to the attached tag).

10. Cake pops!

11. A collection of nail art stickers in leopard print, stripes and French tips.

Now that I had reached the bottom of the bag and exhausted its contents, I was still puzzled over my windfall of good fortune. I took out the camera and looked at the logo again . . . F³. . . . Something about that sounded familiar.

A-ha! Of course! F³ was the new name for Fancy-

FashionFeminist, Jane's style blog! I had the vague rec-
ollection of her mentioning something at the park about
getting some sponsors for the site, but I had assumed
that meant she was planning on going door to door to
collect signatures, like when you run in a charity marathon. I never would have guessed that she was actually
talking about *Apple*. Which I heard doesn't give away
free stuff like, ever.

I went through my bounty again and pinched myself to make sure I wasn't dreaming. Was the re-launch
really going to feature my fairy wings as part of their
rebranding? When Nicole had said she wanted everyone
in NAMASTE to get their own pair, I had no idea she
meant that everyone who read Jane's blog should get
them too! I thought back to Nicole's speech about being
"on-message" and my "personal branding" and couldn't
help but feel a little overwhelmed by it all. I was a fashion icon! And I was already planning what to wear—
something old Lily never would have done, but that I
was doing all the time now because not all my clothes
went with my fairy wings—and started setting up the
iPad when I caught a second glance at the invitation.
The party was happening *this Saturday*. Oh, no.

Harper's birthday.

As in, the most important day of the year, which I'd
been trying to plan for the entire afternoon, and which
I'd resolved to pull off no matter what.

Unless . . . maybe I could come up with a compromise. After all, there I was, unable to come up with any
good birthday ideas, and now an invitation to a super
exclusive party had just dropped into my lap. Wouldn't
that be even better than me scrambling to come up with
something last-second? Plus, it would be kind of cool

for Harper to see me in an environment where I feel comfortable and accepted. (Well, as long as I had my wings on.) Maybe then she would be able to understand why I'd been so nervous and off around her lately. And then I could stop being so nervous and off around her, because she would finally understand what I was going through. Right?

I didn't know what I could do except call Harper and, in what would go down in history as the giddiest display of excitement in my entire life, tell her that I've been planning the most awesome birthday surprise yet. I would tell her that I pulled some strings to score invites to *the* party of the school year, in honor of my favorite PuppyGirl's very special fourteenth birthday. In other words, I would lie, and pretend that Jane's party, which I was obligated to go to, was Harper's party, and I'd be able to make everyone happy all in one fell swoop!

Either that, or I'd just hit a new level of skeez on the Terrible Friend scale. No, I couldn't think like that: I would lie, but I would be lying for a good cause. The cause being the caretaking of both my social identity and my friendship with Harper. I couldn't risk losing both.

This conundrum would absolutely be hashtagged #freshmanyearproblems. How do adults make such serious decisions all the time? It was so stressful.

I had no idea how Harper would react when she saw that most of Pathways had adopted my signature "look." I was also pretty sure that Harper didn't even own a pair of wings, and didn't know if she would be able to get some in time for the party. I was totally spiraling.

I had to act fast. I texted Jane to make sure I could bring a plus-one (yes—thank you Jane!). I couldn't believe I was calling Harper my plus-one when I was usually her plus-one. I know people think plus-one is a negative, but I thought it always sounded so sweet and thoughtful since you were basically being called an addition to a party!

I just hoped Harper would see it the same way. I took the deepest breath in the world as I prepared to press the Number One entry in my Favorite Contacts list.

*Please go to voicemail, please go to voicemail, please go to—*

"Gawkward Fairy!" Harper chirped.

*Dang.*

"PuppyGirl!" I said, twirling my hair so nervously that my finger got caught in it. "So. Do I have a birthday surprise for you."

By the first week in October, it seemed that most people had forgotten about my SchoolGrams debut. Students were no longer stopping to stare at me in the hall, and I hadn't been emailed a "reaction video" of kids watching my SchoolGrams humiliation for the first time for at least a week. (This was definitely in no small part thanks to everyone's new obsession: a viral video of a couple of juniors on skateboards pantsing poor Mr. Sims in the faculty parking lot). Hopefully the whole thing was just going to die down and go away for good. So what if that meant that I had to die a little along with it? That I'd never get to hang out with Derek again? (Even though what he did was terrible and inexcusable, I still couldn't help reliving that stupid kiss in my head every day.) And so what if I wasn't as popular as I'd been all my life before, and if my stomach still did flips every time I saw anything bright pink or mesh coming toward me in the hall? So what if my best friend might be about to abandon me for the fancy new folks at her ultra-cool, alternative high school? At least I wasn't completely alone.

I'd fallen into a pattern at school that, if not exactly fun, was a far cry from the mortification of the first week. After our chance meeting in the park, Stephanie had been hanging out with me pretty consistently during lunch. Tim (who I wasn't just using as a human shield anymore, I swear, though I have to admit I was silently thanking the gods every day for his summertime growth spurt, which made him almost pass for kinda-cute) dutifully walked me to and from every class every day, making sure that I never had to bump into Kendall or one of her cohorts alone in a hallway. In return for this service, he got Lily's former spot in Rachel's car after school.

And though I tried to suppress it as best I could and not get my expectations too high, I was even getting excited for my birthday. When Lily called and invited me to that fashion party, I'd been a little disappointed at first. After we hung up, I looked up the blog that was hosting the party, and, sure enough, it belonged to Jane, aka *Pathways* Jane, aka one of the hip kidnappers who seemed to be intent on stealing my fairy godmother from me. Was Lily really just going to add me as a plus-one to some lifestyle event and consider that a symbol of BFF-ship? But after my initial annoyance, I finally calmed down and found reason. After all these years of friendship, Lily had *never* let me down on my birthday. She also has a history of faking left and going right when it comes to surprising me. Like last year, I was waiting and waiting for her and she still hadn't shown up, and then my mom took me out for what I'd assumed was a pity-ice-cream-cone because my best friend had forgotten about me, but then when we got back there was the most amazing surprise party waiting for me. And then there was the year she told me she'd have to skip the party because she needed to go to San Francisco for the funeral of some great-

great-thrice-removed aunt, and she needed me there for moral support, and she was so gloomy and quiet the whole car ride, but then when we got there it turned out we were really going to this unbelievable dog event that she'd found out about online.

But after a few more sessions of awkward texting with Lily, and after Tim started asking more and more questions about my big Saturday birthday plans, I thought I finally had figured it out: she was planning a surprise party for me, and this "fashion party" thing was just a cover, and she'd even gotten in touch with Tim about it so he could help her cover up the surprise.

Suddenly, it all made sense. I finally knew why Lily was acting so weird and distant (to make the surprise even better!) and why she had bowed out of the Puppy-Bash (so I'd be fooled into thinking she didn't care about me!) Why hadn't I seen that this was the same plan, just updated for a new year? After I figured that out, I was able to relax a bit, and didn't even get upset when Tim would keep asking questions about Puppy-Bash, reminding me that he was going to be there instead of Lily.

It was the day before PuppyBash, and Rachel picked Tim and me up after school as usual. "Still on for Friday night, right?" He'd asked the same question every day ever since I'd invited him, usually while riding home with Rachel and me after school. By Thursday, I was basically treating his question like the running joke it had become.

"What is it with you kids these days?" I tried on my best crazy cat lady voice and waggled my finger at him. Rachel rolled her eyes, the car swerving as if in sync with her sarcasm, yet somehow managed to keep us from veering into traffic. "Always worrying about 'parties' and 'good times'! Pheh! Your generation will ruin everything!"

Tim swatted at my shoulder from the backseat. "I'm just trying to be responsible and confirm our plans! I've got other places I could be on a Friday night, you know."

"Oh, come on," I said, twisting around in my seat and shoving him (not too hard) back. "Like you have anywhere to be. What, am I making you miss a hot date?" I giggled as Tim grabbed my hands and started making them mime the "Cups" song motions in the air. "Stop it, nerd."

"Neanderthal."

"Geek."

"Mega-dork."

"Dweeb."

"Pipsqueak."

"Okay, settle down you two, or I'll have to separate you," Rachel barked. Tim immediately dropped my hands and I, still giggling, turned to face the road. I didn't feel like messing with Rachel today. The last time we got into an argument, she brought up the School-Grams video loudly enough for my parents to hear, and I had to spend the next three days dodging my mom's repeated question of "Harper, what's a 'school-o-gram'?" ("Some kind of new health cracker, Mom," I finally said, to which she just responded, "Oh, that's nice. But careful you don't eat too much gluten.") But then Rachel asked about my birthday plans on Saturday, and I could see Tim leaning forward in the rearview mirror. *Curses, Rachel!* I thought.

"I'm going to a party with Lily," I mumbled, hoping that she would drop the subject rather than start grilling Tim about what *he'd* be doing Saturday. Now that I figured out the surprise, the last thing my Empathy Powers wanted was to feel someone else squirm trying to come up with a lie for my sister, and then I'd have to get into a whole big thing where I'd have to tell her why Tim wasn't invited and then I'd feel like a terrible person and then probably break down and invite him anyway, even though that would make everything totally 100 percent awkward. Or . . . maybe Rachel was in on it, too?

"With people from *Pathways*?" Tim leaned forward and propped one of his gangly arms up on my seat. His eyebrows were knitted in fake concern. Maybe he wasn't in on the party. I wondered if there was a way to tell Lily to invite Tim, without letting her know that I had figured out her surprise plan.

"Yikes, you're partying with kids from that hipster feeder program?" Lately Rachel had become a little *too* enthusiastic about putting down Lily and her new friends. It actually made me want to defend Lily and her artistic, painfully politically correct crowd, but the truth was, I didn't know anything about them or what went on in that school of hers. They actually *could* be terrible people—or brainwashers!—for all I knew.

"Oh," Tim said, dropping his arm to the center console and popping out the retractable cup holder. "So how is Lily doing, anyway?"

Good question. I just wish I knew the answer.

After we dropped Tim off, Rachel sat in the parked car for an extra minute, wiping off her excess lipstick.

"So I guess this is the time we're going to have 'the talk,'" she said, sighing and picking up an e-cigarette from the recesses of her glove compartment, where it was well-hidden from Mom. The tip of the e-cig turned bright blue as Rachel inhaled, a clear sign that she was "thinking."

"Okay. Here's some pro-tip advice, take it or leave it," my sister said, still staring straight ahead. "It's not nice to play with a guy's feelings like that." My sister pulled down her sun visor and stared at her reflection in the mirror, tilting it just-so just to avoid making eye contact with me.

I didn't even know how to respond to that. "Don't be a perv about Tim," I said, doing nothing to hide my snarky tone. "Stick to Jacques-strap."

My sister chuckled. "Trust me, this isn't about me. That boy likes you. Which actually makes me question his judgment entirely. . . ."

"No he doesn't. If anything he still likes Lily. . . ."

"Then why are you two going on a date?"

I couldn't tell if Rachel was just trying to wind me up or if she was being serious, but either way it annoyed me that I couldn't think of an appropriately incredulous response. Of course Tim and I didn't have a date.

Wait. Did we have a date?

I definitely didn't want Tim to think PuppyBash was a date, because I would never want Lily to think it was a date. But I still wanted to hang out with Tim. Oh my god, I couldn't believe I wanted to hang out with *Tim*. It was as inconceivable as suddenly having the desire to spend a weekend away with Rachel and Jacques as their honorary third wheel. I mean, Tim was basically like the equivalent of a gross-cute talking sloth that dressed *marginally* better than he did in sloth middle school.

"Looks like you fixed your lipstick," I finally said, giving Rachel the hint that I was done with this conversation, and that it was time to go home.

"You're right. It's perfect," she said, winking knowingly at me as she backed out of the Slaters' driveway. Less than two minutes later, we were home. Rachel went up to her room for the rest of the night, and I went up to the attic to text Lily about outfits for Saturday, mentioning nothing of the fact that I could not get the words "date" and "Tim" out of my head the entire time.

♥

Friday went by in a blur of classes, gross school lunches, and aggressive avoidance of any sign of both Kendall and Derek. Finally, the last bell rang, and it was time for my favorite thing in the world.

Despite all the Lily-drama surrounding it, I was actually looking forward to doing the PuppyBash this year. The Jacobys and I had spent a month planning out the places we were going to hit. We mapped out an awesome route: the park (again), the Santa Monica farmer's market, the West Los Angeles VA Clinic, the Beverly Hills branch of Bridges to Recovery (a mental health clinic that was really popular with famous people). And last but not least, the Crestwood Hills Co-Op in Brentwood, where preschoolers and their parents could play with the puppies and take them out for walks along the hiking trails.

I had no idea if Tim was actually as excited as I was, so I was surprised to find him already waiting for me in the school parking lot when the Jacobys pulled up in their Mobile Center on Friday, honking their novelty horn that played the chorus of "How Much Is That Doggie in the Window?"

"Excited?" Tim asked, quirking up his eyebrows while trying to help me into the RV. "You ready to play with the big dogs?"

"I don't even know what means," I said, ignoring his offered hand (I'm a modern, independent lady, *thankyouverymuch*) and hoisting myself into the backseat.

"I'm just asking if the dog days are over."

"You're in a chipper mood," I noted, pushing my sunglasses up and onto my head.

"I'm just psyching myself up to play *ruff*. In this *dog eat dog* world."

"Okay," I said. "We're done now." I tried not to pay attention to Mr. and Mrs. Jacoby tittering at our banter in the front of the car.

Finally, we reached the first stop. The park was already pretty packed with young parents sharing juice boxes with their way-too-preciously-dressed children. As we set up the van to welcome visitors, Tim started chatting up the crowd, getting the kids all riled up by asking them how excited they were to bring home a new pet. I realized that I hadn't really explained to Tim that this wasn't an adoption event—that we were here to raise awareness and hand out information for interested families—and there wasn't a prize for the most amount of puppies sold in an evening.

"Young lady," Tim boomed at a small, rapt child in pristine overalls. "You look like you could use a new friend. How about this one here? Um . . ." Tim checked the name tag on a doggy crate. ". . . Cocoa! I know what you're thinking! Cocoa's not a puppy anymore. But Cocoa is the perfect dog for your family. Did you know that Labrador retrievers are known for their even-temperedness and total lack of aggression? Making them perfect for families with young children? C'mon folks! If these puppies are still with us at the end of the night, they'll be in trouble. Please don't ask what we do with the dogs afterward. You don't even want to know." Tim winked at the little girl, who was staring at him with giant, awe-filled eyes.

"Tim, knock it off!" I said, trying to act less neurotic than I felt. I turned to the crowd gathered behind us and forced a smile. "Ha-ha. Sorry everyone. That was, um, a joke. He doesn't even work with us, normally. We are *not* a kill shelter. I repeat: we are definitely not a kill shelter! We care for all of our animals humanely and with kindness."

"So." The father of the little girl stepped forward; he was trying to get to his wallet but was having a little trouble due the sheer tightness of his cool-dad jeans. "Are you telling me this little guy is for sale, then?"

"Oh, um," I coughed. "We don't *sell* the dogs, sir. This is more of a rescue and adoption service. We pay for the neutering or spaying and the basic shots. . . ."

Hipster Dad was running out of patience. "Great. So you can just give us the dog, then. We'll take her. Him. Whatever."

"Uh." I was imagining this guy going home to his unsuspecting wife with a new dog. This was exactly how animals ended up cycling through the rescue process multiple times. "You still need to fill out your application and adoption forms, and we'll have to check out your references. The whole process takes two to three weeks."

The dad stared at me. I couldn't tell if he was confused or annoyed, and to be honest I don't think he knew which was the dominant emotion, either. This really wasn't the way PuppyBash was supposed to go down. When it was Lily's and my pre-birthday ritual, we had a whole system in place on how to get people interested in PuppyTales. We'd show them the dogs, encourage them to play with the dogs while we supervised and told them stories about the absolute cutest thing Bonezilla the Basset Hound did when we first took her swimming, or how Kevin the Pekinese makes this adorable little oinking noise when he sleeps. None of these "Step right up!" shenanigans that turned the puppies into sideshow stars. Adopting a dog was serious business!

"Tim," I said after clearing my throat with authority. "May I speak with you when you have a moment?" I wasn't sure if he could hear me over my grinding jaw. Tim shrugged at Hipster Dad and shooed Cocoa off back into the RV. It was time to go to the next stop on the itinerary, and I would have to set Tim straight on the way.

"Okay, so how did I do?" Tim asked after we'd packed up the van to head for Laurel Canyon. He looked so pleased with himself, which annoyed me even more.

"Not great," I said. I licked my finger and tried to get a white smudge out of my black shorts. I tried to wear only dark colors during my volunteer work, but somehow they still always ended up dirty. "You should really be following my lead, and maybe just stick to handing out pamphlets. This isn't some joke, and you don't know what you're doing." Was I being too harsh? Maybe. But this was my passion, and even though Tim meant well, he was just barging in on it like a Great Dane in a delicate figurine store, messing everything up.

"Okay," Tim said, looking appropriately abashed. "I'm sorry Harper. But I was just trying to be funny, you know? Entertain people. Make them want to take home the dogs. That's the whole point, right?"

I could have given any number of reasons why he was wrong. That the PuppyBash wasn't about unloading shelter dogs onto people who make decisions based on a whim or a charismatic salesman—that's exactly how these dogs end up in shelters in the first place. Or I could have told him that, despite his joking around, there wasn't going to be a happily ever after for any of those dogs if a place like PuppyTales couldn't raise enough funds to sustain itself, which was 90 percent of the purpose of our community outreach tonight. Hell, I could have told him he had no right to argue with me, and that tagging along for this thing was HIS idea.

Instead, I just snapped. "No, the point, Tim, is that this isn't about you. It's about the fact that Lily and I always spend the night before my birthday doing something that she knows means a lot to me. And instead of her, I have to do it with *you*." It was the worst possible answer, since it was the one that was the closest to how I really felt. I felt the warmth in my cheeks spreading down to my neck. *Rein it in, Harper*, I thought. I took a breath, closed my eyes, and found my center. In and out, in and out, breathing with my lower diaphragm. Just like mom's trainer/nutritionist/breathing coach Raoul taught me. Finally I felt calm and relaxed.

"So," said Tim, leaning against the truck but no longer smiling. "This is really about you and Lily."

My eyes flew open. "THIS IS ABOUT THE DOGS!" I scream-splained.

Buffy and Georgie and Bruschetta and Dottie and Bandit howled in agreement from their crates.

I looked at Tim. He was already looking at me. I

know one of us was the first to crack, but I can't remember anymore, because soon it was a rolling wave of unending, howling laughter.

The rest of the night went better. On Mulholland in Laurel Canyon, we introduced our buddies around the park, gave away some literature about PuppyTales, cleaned up our fair share of dog poo, and finally shooed away those scam artist "dog walkers" who ignore their fifteen plus charges as soon as they're fenced into the park. Then we were off to Lake Hollywood Park, right in the shadow of our most famous sign. We were there for no more than five minutes before a giant German shepherd bowled Tim over—literally—while making a play for his sweaty handful of Snausages. Instead of freaking out, BoyWonder just giggled that new Matthew McConaughey laugh of his—heh-heh-heh—and let volfehounder perform an intensive cavity search. All right, I told myself. All right, all right, *all right.*

"Hey, so . . . sorry about earlier," I told Tim when we were finally on our way home. It was after dark and the dogs were happily pooped (literally and figuratively). From the front of the Mobile Center's cab, we could occasionally catch snippets of the Jacobys murmuring their gratitude in our general direction. "I know you've been really cool to me and I appreciate it," I went on. "I just . . . I'm just used to doing this only with Lily, you know? I still can't believe she bailed on me."

"I can't believe it either," Tim said. "That doesn't seem like something she'd do."

Then, the Mobile Center took a sharp left turn, causing me to lose my balance and practically fall into Tim's lap. Even in the dark I could feel him blush, and he quickly angled his arm out from under where I was splayed, resting it on my shoulder in an awkward, one-arm hug, his chin resting on the top of my head. He smelled nice, like laundry detergent and . . . firewood. Is firewood even a scent? I don't know, but whatever it was, I liked it, and for once I wasn't going to question how I felt or what it would look like to anyone else. I closed my eyes, feeling myself drift a little bit over to Tim. In the front of the RV, Mr. and Mrs. Jacoby were singing along to Crosby, Stills and Nash.

"This part is nice," I said groggily, letting my head rest on his chest.

The hand on my shoulder relaxed. "Wuzzat? The song?"

"Sure, the song, the drive . . . it's all nice." I held my breath, but Tim didn't respond at all. In fact, his breathing had slowed down considerably.

"Tim?"

There was a beat, and then a loud snore. Tim had fallen fast asleep. The dogs in the back howled.

The day of Harper's birthday and the F³ re-launch party, I spent an inordinately long amount of time picking out my outfit. It had to be just perfect, and I went through a bunch of options, frowning in the mirror at each one. Vintage Girl Scout uniform? Too drab. Coral sleeveless silk top paired with blue culottes? Too formal. Floral print midi dress? Too young. Oversized chambray shirt, belted, with black leggings? Too *stylish*.

Ugh, fashion was the hardest thing in the entire world and I hated it and I wished Nasty Gal and Man Repeller had stayed Nasty and Repellant, instead of making alterna-wear a "thing." I wished I had never found WhoWhatWear.com and I wished that I could go back to the time when I thought "street fashion" meant something you actually saw on the street, not the Internet. Finally I settled on the first thing I'd tried on: a Free People layered tulle tutu in soft pink, paired with a cream-colored leotard. I tried to wrestle the pink tutu skirt over my head as I heard the doorbell ring. Ugh, why could I never remember to step *into* these things? The skirt was scratchy against my bare legs. I could already tell it would be itchy all night, and that I was definitely going to get hives. I wished that I hadn't made a pact with Harper about staying true to ourselves, when

I didn't even know what that meant anymore.

I muttered something to myself that even I didn't catch and threw my phone on the bed, right in time to hear a knock at my door.

"Come in!" I said, wincing as the girl I saw in the mirror put on a too-bright smile. Harper entered almost shyly, wearing a dark red dress that fell around her shoulders in a cowl. She had arranged her hair in a messy up-do, and was wearing smoky eyeliner, like an adult. She had done something (or Mrs. Carina had) to her cheeks as well: they now had capital D Definition. I cringed, and not only because I suddenly felt like a kid next to a well-dressed adult: I wondered if Harper knew how inappropriate she looked for a Pathways party. Not to mention the fact that she didn't have any wings. Darn it, had I forgot to mention those over the phone? I must have been too busy planning this whole party, which actually should technically count as planning Harper's party, so who cares if I forgot a detail or two?

"Wow, you look amazing! Let me get a good look at you!" God, I sounded like a daytime TV host. "Happy birthday, birthday girl! How are you?"

"Thanks," Harper said. "Fine." She was looking at me oddly, like she was expecting something. It made me nervous, so I pretended to rummage through my bag for something I didn't need: gum, a Band-Aid . . . anything. Unfortunately, all I had in there was some lint and three citrus flavored Tic-Tacs that had fallen out of their plastic container. I put one of them in my mouth anyway, because I'm disgusting.

"So, are you excited about tonight?" I couldn't think of anything else to say. *Why couldn't I think of anything else to say?*

"Sure." Harper coughed. "Um, if that's really what we're doing. Going to your friend's party, I mean."

"Of course it is!" I said, as brightly as I could. "Where else would we be going?" Harper seemed to sag a little bit when I said that, so I tried to pump her up. "Isn't it great? I scored us an invite to the hottest party in town! The F³ rebranding is, like, the biggest event this season!" Whoa, *hello*, where did that come from? Was I on some terrible scripted show about my own life?

"I don't know, Lily." Harper sighed as she drifted toward my dresser, absentmindedly picking up and putting down random objects: my crocheted tea cozy, my porcelain rocking horse, my mirrored tin with all my jewelry. "This seems like a whole . . . thing."

I gritted my teeth and tried to smile. "That's the point, Harper," I stressed, sitting on my bed. "It is a *whole thing*. We're going to change it up for once. And you said you wanted to meet my friends . . . I just wish you could have gotten more in the spirit of things! Like, do you maybe want to borrow something of mine to wear that's a little more . . . fun?"

"Fun?" Harper sounded doubtful. "Since when do you care what I wear? Plus, Lily, I know you put a lot of thought into this, but I was thinking we could maybe just stay in this year? Hang out? Just the two of us?" This was totally not a Harper-like reaction to the idea of going to a cool party. She was usually the one who got pumped about meeting new people, and I was the one who was always begging to stay in and eat cheese and watch weird movies. I had to shake her out of her funk. What would Nicole do?

"Oh, come on! It'll be fun! There is no 'I' in 'Us,' Harper!" I walked over to my dresser with more determination than I'd ever had and spun Harper around so she was facing me. "But there are three of them in 'Individual!'"

"What are you talking about?"

"Uh, well, it's just that . . . maybe this year, we could try to do something a little more . . . unique. I was really hoping we could try being, uh, real. The real us. By not following the crowd, and doing something, you know . . . unique?" This kind of stuff sounded so much better when it came out of Nicole's mouth.

"Wait. You want us to *not* follow the crowd by going to . . . a party?" Was it just me or was Harper starting to sound a lot like her sarcastic sister these days? Nothing was ever going to be easy with Harper, even when I was . . .

"*. . . trying to help her . . .*"

Harper looked confused. "Lily, what did you say?"

"Nothing!" I threw my hand over my mouth, all of a sudden feeling totally overwhelmed. Sometimes it was like my brain couldn't think about stuff without having it also come out of my mouth. I would have to watch that little tendency of mine tonight, while Harper and Nicole were in the same room together. I tried to regroup.

"I'm just . . . trying to help us—*help you*—become the best possible version of yourself," I said, making sure no extra words were getting out. "I put a lot of thought into this . . . and . . . I just think, you know, we need to put more Energy and Art and Nature and Magic into your birthday this year." I left out Sheganism and Alienation, but managed to throw out the other core tenants of NAMASTE in my Hail Mary speech. I crossed my fingers and toes and prayed for it to work.

"Fine," Harper finally said, looking down and

fidgeting with her cowl collar. "Lead the way, oh brave fashion pioneer."

I tried not to take that as an insult and instead practiced harnessing my good vibes. "Great! Oh my god, you're going to adore Jane! And Drew! And my friend Nicole, she's the president of this club I've told you about . . ." I reached behind Harper and pulled the finishing touches to my outfit out from my top dresser drawer: a cool floral crown that I'd found in an excavation of my attic, and of course, my wings. Can't leave home without them. At least not to any event planned by my Pathway friends.

I really hoped the party would live up to my hype. I hoped Nicole and my Pathways friends would really love Harper the way I did. But the thing was, I was worried. As much as I loved being accepted at my school, my new friends weren't really *accepting*. I used to think that the word "intolerance" referred to bigots and racists and bros (and lactose and gluten, obviously), but it turns out that the most open-minded people can also be the least forgiving. At Pathways, if you're not unique, you're "basic." If you like anything that's accepted by the mainstream culture, you're "brainwashed." If you don't wear your originality on your sleeve, literally, every single day, then you are being a conformist and not thinking for yourself. You're Beth-Lynne, and you end up in tears in the middle of a hallway filled with judgmental classmates.

No. It didn't have to be like that. I was sure my new friends would love Harper, I decided. Of course they would. They had to.

They had to.

Right?

# Harper

Lily was really quiet on the way over to the F³ party, which was fine, because I didn't feel much like talking either. On the seat beside me was the birthday card that Lily had absentmindedly handed me on the way out the door. I was sure I had seen the card at Walgreens the other week—it featured an owl asking "Who-who-whose birthday is it?" (Uh, it's my birthday, owl. Do your homework.) Inside, there was a dashed-off note in Lily's chicken scratch. "Happy birthday!" It read. "To my bestie!"

Thinking about it again, my hands flew up to my neck, feeling for the present Lily had just given me: a vintage BFF broken heart necklace that came in a pair—Lily had the other half. It felt gold and old and pretty heavy. I probably would have loved it, except that, as we rode in the car toward a party that I had assumed was a jokey cover for my real birthday surprise, I couldn't help thinking of it as a consolation prize.

Plus, it totally didn't match my outfit.

Maybe I was too overdressed? I figured since this was a fashion party, I could borrow something from Rachel's pre-goth-phase wardrobe. I picked out a beautiful red BCBGeneration cocktail dress that was a little shorter than what I'd normally wear, paired with gold strappy sandals. The dress flared out from the waist and gave my usually straight figure more curves. It was also really adult-looking, especially after I put my hair up in a sprayed bun and lined my eyes with kohl. If I was going to blow this thing up, I might as well blow it up *right*. I actually felt good about my outfit tonight, until I saw Lily's.

She was wearing a costume. Well, Lily was always a little bit in costume, but this was Halloween-level, even for her. She was wearing a tutu! And of course, her wings, which had so many new scraps of fabric tied around them they made her look like a hunchback. She had a flower crown in her hair, which would have been cute if I wasn't almost positive that it was the same one she debuted back in fourth grade gym class. (The dust bunnies scattered among the fake peonies gave it away.)

"Is this a Halloween party?" I had asked as we left the house, Lily shrugging on her wings with a kind of resigned determination. "Or does it have some kind of retro theme?"

"No." Lily shrugged. "Why? This is just called 'looking good on a Saturday night.'"

"Okay," I said. "Just asking." I didn't bother following up on that, and so resigned myself to staring dejectedly out the car window as we drove, wondering when it had become so hard to make conversation with my best friend.

"By the way," I said, hoping to guilt Lily about Puppy-Bash, "I saw the Jacobys the other night. They said they missed you. . . ." They hadn't said any such things, but I saw Lily's shoulders tense as if shocked by a cattle prod.

"Oh," she squeaked. "Was . . . did you see Beth-Lynne by any chance?"

I scowled in the backseat. What did Beth-Lynne have to do with any of this? I hadn't even seen her since my last birthday party.

"No," I said curtly. "Why, have you?"

Lily mumbled something I couldn't catch, but it was possible she was just talking to herself again.

I think I was still holding out hope that this was going to turn out to be some epic prank, right until the moment that we pulled up to Art Rebel. The building was a giant warehouse, the kind some witty detective might find a body in in an episode of *NCIS*. Except usually those buildings didn't have a red carpet outside. There was a line round the block; a sea of improbable hair colors, asymmetrical clothes and thick glasses. But the most insane part was that everyone was wearing wings except me. It was like we had wandered into some strange Disney-sponsored tween nightmare.

"You girls have a fun time!" Mrs. Farson purred as she unlocked the doors. I considered making an argument for staying in the car—lady cramps were probably my best bet—but Lily was dragging me by the hand and out the door before I could protest.

Even from outside, the scene was chaos, like some end-of-the-world apocalypse scenario meets a Zac Efron premiere. Kids were shouting and there were light bulbs flashing everywhere. Loud bass-heavy music was booming from the entrance, where a linebacker-sized bouncer stood holding a tiny clipboard. It would maybe have been funny if I wasn't so disoriented by the myriad of Tinkerbells (and Tinkerboys!) thrumming outside the entrance.

"So, these wings, is that something you started?" I asked. "It's a little . . ." I didn't actually know how I planned on ending that sentence. It wasn't *a little* anything. It was a *lot*. Much to the Muchness. Instead of responding, Lily squeezed my hand tighter as we approached the door. Either she hadn't heard me or was pretending not to.

"Lily!" There was a loud screech near the door, and suddenly the giant bouncer stepped back to reveal the pink-haired girl from Lily's first day at Pathways. Except tonight her coif was silvery white, and she wore a black, shapeless tunic with a gold braided sash. Neon plastic bangles ran up one arm and down the other, and her nails were bright orange. Though I'm sure she thought she looked oh-so Warhol-era, the effect was less Edie Sedgwick and more raver Scarlett O'Hara.

Oh, and one other thing: Her back was sprouting a large tuft of angel wings. Each feather was dyed the same metallic blue-gray as her hair color, and her wingspan ran all the way to the tips of her fingers when she spread them to point to us.

"*She's* good, Julio," Nicole said, unlatching the red velvet ropes and beckoning Lily with one pumpkin-painted nail. "And so is her, uh . . ."

I smiled grimly. "I'm Harper."

"Of course, Harper." Nicole's voice could have been sponsored by Splenda for all the artificial sweetener she'd put in it. "We've heard so much about you! Though didn't Lily tell you about the dress code tonight?" I frowned at Lily, who was suddenly looking anywhere but at me. *No*, I thought, *I had definitely not been told about any dress code.*

Nicole pursed her lips and shrugged benevolently. "Oh well, I'm sure we can't all find a pair of wings quite as stunning as our Lily's on such short notice. It's natural that you would feel a little, shall we say, *less motivated* to

be your true self, what with that upbringing you've had."
Nicole moved in between me and Lily, pushing us apart
and snaking her arms through ours as she bulldozed
through the entrance, leaving me to wonder just what
Lily had told her about my home life. What did she mean
about my upbringing? Sure, my parents weren't perfect,
but I loved them to death! (And so, last time I checked,
did Lily.) I couldn't imagine what Nicole was referring to,
but it sounded nasty. I needed to talk to Lily, ASAP.

The warehouse opened up to a giant makeshift
runway on which uncomfortably skinny girls were
losing their balance on treacherously high heels and
were being weighed down by what looked like welded
metal angel wings in different shades of black and red. It
was like a carnival sideshow sponsored by Lady Gaga's
costume company.

"These wings were made with a 3-D printer, using
only organic plant synthesis," Nicole intoned like a tour
guide, unlocking her arms and sweeping them toward
the girls teetering around with frantic looks toward the
audience. "The process is completely cruelty-free."

I caught Nicole's pointed stare at my patent leather
sandals. "Oh, these are faux," I said, probably too quickly.
Lily looked embarrassed. Nicole gave her an impercepti-
ble nudge in the ribs that I wasn't supposed to see, and
then Lily cleared her throat. "Oh, um, even faux leather
promotes the animal slaughterhouse industrial com-
plex," my supposed BFF said in one breath, not meeting
my eyes. Nicole's grin got even wider.

"Oh," I said coolly. "That's really interesting." I shot
Lily a look that I hope said, *Best birthday ever??*

"Fascinating, isn't it?" Nicole grabbed a passing plate
of spring rolls from a black-clad waiter. "You know," she

crunched, "I actually grew up near Brentwood. That's where you're from, right Harper?"

I nodded, shifting my gaze back onto Nicole. It took all my concentration to remember the MomTips to use when confronted with hostile and undermine-y people, such as "Maintain eye contact at all times" and "Minimize anxious babble."

"Shrimp roll?" Nicole asked flippantly as she tossed two in her mouth. *Shrimp roll, Miss She-gan?* She seemed to realize her mistake immediately.

"I thought you were vegan!" Lily sounded so shocked, I felt bad for smiling.

For once, Nicole's placid kumbaya exterior seemed to crack. "Well, shrimp don't count," she shrugged defensively. Despite being momentarily thrown off her game, Nicole barreled through, her garish silver hair catching the light dully like antique shards of iron. "I mean, shrimp don't even have brains. They're disgusting. They're basically insects."

"Oh," Lily nodded, as if she actually believed that Nicole wasn't spewing complete BS. "I get it."

I'd had enough. "Excuse me," I interrupted, aware that I had my hands on my hips as if I were a superhero trying to puff myself up to be as large as possible. Or a blowfish expanding into a giant to scare away predators. "Nicole, it was so lovely to meet you, but do you think I can have two seconds with my friend here? I'd really like to . . . look around the space with her."

Nicole's eyes narrowed and she removed her arm from around Lily's shoulders. "Of course," she said. "*Namaste.* That means 'go in peace.'"

"Thank you soooo much!" I chirped. Even I could hear how fake and bitchy I sounded. Nicole nodded and, after one more steely-eyed appraisal, walked off.

"So, what do you think?" Lily whispered once we were out of earshot. "She's awesome, right?"

"Oh, she's the best," I said. "I really like the part where you and she emphatically agreed that my shoes are the downfall of Western civilization." If Lily caught any of my sarcasm, she didn't show it. Instead, she waved to the backstage area, where a girl with a sizable 'fro stood next to a lanky guy in a tie suit. Like, the suit was made out of ties.

"Hey, I've got to say hi to Jane and Drew. Wanna come?" I shook my head—had I not just told her I needed some time alone with her?—and Lily looked torn. I decided to make things easy for her.

"I'm going to get us some drinks," I said, marching away before she could protest. "I'll come find you guys."

Somehow, it was even more insulting that she didn't chase after me. But what did I want? For her to realize how upset I was, throw herself at my feet, and beg for forgiveness?

Actually, yes, that is exactly what I wanted.

I situated myself by a table of gluten-free cookies and wheatgrass shots. Gaggles of kids walked by in all manner of perfectly scrappy apparel, some of it obviously crafted by big-name designers to give it that hobo-chic look, other outfits appearing as if they were actually assembled out of the contents of a neighbor's trash can. And as far as I could see, all of them were wearing variations of Lily's feathery trademark quirk. If this party had a theme, it would be What Pinterest Puked, I thought while trying not to stare. Or *D-I-god-Y?, Craft Store Horror, Say it Ain't Sew.* . . . The list went on in my head as I angrily downed wheatgrass shots, which I don't even like.

Then a new voice sounded out from behind me, almost causing me to spill a grass-green concoction down Rachel's dress. "'Etsy atrocities'?" I was surprised out of my thoughts to see a red-haired, freckle-faced boy smiling crookedly down at me.

"Sorry, I didn't realize I'd said that out loud," I mumbled, thinking that, gee, I must be losing it as bad as Lily had if I was talking to myself. Red grinned, and I was relieved to notice that he was dressed like a normal person. Well, at least in the ballpark of normalcy: green denim jeans, a brown long-sleeve shirt, a bright pink bow tie, and an overly warm coat that he had draped across his forearm. He had Harry Potter glasses but a face like Snape's, lending him the look of a large, somewhat ridiculous-looking bird with ginger feathers. He peered at me unapologetically, though somehow managed to avoid any eye contact: It was a look I'd come to know as the "Pathways Appraisal." At least he wasn't wearing any wings either.

"I'd ask if you come here often, but I feel like I already know the answer," Red said, still grinning and pointing to my lack of fairy apparel. "So how about the next cheesiest line I know . . . what brings you here?"

"It's my birthday," I said, surprised by how angry I sounded. I sought out Lily in the crowd of bodies crammed near the catwalk until I finally caught a glimpse of her shimmery wings as they fell into step with a harsh halo of silver and a swatch of metallic feathers. "Though this isn't my party, *obviously*. My friend invited me, and I think she just kinda forgot about my existence."

"That's a bummer." Red followed my gaze. "Are you

talking about that fairy girl? She's a big deal around here. I hear her band is supposed to be excellent. I can't wait till they finally play a show."

"I wouldn't know," I sniffed. "I'm more of a pre-Pathways friend."

"So you don't go there? I noticed you were wingless."

I shook my head. "Nope. But I'm assuming you do?"

"Only school I've ever attended." He puffed out his scrawny chest with mock pride. "I'm the president of our chess club and the corunner of our pickling and canning cooperative. I'm a unique frickin' snowflake, blah blah blah."

I cracked a smile despite myself. "What, Pathways isn't turning you into the best you that you can be? Or whatever nonsense they tell you?"

"Oh yeah, there's some of that," Red said, running his hand through his mop of hair. "But there are also people like her." I followed his gaze past Lily to Nicole, who was flapping her arms aggressively at a waiter.

"Oh? Who's she?" I said, not letting on that I knew exactly who she was.

"My ex." Red sighed and adjusted his glasses. "Worst three months of my life. That girl is a sadist, pure and simple. You could tell by middle school. I mean, who tells their entire eighth grade class that her boyfriend is suffering from a case of 'facial gonorrhea' just because he doesn't want to take her to see *Perks of Being a Wallflower*?"

"Is that even a thing?" I felt bad giggling, but I couldn't help it.

"Yeah, it's this totally overly precious movie based on a totally overly precious book that's basically girl porn." Red stopped when I gave him a *duh* look. "Oh, you meant is facial gonorrhea real? No. But try telling that to a bunch of grossed-out middle school girls. I was a pariah for the rest of that year, and then my entire freshman year after that." I could tell this was obviously a sore subject for Red, because he then shoved two cookies in his mouth, spraying gluten-free macadamia nut crumbs into the stratosphere as he continued to rant. "The thing is, it would be almost okay if Nicole was this *obvious* mean girl. Like if she was a juice-cleanse-obsessed cheerleader or some spoiled actor's kid with a Bentley and a chauffeur vetted by her fellow Scientologists. But instead she walks around campus like a goddess, preaching all this peace, love, and NAMASTE nu-hippie crap, and everyone assumes that she's *nice* and *good*. And now that she's totally coopted your friend's 'wings' look . . ." The gangly boy blanched, seeing my expression darken but misunderstanding why. "I'm sorry, I know I sound mean. I'm not sure if I'm explaining this right."

Unfortunately, he was explaining things exactly as I feared they were. I knew exactly what Red meant. Nicole was a bully, plain and simple. Sure, she might be artistic, creative, and "vegan," but she still used the same torture techniques found in the handbook of any run of the mill cafeteria despot. She didn't even have any creativity herself . . . she had stolen Lily's idea and made it part of her *image*.

Divide and conquer. Belittle and undermine. *Pressure others to do the same.* And push anyone out of the way who might be *even the least bit* threatening. Like me, for instance.

Over Red's shoulder, I could see Lily laughing with her new friends and felt a rush of ice-cold anger race through my veins. Not just at Lily, but for her, too. She had put so much faith in Nicole, seemingly sacrificed so much of who she really was, and what was she getting in return? She had been relegated to lackey status, like one of those sad eels that follow Ursula around in *The Little Mermaid*. Not even the main villain, just a disposable sidekick, there to do the dirty work, like calling out people who've kept your deepest darkest secrets for wearing fake leather.

"No, you've actually been really helpful," I said through gritted teeth. "I think I'm going to find my friend now."

"That's a good idea," Red said, fluffing and fussing around with his coat as if it were made of feathers. "I hope it's not too late. Oh, by the way." From underneath his coat appeared one freckle-spotted hand. "Minerva."

My hand froze halfway out to shake. "Sorry?"

The boy rolled his eyes behind his glasses. "My name. Yeah, it's lame . . . and kind of girly. I guess my parents were really into Greek mythology or something. Most people just call me Min."

"Roman," I said, feeling my stomach plummet into free fall. "Minerva is Roman, but the owl is Greek." Nearby, someone had started running a fog machine, or maybe it was a broken bubble machine. Soon the room got so smoky that it was hard to see anything not right in front of our faces.

Min shrugged. "Cool. Anyway, I hope it's not too late for you to help your friend." Min gave me one last, ponderously curious look, and then disappeared into the machine-generated fog, leaving me alone, birthday-broken and too late to save even myself.

I wasn't even mad when Harper humiliated me in front of Nicole by acting so weirdly snotty and stuck-up. Even though I knew Nicole was just trying to help her be more conscientious about her footwear choices, it probably came off differently to Harper, who just stuck her nose up at her. Honestly, that one was on me. As a NAMASTE representative, I should have spotted Harper's shoes before we even left the house, but I'd been so distracted.

I was still hoping that we could work things out when I introduced Harper to Jane and Drew. They were less intense than Nicole, and I'd even thought about how much Harper would love talking fashion with those two. So when I saw Harper coming up to me, Jane, and Drew, I made a big production about introducing my really, *really* good friend from Hollywood Middle. I felt a little embarrassed that Harper was dressed so . . . low-key. Especially since Jane and Drew had really gone all out with their wings. Jane's were aureolin yellow and pointier than mine, made out of this beautiful beaded muslin fabric her dad had had shipped over from India. Drew's were cerulean blue and orange, aerodynamic and made out of plastic or plexiglass, so they looked like hard, shell-like wings, like the kind you'd find on the first lightning bug of the summer, rather than on a fairy. But I guess that still counted. I made a mental note to check that by Nicole . . . we couldn't have Drew bringing down the NAMASTE/Gawkward Fairy collaboration with something as innocently off-message as the wrong pair of wings!

"Hi," said Harper, barely giving them a glance as she shoved a red plastic cup at me, nearly spilling it down the front of my dress. "Lily, I need to talk to you. It's important."

I caught Jane cocking an eyebrow at Drew and translated the little accompanying thought bubble that I just knew was hovering above her head: *Basic*.

"Um, one second Harper." I smoothed down my skirt and tried to bury the deep thoughts that were burning their way to the surface of my face. "Jane and Drew are the other members of our band."

"Oh, right," Harper said, shooting me a look while shaking Jane's bedazzled denim gloves.

"It's nice to meet you, Harper," Drew said, sticking out an onyx-ringed hand. "Lily has told us so much about you!"

Lie.

"Lily, I really need to talk to you." Harper ignored Drew's out-stuck hand and I felt a flash of something bigger than annoyance. "Can we just get out of here for a minute?"

Well, two could play her ignoring-people game. "Oh, and, duh, how could I forget? Jane is the woman of the hour! This party is for her blog, and she is our hostess with the most-est." I waggled my shoulders, pretending to be sillier than I felt inside. Along with her wings, Jane was wearing a crocheted white minidress with a tangerine slip that matched her lipstick. I doubted anyone else in the world could have pulled off that look, but Harper barely offered her a glance.

"Right. FancyFashionFeminist. Cool," said Harper in monotone.

"Actually," said Jane, "we're just going by the new name now." She pointed at her laminated 3-D button with the $F^3$ logo of my fairy wings. "We might start selling these at Urban Outfitters."

"Wait, really?" I asked, confused. "That's news to me. I mean, are we really trying to sell stuff to the general public?" I knew that Jane was a much savvier businesswoman than I'd ever be—Nicole didn't call me the "creative" in our group for no reason—but I felt uncomfortable with the idea that soon anybody with a credit card could purchase a piece of my grandmother's personal history. I didn't want to become mere merchandise.

"It was Nicole's idea," Jane shrugged. "She said you'd be okay with it."

"So . . . how do you pronounce that?" Harper asked, cutting in before I could ask anything else. "You know, when people ask? Is it F to the power of three? Or F-three? Or Eff-Eff-Eff?"

Drew grinned and acted like Harper had just said the most delightful thing in the world. He closed his eyes and swayed a bit to the music with a slow grin.

"Or what if it was like, Eff-Eff-Eff-Eff-Eff and it just went on forever?" he asked dreamily. "Like when your keyboard gets stuck?"

"Maybe I should just change the name to 'Sound of Drew's Broken Keyboard,'" Jane said, poking him with an orange fingernail. Drew's hands flew to his sides in mock pain.

"Oof," he said.

I took a deep breath and started to relax. The thing about Jane and Drew was that they weren't so serious about everything, the way Nicole and the NAMASTE "bbs" (our name for the younger kids who worshipped the ground Nicole walked on, and who I was sure had parents who bought into Karen "MomTips" Carina and her lecture series) were. Jane and Drew knew how to keep themselves entertained, so there wasn't as much pressure to make a good first impression. Which was good news for Harper—as soon as she stopped playing Alice in Wonderland, I knew everyone was going to love her.

"So, Harper," Drew said. "Where do you go to school? Lily said you guys met in, like, second grade or something."

"Actually it was fourth," I mumbled, not loud enough for anyone to hear me.

"You tell me," Harper said. "You're the one who has heard so much about me." Harper was sucking in her cheeks in that way that made her look exactly like her mother. "I guess you're the expert." Jane raised an eyebrow and even Drew, ever the peacemaker, took a step back to avoid Harper's venom.

It was like watching a train wreck in slow motion. I wanted to clap my hands over Harper's mouth. I wanted to travel back in time to before I ever tried to meld my two friend groups together. I wanted a button that would erase everyone's memories. Unfortunately, none of those things were in the Gawkward Fairy's bag of tricks. So instead I just did what I do best: make everyone so uncomfortable that they stop fighting.

"I have to go to the bathroom!" I yelled over the very loud music . . . that had stopped playing the moment I opened my mouth. If my life had a soundtrack, it would just be a series of *womp-womp*s.

"Come on, Harper," I said, grabbing her elbow. "I need you to come with me to the bathroom."

"To do *what*?" Harper protested.

"To do . . . whatever it is that girls do in the bathroom together!" I exhaled impatiently. "Tampon fights. Cuticle selfies. Whatever!"

I turned to Jane and Drew and smiled extra wide. "Guys, I'll catch up with you in two seconds!" I dashed off with my BFF—if that's what she still was—at my elbow. Hopefully I hadn't just ruined my entire life at Pathways by bringing Harper to this party.

Once I'd managed to drag Harper into the bathroom, I took a breath and surveyed the room, which was decoupaged with old food magazine photos, a lot of which featured a sort of meatlike substance suspended in gelatin. *Cool,* I thought.

"Gross," Harper said, surveying the same walls with judgmental eyes. "This place is just too much. I'm getting a headache. I think I'm just going to go home."

"What?" I sputtered.

"I'm not having a good time," Harper said, making eye contact for the first time in . . . forever, actually.

"Well, that's because you won't give anyone a chance!" I heard myself pleading, and prayed that no one would have to use the bathroom anytime soon. I knew Harper was having a terrible time, and that I'd really messed up on her birthday, but she couldn't just leave me here alone!

"Look, I don't want to take you away from your friends," Harper said. "And you're obviously *really* popular at school, and that's great. I love how your . . . *look* . . . has really caught on. But I don't really think this is my scene, and it's getting late, and I really don't want to . . . *burden* you with having to keep *babysitting* me all night. *On my birthday!*"

I knew Harper meant this whole speech to come off sarcastically, but it actually made a whole lot of sense. I was feeling torn between my two worlds, the one that Old Lily used to call home and the one that New Lily was trying to make for herself. If Harper left, then I could just be New Lily, and never look back. I wouldn't have to worry about that stupid pact we made on the beach, the one I'd been dreading thinking about ever since I had entered Pathways. The one where I said I would never do anything to fit in, that I'd never be a bully to someone like Beth-Lynne (forgive me, Beth-Lynne!) to make friends.

But . . . the idea of facing those crowds—and Nicole—alone seemed really overwhelming right now. Plus, it was *Harper's birthday.*

"Don't leave me," I said. "Seriously, I need you here. For emotional support, if nothing else. Can you wait just a little while and we'll do a little birthday thing after? This night is really important for me . . . and for us! Please, PuppyGirl, help out a gawkward girl in distress!"

Harper shook her head. "I think we're getting a little too old for nicknames. And just so you know? My birthday never had to wait before."

I was so stunned that I couldn't come up with any response, but it didn't matter, because before I could say anything, she streaked out of the bathroom like an *haute couture* blur.

And now for a recap of this crappy evening thus far, folks: I was now stuck in a bathroom stall, friendless, and too chicken to go out and face the party alone. Like I was some friendless Gawkward mascot, instead of a real person.

And I didn't even have to go.

I left the bathroom and wandered over to a table piled high with bright red cups and poured myself a glass of punch, making sure to sniff it first. As alternative as this party was, I wasn't going to risk it: getting wasted is the kind of stupid activity that can cross all social barriers. Luckily, the punch was clean. I stood and waited for Lily to run out of the bathroom and up to me with tear-stained cheeks.

After a couple of minutes, I poured myself another glass of punch. And then waited some more.

And some more.

And some more.

By the time I'd drained my fourth cup of vicious red Kool-Aid, a half hour had passed and I had to go to the bathroom—for real this time. Maybe I would find Lily still in there, quietly sobbing in a stall. I felt a stab of guilt. I hadn't wanted her to be that *upset*.

I shouldn't have worried. The moment I swung the bathroom door open, I heard a familiar voice speaking animatedly, clearly mid-rant.

". . . don't know what's gotten into her!" Lily's back was turned toward me, but the group she was talking to—Nicole, Jane, and even Drew—all stood facing the ladies' room door. They were all clearly surprised to see me, but when Drew perked up and tried to alert Lily to my arrival, Nicole subtly tapped him and hushed him up. "But, I promise you, Jane, Harper's super grateful for the invitation. I know she's having such a good time. She can just be kind of . . . not the best, socially. And I really didn't want to embarrass her by mentioning the dress code, especially when I saw that what she was wearing was so . . . *conceptually challenged*. But really, thank you thank you thank you so much for inviting her. I couldn't think of anywhere else to take her for her birthday, so you really saved me."

Part of my brain was telling me to go, just leave it be. But I was stuck; rooted like one of those ancient mosquitoes caught in amber from *Jurassic Park*. Drew let out a nervous, uncomfortable laugh, and Lily finally turned around. The shock on her face was enough to let me know that she'd assumed that I'd left the party entirely, and that I was the last person she was expecting to see. Her friends looked embarrassed and started making their way to the door to leave us alone in our own personal version of bestie hell.

"Er, well . . . good chat," Nicole said, breezing by me, her steely wings cold on my shoulder. "I've got to go mingle. See you later, Lily!"

Jane and Drew followed, looking at least a little apologetic, and the door swung shut behind them.

"Hey." Now that we were alone, the echo of my sullen greeting rang dully against the linoleum floor.

"Hey, lady!" Lily was laughing nervously, pretending to do her hair in the mirror. "There you are! I was about to come looking for you. But then I got caught up talking to Nicole, and . . ."

"Save it," I cut her off. "I was just coming to see if

you were okay. But I should have gotten the hint a long time ago. You are doing just fine without me."

Lily's eyes started to water, but I threw out my hand, palm up.

"No! Just . . . no." I felt ice cold. "You can cry later. I am really sick of protecting you from all the bad feelings in the world, Lily! Especially right now, because those bad feelings you're sensing? They're coming from me."

She still wasn't looking at me, but I could see her reflection in the mirror above the sinks. Her lips were moving, and I knew she was just drowning me out with whatever whispery mumble-jumble she was reciting to herself. I pressed on anyway.

"I can't believe you were talking about me. That's such a mean-girl thing to do." I folded my arms and tapped my toes impatiently, blocking the bathroom's exit. If this was about become a toxic drama zone, then so be it: Get out the quarantine gear, don't let anyone else inside, because this was going down. "It's like this school has totally changed you into this completely different person, and I don't recognize her at all!"

"I wasn't . . ." Lily interrupted.

"Stop it!" I forgot myself and yelled . . . and I'm not a yeller. "Don't do your ditzy little 'Oh I didn't know what you were feeling because I live in my magical world of la-la fairies!' thing! You know you haven't been there for me since you started Pathways. Did you know that I had my very first kiss with Derek Wheeler? I mean *Derek Wheeler*? The *smelly kid*?! And everyone at school has seen what I look like pretending to be drunk, and it's not cute! Like Derek 'Smelly Kid' Wheeler gets to look down on me with his stupid girlfriend Kendall, and I can barely get anyone to talk to me. And it's *not okay* that you're my best friend and don't know any of this because every time we text or talk on the phone, you just respond to everything with these fake-cheery replies that just gloss over everything real, and prevent us from having an *actual* conversation about real feelings. It's like you're avoiding me without actually avoiding me and it drives me crazy! And it's also not okay that I have to feel weird about the fact that I'm hanging out with Tim without you. And it's not okay that all you care about is that bully Nicole and her stupid NAMASTE club! *We had a pact about not changing to fit in!* Or doesn't that mean anything to you anymore?"

"Don't you *dare* put this on Nicole!" Lily's eyes flashed. "Look, I am sorry that I've been, like, a less attentive friend than I could have been. But Pathways is making me feel really good about myself! You say that I've changed, but this is the real me! For once, I finally feel like everyone likes me for *me*, and not just for being friends with *you*!"

I could see I was pushing Lily farther away, and I could hear how jealous and paranoid I sounded, but it was like I was having an out-of-body experience, unable to stop myself from barreling down this toxic route. "Nicole is a garbage person, Lily! And she *is* a *bully*! She's just stealing your look and using it to bully everyone to dress exactly the same! She's turned something creative and unique into a "brand" to sell a product . . . you! And she's a vegan who eats shrimp! *SHRIMP!*" I was on the verge of a full nuclear explosion, and I didn't care who heard. "Are you really going to stand here and tell me you don't see a hypocrisy problem with that?"

"They're barely animals." Even Lily looked a little confused by her logic.

"Shrimp is meat, I don't care how small their brains are! And," I continued, unsure if I would ever be able to stop, "no offense, but her entire *ish* is phony! This whole NAMASTE thing? It's not about anything! It's just an excuse for her to lord over a meaningless club, like they have in any other school. It doesn't put you above anyone else, and it doesn't give you the right to start treating your real friends like compost!"

Lily snorted and turned away to face the mirror instead of me. Wasn't that just a giant metaphor for our friendship now? The thought had me digging my nails into my palms.

"You know, you don't just get to win fights because you're good at crying," I said, turning my heart to stone.

"You say I treat my friends like compost?" Lily turned on me, eyes blazing through her tears. "What about you? Here you are complaining about how alone you've been this whole time, when you've just admitted that there's been one very specific person by your side this entire time. Or are you so busy feeling sorry for yourself you can't even stop and see that Tim, my *ex-boyfriend,* is totally in love with you?"

I heard someone push open the door to the bathroom. "Occupied!" I screamed. "Use the boys' room! Or hold it in!" Whoever it was fled pretty quickly. "So that's what this is about," I said, shaking my head. "You're still not over Tim. And you're blaming me? What, because a guy I've known my whole life is the only person in my entire school who will deign to hang out with me?"

"No! That's not what I meant! I don't even know why I said that." Lily groaned and pressed her head against the wall, slightly banging it in frustration.

I took a breath to keep my hands from shaking. "Here's a quick question Lily: Why are you so scared what everyone is going to think of you if they find out you hang out with a lame, *normal* person like me? Because I never cared what people thought when I hung out with you!"

That finally got Lily away from her mirror, and she came stalking up to me so fast I took an accidental step backward.

"Oh, so you should get a medal because you were *so brave* for being my friend all these years? You think that I'm like one of your stray dogs and I need you to take care of me? Is that how you think about our friendship? That it's just some *chore*?"

I folded my arms in front of me. "Well, it's certainly not been very fun recently, has it?"

Lily drew herself up tall, to the highest height of her tiny, fairy-girl frame. "If that's how you really feel, than maybe you should just leave," she said in a calm voice that didn't match her tear-stained face.

"Fine. Stay blind," I sputtered. "I'm out of here. Tell your mom I took an Uber home. Thanks for the awesome birthday party, *Gawkward Fairy*. I hope you and your new friends will be very happy together."

No reply, though this time I wasn't going to wait around for my former best friend to revert to her old, quirky self. I had my phone out of my pocket and was booking a taxi before I'd even turned to the exit. But I didn't leave before taking off Lily's "thoughtful" gift and throwing it at her feet. She could jump up and down and tear that necklace to pieces—what was it to me?

Five minutes later, I was speeding down the 101, asking the driver to put on some music—any music—to drown out the thoughts raging through my brain. He responded by flipping on a Ukrainian Sirius channel, which actually served as the perfect distraction.

I didn't even look back, not once, and didn't even let myself cry until we were safe on the freeway.

It had been fourteen hours since my big fight with Harper, and I was spiraling down a dark, endless-seeming rabbit hole. It had been half a tortuous day since the party, in which exactly zero bytes of information had been traded between us. Maybe there were some messages lost up there in the cloud somewhere, but I had no idea what kind of *Inception*-level security was necessary to enter the incorporeal info-cloud. Does it involve Google? Because I do know how to Google.

I clung to my hope that this would turn out to be just a Wi-Fi-based issue of miscommunication, two ships filled with emojis, passing in the night, buoyed by the soft caress of the information waves of the . . . cloud.

I really, really needed someone to explain to me what *the cloud* was.

But as morning turned into afternoon, my emotions churned through a whole life's worth of cycles. At first I was furious at Harper for saying those terrible things about me and my friends, and mad that she didn't even try to listen to what I had to say. Then I was annoyed because she refused to answer her phone all night when I was calling to ask if she was all right. Like I'm sorry we had a fight but we're not *animals*. We need to let one another know that we got home safely!

Then I was scared: What if something terrible had happened to her? What if our fight was the last conversation we'd ever have together? Then, guilt: I shouldn't have let her take an Uber home by herself. What if her driver didn't have his license, or abducted her and took her back to the headquarters of his weird Manson cult! Then I felt so much shame for being so snappy with her in the bathroom, which led to me feeling angry again that she had ridden me so hard about Nicole and my new friends.

I was totally spiraling. I needed a break before I went completely insane.

That afternoon I decided to give Mom a break from my frantic pacing and headed out for a ride on my bike. I debated riding by Harper's place, but I didn't want to look like a stalker, so instead I veered right and went to the only spot in Los Angeles where I knew I could find my Zen: Yogurt to Be Kidding Me.

Okay, so I'm just like everyone else. I love fro-yo. Sue me for being *obvious*. I used to be a big Pinkberry-head, then for about six months I went through a brief love affair with Menchie's iced-coffee-flavored confection, with little chocolate sprinkles dotted on top. After that, it was Yogurt Stop because of all the flavors and glittery names ("Hallelujah! It's Raining Red Velvet Men" and "Shake Your Salted Caramel Booty" were my two favorites), but that place became a paparazzi feeding pool after a bunch of the *Real Housewives* and Rachel Zoe started bringing their kids in for treats and some quick and easy paparazzi exposure. Plus, eating all those thick concoctions almost daily eventually made me gain five pounds—it might as well have been real ice cream. My backup fro-yo stop those days was Yogurt

Piazza for red velvet and original mixed in with banan-as, berries, and drizzled with some chocolate. And The Big Chill, and, oh, Studio Yogurt, which closed and it was so heartbreaking because they had the cheapest prices and the biggest portions and it was amazing.

Which was why it was no less than a small miracle when I found Yogurt to Be Kidding Me over the summer. I thought I'd died and gone to low-cal frozen treat heaven. Yogurt to Be . . . was owned by this cute Korean couple who ran the shop out of an unassuming basement in the Brentwood Place Shopping Plaza. Warm, low lighting glowed from the Edison bulbs strung around the dispen-sary, and the tables were made from dark cherry wood instead of the usual glaringly white Formica. The *ambi-ence*, to use a Yelp term, was quiet. I liked how no-frills it was, because it added to its magical hideaway charm. It wasn't self-serve the way that most yogurt shops are these days. Instead, you just told one of the owners what size you wanted and picked from the mercifully brief list of toppings, all of the natural fruit and nut vari-eties. The only sauce they offered was honey, and they only served one flavor of yogurt: original.

But best of all, the place wasn't even listed online, and it had very little foot traffic—which was why it was especially strange to walk in on a Sunday afternoon to find Stephanie Adler sitting in one of the shop's four seats, her blond hair framed by a halo of soft sunlight filtering down from the lone small window above the door.

*Great.* The last thing I needed right now was one of

Harper's friends giving me the stink-eye, so I ordered a small, unadorned fro-yo and sat as far away from her as I possibly could. Which wasn't very far: the one thing Yogurt To Be . . . had in common with its competition was its lack of space. I pretended to study my required NAMASTE text, *Be Here Now*, but it was just a confusing bunch of nonsense (*where else was I but here? Now?*). I really liked the pictures, though. Maybe it would make more sense once I was fully enlightened. Then, a voice cut through my attempt at meditation.

"Original?"

Sure enough, Stephanie had noticed me.

I frowned and exaggeratedly put my finger in the book, trying to give her the impression that I was too busy to talk, and swiveled my head in her direction. "Excuse me?"

Stephanie motioned to my fro-yo and quirked her eyebrow.

"Oh, yeah," I said. "It's the only flavor they have." I put my nose back in my book; I wasn't in the mood to talk, but my body language didn't deter her at all. I could hear the rustling of her backpack as she got up to sit across from me. Funny, I always thought of Stephanie as more of a purse person, but when I finally did look up to meet her gigantic smile, I saw that she'd made some major changes to her style, even since the last time I'd seen her in the park. She was wearing boy shorts and a wifebeater and was sporting the beginnings of some serious dreadlocks.

Still, underneath all that skater girl grunge, Stephanie was still as bubbly as ever. Out of Harper's pre-Us friends, I had always liked Stephanie the best. But it was hard to think of Steph without thinking of Jessica, but Jessica had always been removed and cold and a little robot-y. Stephanie, though, was the first to follow Harper's lead and join in on any group activities. The only reason we weren't better friends was that she had been so glued to Jessica's hip all the time.

"I really like that they only serve one flavor here," she said, sucking on her plastic spoon. "All those other places try to give you every possible flavor choice that you'd never want, like Strawberry Bourbon Cheesecake, or Mojito Kale or . . . Lobster. You can't even find anything resembling just plain-style anymore. It's all 'Bitter Tart Vanilla Bubblegum.'"

"Sometimes Original is the most original." I thought that was a very Zen comment, but when I saw the crinkle-confused look on Stephanie's face, I realized how pretentious I sounded. "Sorry, that made much more sense in my head."

"No," she said. "That's exactly what I meant. You nailed it."

For the first time in a while, I could feel my face relaxing into a real smile, one that Stephanie beamed back at me with the ease of a native Californian.

"It's like those perfumes I see sometimes, there's this whole line with normal stuff like 'Apple Cake' and 'Vanilla Candy,' but then there's 'Play-Dough,' and 'Fresh Sheets,' and 'Dirt' and 'Library Books.'" Stephanie made a face. "Who would want to smell like an old book?"

"I actually think that sounds romantic." My phone chimed, and I grabbed for it, thinking it was Harper.

Jane (5:05pm): Where are you??

Shoot! Band practice! I had forgotten all about it! I shoved my book in my bag—luckily, I had stashed my Lily-Fairy wings in there the night before—and looked longingly at my half-finished fro-yo.

"Was that Harper?" Stephanie asked. "Are you guys hanging out still? I never see you around anymore."

"Um . . . no." It was too long of a story, and the last thing I wanted to do before getting together with my Pathways friends was rehash Harper drama. I grabbed my bag, my chair making a scraping noise as I stood up too quickly. Oof, brain freeze.

"Hey, do you need a ride somewhere?" Stephanie pointed outside. "My older brother is going to be here any second. We could drop you off."

"Actually, yeah, that would be great. Thanks," I told her, grateful. "I'm going to my friend Jane's for band practice. She lives right around here."

"You're in a band?" For some reason, Stephanie's look of surprise made me smile. "That's awesome. I'd love to hear you play."

"Sure!" I spoke before I really thought it through, but Jane wouldn't mind if Stephanie came to rehearsal, right? And maybe Stephanie would go back and tell Harper how relaxed and happy I seemed with my new friends, who were all wonderful and accepted me, and then Harper would come to her senses.

Stephanie's brother Jack turned out to be way older, like in his twenties. He had Stephanie's blond hair and giant smile, but compared to Steph's unkempt dreadlocks and accompanying skateboard, he was as clean-cut as a Ken doll. His red surf shorts and yellow tee coordinated perfectly with both his Lightning Bolt surfboard and his crimson convertible. He belonged on a Tumblr called "Cute Cali Boys" or something.

When we drove up to Jane's split-level ranch house in Bel-Air, I thanked Jack and was about to jump out when Steph twisted around in her seat and watched me struggle to put on my fairy wings. "Do you need help with that?" She asked, laughing.

I felt a little embarrassed as she tightened the straps on either side. The wings were a little . . . no, at this point they were *beyond* gawkward. They were way bent out of shape and they didn't even make me feel like *me* anymore. It was more like a "Lily" costume I had to put on to go to school and for NAMASTE activities. On the weekends, I rarely even carried them on me, unless I knew I'd be running into Pathways people.

Jane was waiting impatiently by the door as we arrived. "You're late," she admonished, wagging one matte fingernail at me. I hated being called out, for any reason, and Jane looked particularly annoyed this afternoon. She looked behind me, to where Stephanie was standing.

"Stephanie, Jane, Jane, Stephanie. Steph and I know each other from middle school. She wanted to hear us practice."

Jane leaned in the doorway and exhaled slowly, looking Stephanie up and down.

"Hi," Jane said to Stephanie. And then to me: "Nicole is not going to like this." She shook her head and beckoned us in. Stephanie shot me a quizzical look, but I was just as confused as her. Why was Nicole at band practice? She didn't even approve of non-NAMASTE activities.

Jane's parents had the best basement for practice, which made total sense: Once upon a time, it had actually been part of recording studio, built after Jane's mom decided to quit modeling and self-release her first (and only) album of Afghan rubab music. Jane, Drew, and I had listened to it once, and I didn't think it was all that bad. I had especially liked the part where Sting came in to sing backup vocals on the Pashto track.

As we descended the stairs, Nicole came into view. She was sitting with her back to us, her hair as gleaming and as silvery as the dials on the control board she was jabbing. She was wearing the same wings from the party, though they had lost a little bit of their metallic luster . . . now they just looked like they were molting.

On the other side of the glass partition was Drew, sitting on a stool and balancing his jug xylophone on his lap. His wings lay on the group in a heap: he'd apparently taken them off to jug more freely.

"You're late." Nicole didn't even bother to turn around. "And? Not to dump all my truth on you at once, Lily, but you were very rude last night. You didn't even participate in our closing meditation service at the end of the party."

"Sorry." I could feel Stephanie shifting on her heels behind me. "I was distracted."

Nicole swiveled in her chair and regarded us, eyes narrowing at the new visitor.

"I'm sorry." She smiled at Stephanie, barely looking sorry at all. "But this is a closed session. Members only."

I cringed inwardly, but Stephanie just smiled and extended her hand like nothing was wrong.

"Hey, I'm Stephanie," she said. "I'm Lily's friend from . . ."

Nicole swiveled back around as if she couldn't be bothered to hear the end of the sentence. She snapped at Drew through the microphone hooked up to the recording studio. "Okay, Drew! Let's try it again. This time, I really need to hear the soul!" Drew winced, his wings shaking a little. "You need to make *love* to the jugs. Otherwise we're just listening to a guy tooting into a water bottle. You have to stop. Stop tooting!"

Stephanie laughed, muffling her mouth with her hands. I could tell from the way Jane and Drew widened their eyes that this was the most sacrilegious thing she could have done. In all fairness to Steph, the scene was ridiculous: four kids dressed up like DIY pigeons, looking like rejects from a hipster cosplay convention, yelling about making love to jugs and *tooting*. I had to work to suppress my own giggle.

Nicole wheeled back around and once again fixed on us both with a stare as steely as her plumage. "Lily, I thought I asked your friend to leave. I cannot abide anyone mocking our expression of self through music." Stephanie grabbed my arm, and I knew if I looked over at her we'd both lose it completely.

"Come on Nicole," I said, temporarily insane with endorphins. "No one is making fun. It's just . . . *funny*. In a good way. I promise."

"I can call my brother," Stephanie said. Somehow, she was still effortlessly composed, as if Nicole's withering stare and demands that she leave didn't make her feel subhuman. "I didn't know it was going to be a problem."

"No!" I cried, surprising myself with my own forcefulness. "That's not fair. I want you to stay." I turned back to Nicole with pleading eyes. "Come on, she can

243

stay, right?"

"Band members only," Nicole said. "Sorry. Them's the rules."

"What rules? You're not even in the band!"

I had overstepped, and I knew it. I could feel Nicole's chi shifting the room into majorly negative NAMASTErritory. "Lily." Nicole said my name in the key of a disappointed school teacher. "I am lending my services today in a managerial-slash-producer capacity. Music is always a collaboration, and no role is more necessary than that of the person who tells you when something is not living up to its fullest potential."

"Well, can't an audience do that, too?" If I was going to alienate every single one of my friends in the same weekend, I might as well finish the job now in one broad stroke. "Stephanie can offer feedback as an audience member! Seriously, she just wants to hear us play!"

"I *so* highly doubt that. I mean, look at her." Nicole waved her hand dismissively at Stephanie, whose outfit was so far from offensive it could have been in a *Teen Vogue* spread for "How to Appear Nonthreatening": white tee, shorts, Vans, beanie.

"She just looks so . . ." Nicole groped for words.

Nicole snapped her fingers at Jane, who had somehow materialized behind me, in the middle of the staircase, where she was balancing a tray of chilled Kombucha tea. "Jane, what does she look like to you?"

I could tell Jane's blank stare of incomprehension annoyed Nicole even more. "I guess she looks . . . normal?"

Nicole nodded. "Very *normative*," she said, misusing the word completely. "There's no imagination there. This outfit is afraid to tell us anything. It's the uniform of the herd of the rich, popular kids who never question authority or try to broaden their horizons. It's totally *off-message*." Nicole grinned savagely. "I mean, of course I'm not talking about you . . . um . . . Stacy?"

"Stephanie," I said dully, answering for my friend.

"Right. Well, I'm just talking about your fashion statement, *obviously* . . ." Nicole's smile made it obvious that she was doing no such thing. Jane and Drew hadn't made a peep yet, which made me a little angry at them, but then I realized I hadn't really stood up to Nicole either. This whole situation made me want to curl up and die, in an all too familiar way.

*Bully.*

Harper's description of Nicole floated through my head like a bouquet of giant, green, sickly balloons. *Phony.* She had called NAMASTE a meaningless club, a clique, just like the kind you'd find at any other school. But how was that possible? Nicole didn't look like a bully. Her philosophical ideas about being yourself and expressing your creativity didn't fall in line with classic bully-speak. But if Nicole was treating Stephanie like poo just because of how she dressed, what else do you call that besides "bullying"?

Oh my god. Had Harper been right all along?

While all this was short-circuiting my brain, the room's bad vibes had only increased. Stephanie calmly began to collect her skateboard from where she had stashed it under the stairs. "Well, I better be going and let you guys go back to it," she said cheerfully. "It was nice to meet you all!"

She sauntered up the stairs and I followed behind her. "I'm just going to go . . . walk her to the door," I mumbled. Nicole scowled, but turned back to the control board without a word.

"Sorry about that," I whispered, feeling a dark pit in my stomach as I funeral-marched Stephanie out of Jane's house. "Nicole can be intense sometimes."

"It's no problem. I've dealt with girls like her before." Stephanie really did look unfazed as she rifled through her bag for some ChapStick. "I can never find anything in here," she sighed, faux-exasperated. "You know how it's always the one thing you need that's never in you gigantic purse?" She finally found the little tube and blotted a layer onto already perfectly shiny lips.

"Sure," I said. "Kind of."

"Take Harper." Stephanie capped her ChapStick and zipped up her bag in the practiced way of someone who never had to look for anything, ever. "Every day when I see her in school, she's bugging me to borrow my phone charger. She is, like, constantly losing hers. And she's afraid of her phone dying and she won't turn it off during class, she told me, because I guess she's worried that she might miss a message from you."

"Really?" My voice came out scratchy.

"Yeah." Stephanie shrugged, one hand on the door. "I told her, they're not like dropped phone calls. Verizon can't just make a text disappear. It's always *there*, waiting for you. You know?" She paused. "Anyway, it was good to see you, Lily. I hope you have fun with your band. They seem very . . . creative."

I gulped and nodded and closed the door behind her. Below, faintly, I could hear music playing, and Nicole yelling above the din.

"Okay," she shouted. "This time, let me really hear you jug!"

"How much does a smoothie cost?" Rachel had stationed herself on my floor, propped up by rugs and throw pillows. In the past couple days she'd created a proper nest in my bedroom where she liked to use her laptop.

"I don't know," I mumbled, head under my covers and pillow. "Eight dollars maybe?"

Rachel snorted. *"Eight dollars* for a smoothie? That's ludicrous. That's, like, the cost of three meals, for just one smoothie."

My sister had been trying out some sort of paleo-keto-gluten-free-cleanse thing for the last couple of days, a side effect from her sudden "break" from Jacques. ("Jacques said we need to take time to explore other people," was how she'd described it. "I totally agree with him," she lied.) As much as I dislike Jacques-attack, I dislike Rachel-on-a-diet even more. The plus side of the breakup was that she was now fully available on a Sunday to tend to her depressed and lonely little sister. But another downside: For the first time in my life, I couldn't care less that Rachel was being nice to me.

"Ew, it says here that one large Jamba Juice contains the calorie and sugar equivalent of twelve donuts. Who would eat twelve donuts?" Rachel's eyes were glued to the screen. "Did you know that for two hundred and

247

fifty dollars we can buy a pretty decent smoothie maker? If you drink two smoothies a day, that would pay for itself, in like. . . ." She turned and caught me looking catatonically right back at her. I shrugged. Math was neither of our strong suits.

"A week? Or no, a month?" Rachel went back to clicking. "I'm hearing a lot of good things about superfoods. Maybe we should get really into baby bok choy."

"Okay, GOOPster." My phone buzzed from the drawer of my bedside table and I groaned. I had turned it off when Lily wouldn't stop calling after I left the party, but I'd forgotten how itchy my fingers got for CandyCrush if they went too long without it, so I broke down and turned it on again in the morning. You win again, apps!

"Who is it?" Rachel asked, prying her eyes away from zoomed-in images of overpriced blenders.

"Tim wants to know if I want to go to something called Wacko with him." I leaned over to Rachel. "Hey, can you actually Google, 'What is a wacko?'"

"Harper! Wacko Soap Plant! I love that place!" Rachel jumped out of her blanket fort, making pillow shams and poufs rain down like she was Godzilla trapped in a Jonathan Adler store. "It's like this insane toy-store-slash-punk-rock-explosion emporium. I can't even describe it! Tell him we'll be there in twenty."

"We?"

Rachel grabbed me by the arm and gave me a tug. I barely budged, which was an appropriate response since at the moment I was officially a wet lump of nothing.

"Stop, I feel like one giant bruise." I yanked my arm away and buried myself even deeper under the covers.

"Your life is one giant bruise," Rachel said, throwing on her favorite black hoodie, the one that said "Hug

Life" in bedazzled letters. "Get up, we're going. I can't watch you mope around like a *Twilight* vampire just because you got into a fight with Lily."

When I got home the night before I ran straight up to my room and practically ripped my stupid dress off. Moments later, Rachel knocked on my door, quietly asking if I was okay or if I wanted anything. When I didn't reply, she padded away, but in the morning she showed up at my door with a box of tissues and two bowls of cereal, suggesting a Netflix marathon of an obscure British comedy.

"Fine," I grumbled now, remembering how thoughtful she was being. "We'll meet him. But you're buying me something adorable. Preferably Hello Kitty related."

"Yay! Tell your *boyfriend* we'll be there pronto. Unless you want me to tell him, but watch out, I might start texting loooooove poems from your cell phone." Rachel made a swipe for my phone before I could stop her, and held down my flailing attempts at recovery with one hand.

"'Hey, how did it go last night?'" Rachel read from my phone in a fake-deep voice. "'Hey, just checking in to see if everything with Lily went okay, plz text me back. I have something 4 u.'" Rachel waggled her eyebrows suggestively at that one. I groaned and flopped onto my back as she read the last message before the Wacko one, from this morning, out loud. "'Okay, well what I wanted to say last night is that I hope Lily threw you an excellent birthday party and it was all you ever wanted, because you are great and deserve it. That's all.'"

Rachel looked properly mollified, and handed me back my phone without another word. "Okay," I shouted as if she were still twisting my arm (which she kind of was). "Enough. Let's go to this stupid toy shop."

♥

Because it was a weekend, it took us an extra twenty minutes to find parking on Hollywood Boulevard in Los Feliz, so we were a little late to arrive at Wacko Soap Plant, which was sensory overload from the moment we walked in. It was like Willy Wonka's Chocolate Factory, but for weird Day of the Dead totems and porny robots instead of chocolate rivers and Never-Ending Gobstoppers. I tried to mentally catalogue all the oddball stuff I saw, but gave up after I found a taxidermy alligator head next to a product that accurately billed itself as "Hot Dog Earbuds." A vintage *My Little Pony* lunchbox was mounted on one of the claustrophobically tight walls, next to a hologram poster of the Hindu god Ganesh, whom I recognized from that one Simpson's episode. I spotted a *Doctor Who* TARDIS ice bucket (because yes, I do know about nerdy things!) buried under two throw pillows shaped like a red Converse sneaker and a bag of potato chips, respectively.

"Hey, you're here!" Tim raced down the aisle pushing an overflowing shopping cart, grinning like a kid in a candy store (that also happened to sell Batman plushies). "How are you feeling?"

"Fine," I grumbled. To prevent Rachel from eavesdropping, I grabbed the cart from Tim and began pushing it back the way it came. I could hear Tim as he panted to catch up behind me.

"Hey, what's up? Harper?"

I didn't slow down till we reached the novelty gag section, all fake farts and spitting ink pens.

"Are you okay?" Tim stood in front of me with his hands on my shoulders. "What are you so upset about?"

"Nothing," I muttered. "I just had a bad night." Tim gave me a sympathetic look, as if he already knew.

"What are you, a psychic? Or am I just always having terrible nights so it's the go-to explanation?" I suddenly had this image of myself as baby rattlesnake, just snapping and biting and releasing all my bad feelings.

"No, I just figured . . . you usually text me back," He scratched the back of his neck. "I was worried." I thought about the millions of texts Lily had sent me since last night, filled with more emotion than all of the ones she'd sent since school started combined. Of course half of them were in all caps and totally shouty, but a couple had made it seem like she was genuinely concerned.

"There's nothing to be worried about. I'm totally fine. Last night was fine." I grabbed the first thing I saw off the shelf and pretended to study it. "Yikes. What is this?"

Tim studied the label earnestly. "Cat Butt Gum. Looks legit. Should we get it?"

I immediately dropped it back on the shelf and wiped my hands on my shorts. When I looked up, Tim was staring at me with knowing eyes, practically willing me to tell him the truth about my birthday disaster.

"Okay, fine," I admitted, no longer able to distract myself with juvenile candy packaging. "Lily's party was terrible. It wasn't even *for me*. She just dragged me along as a plus-one to one of her stuck-up Pathways friend's parties. And they are all such suck-tacular Vampires and Murderers going around pretending they're hippies. You should have heard them, Tim, they were so fake and condescending. And then Lily and her new BFF Nicole told me that my FAUX LEATHER shoes were responsible for, like, genocides and the decline in adult literacy or something."

"Huh." I waited for Tim to continue his thought. I fully expected him to be outraged on my behalf, but apparently I wasn't doing a great job describing how terrible it had been. I went on.

"So, I tell Lily it's *fine* to leave me alone at this party with the approximately zero people I know, and then she's gone before you could say 'traitor'! Oh, and I met this guy who said Lily's friend Nicole is pure EVIL."

"Huh."

"So, wait, the worst part? When I go to talk to Lily, she's in the bathroom, apologizing to all her new, cool friends for bringing *me*! She's totally changed, and I don't even recognize her. And I tried to tell her how upset I was but she just told me I should leave if I didn't like it and so I did and she didn't even try to stop me!"

"Uh-huh."

"Stop saying that!" I exploded. "I need you to be more sympathetic! You're my shoulder to cry on!" I meant that last part as a joke, but Tim took his hands off my shoulders and looked embarrassed.

"Sorry," I said, quickly backtracking. "That was just a bad joke. But I could really use some friendly support right now, is the thing."

Tim reached behind me and picked up a plastic box. "Do you know what this is, Harper?"

"A dorky toy?" I asked.

"No. This is a vintage edition Antman figurine. They only made one batch of these, in the nineties, when Marvel was merchandizing all their characters up the wazoo. At the time, a lot of stores didn't think they would sell, because who cares about Antman, right? Except today there's this total surge of interest in those old characters, and now it's the totally random heroes with the really ridiculous powers that are worth a fortune."

"Okay . . . ?" I had no idea where Tim was going with this.

Tim blew his cheeks up with air and then slowly exhaled. "I'm just saying, did it ever occur to you that maybe being at Pathways helps Lily feel like she's valuable? That she's not just some novelty product"—he motioned to the junk surrounding us—"but that she's actually talented? And that it might feel good to have people appreciate her for all those same little quirks that made her an outsider before?"

"But I liked Lily the way she was! I always appreciated her!"

Tim had the ghost of a smile. "Right. And that's great. But maybe what she's expressing—albeit terribly and maybe a little misguidedly—is that she finally feels like other people, besides you, finally get what she's about. That her creativity is being appreciated exactly because it's not like everyone else's?"

"But where does that leave me?" I asked. "I feel like I'm being left behind. Everyone else I know can do stuff. You draw, Stephanie skateboards, Lily . . . well, Lily creates these entire worlds to exist in. And what's my thing? What am I good at? Liking animals? Having friends and losing them? Peaking in middle school? Are those my superpowers?"

Tim looked serious. "What's your 'thing,' Harper? What's your 'superpower'? Do you really not know?"

I really didn't. I did notice, however, that Tim and I were standing really, really close to each other.

"The way you believe in us is what makes you special, Harper," Tim said. "You bring out the super in everyone."

I wanted to cry, but I was too busy not breaking eye contact with Tim, who was less than a freckle's width away from me.

"No, I can't do anything," I whispered. "I'm not special."

"That statement is so far from true I'm not even going to dignify it with an answer." Instead, Tim bent down and I stretched myself up, and then his arm was around my waist, pulling me closer into him and up against a rack of half-priced Edward Gorey piñatas. His breath smelled like peppermint. Were we going to kiss? Was I about to get my second kiss ever? From Tim Slater? Literally the only person more unfathomable than Derek Wheeler? *And* Lily's ex-boyfriend? Would I even be able to tell Lily? Would I ever be able to tell Lily anything again, ever, regardless of this? My brain knotted itself into a confusing jumble of thoughts that were all yapping at each other's heels like pent-up Pomeranian puppies.

*"Ahem."*

Rachel cleared her throat at the end of the aisle, where she stood tapping her toes and smirking. Tim blushed and pretended he was reaching above me to grab some black soap (which I really shouldn't be imagining him using all over his broad shoulders and sandy hair and—NO! BAD HARPER!).

*"Pardon me.* I just wanted to see if Tim needed a ride home," she said.

"Uh," said Tim, backing away from me even more. "That would be great. Thanks. Just need to pay for this and then I'm ready to go," he mumbled, then trotted off past me and my sister to the register.

Rachel raised an eyebrow at me and put on a goofy, mocking, lovey-dovey grin.

*"Don't even,"* I warned, walking away to meet Rachel and Tim at the exit.

I didn't so much as glance at Tim as we sheepishly made our way back to the car.

*He's my dorky friend,* I kept on having to remind myself as Tim clambered into the back of the truck. Even if he inexplicably looked like a young Brad Pitt these days, Tim would always be a Sponge: the kind of guy who just absorbed all your emotional drama and neuroses, who listened patiently and gave good advice. Sponges were the opposite of Spirals, Murderers and Emotional Vampires. They were nice. Unfortunately, no one has ever talked about the sexiness of a Sponge in the history of humankind.

"So . . . are you going to call Lily now?" Tim asked quietly from the backseat. He was holding on to the back of my seat as he leaned forward, and I couldn't help but notice how his hands brushed my shoulders every time we hit a bump.

"No," I shook my head and stared out the window. "Even if everything you said makes sense, I still can't just pretend like my birthday never happened. Even if she can."

"Maybe it's not about forgetting," Tim said. "Maybe it's about something else?"

"What?" I turned around to face him.

He shrugged. "I don't know. Growing up, maybe?"

I turned back to the passenger side window and let my head rest against the cool glass. "I don't really feel like doing that right now, either," I said, but I'm not sure if he could hear.

There is nothing more depressing than an empty Inbox. Which was exactly what was staring me in the face when I logged into my email after getting home from Jane's, racing upstairs, and throwing my wings haphazardly in the closet. If I could have, I would have ripped those wings apart with my bare hands right there in the recording studio—that's how angry I was at Nicole and even Jane and Drew. How angry I was at myself, for being so blind to how undermine-y and negative and cliquey they were. When I imagined the Jug Judies now, I didn't see the image that I used to, of bright, shining stage lights behind us, all three of us playing our hearts out in some honky-tonk Texas town. Instead, I saw a group of evil sprites bearing a faint resemblance to Nicole, Jane, and Drew—and to Maleficent, but without Angelina's cheekbones—and they were dangling me and Harper above a bubbling vat of acid. And on the side of the vat, it said NAMASTE, in blood red writing. I saw the F³ symbol stamped onto a million vinyl records of the Jug Judies first mass-produced album, bought by a bunch of confused kids all over the country who confused kitsch for originality. I saw my Gawkward wings turning into an empty symbol, instead of what they were: a personal tie to my grandmother and to my friendship with Harper.

But what was really getting to me was the fact that an empty Inbox meant no emails from Harper. She hadn't texted, and I had even sent an iMessage to myself to make sure my data plan, or cloud, or whatever, was still working. It was.

If Harper messaged me, I'd told myself on the way home from Jane's in mom's car, I would apologize for the party. I would make it up to her, a billion-fold. I would claim responsibility for stealing her favorite lemon-scented hand creme in the eighth grade. I'd beg her forgiveness for missing the PuppyBash, and I would throw her an all-new rain-check PuppyBash that would blow all other PuppyBashes out of the water.

But the problem was, as guilty as I felt—for probably breaking our pact by wearing my wings when my heart wasn't in it, for being so mean to Beth-Lynne just because Nicole told me to—I was still mad at Harper, too. Yes, I was responsible for neglect; I *hadn't* been thinking about her birthday. I'd been too busy getting swept up in Pathways and NAMASTE and . . . okay, my own crippling fear that if Harper knew how I'd been acting with my new friends, she'd never want to speak to me again. If Harper would just listen to me, I'd rend my garments and gnash my teeth and pull my hair and swear it had all been a giant mistake. I'd acted so terribly because I had no idea what I was doing, not because I was a terrible friend. I would apologize for everything. But I still wished she could see how happy I'd been—or at least, how happy I'd *thought* I'd been—at Pathways, extending my wings. (Even if those wings were attached to my body by force.)

Now I never knew if I'd be happy again.

I was spiraling so hard that I was basically a human vortex. I had to tell myself that best friends never really stop being best friends, no matter what. But what if one best friend had recently found herself trapped under the reign of an organic-food-obsessed dictator?

Still no messages from Harper. No emails, no texts, not even a regular voicemail. I checked Instagram, which I'd lately only been using to keep up with Jane's F³ account, but which also made a convenient Harper stalking tool. She was usually a regular poster, but, hmm . . . she hadn't posted since before last night. Most of her recent pictures were of her and Tim or Stephanie, sticking out their tongues for the camera or making duck faces and throwing up fake gang signs. They all looked really happy in every shot. I knew I must have been in deep BFF pining mode, because looking at the pictures, I didn't feel one hint of jealousy—even the irrational kind—over the way Tim was looking at her in some of the photos, which to me looked a little lovey and pine-y . . . I just felt left out.

Once again I checked my phone and frowned at my slew of unreturned texts, all sent within the last few hours.

> **Lily (2:46 pm):** Harper, will u call me back?? plz bb!

> **Lily (3:45 pm):** u r making me feel like a stalker just texting into the ether. i tried your house no response and rachel let her phone go to voicemail plzzzzzzz call me

> **Lily (4:45 pm):** this is crazy!!! ur so frustrating im trying to say sorry!!! very immature harper!

I felt another wave of annoyance at Harper. Sure, she might have been right about Nicole and NAMASTE, and she didn't even know the worst of it, but Pathways wasn't all bad, and it was unfair of her to act like this great thing to happen to me only existed to make her life difficult. Harper had been the one to flip out and leave in the middle of the party. *She* was the one who wasn't answering my texts or calls now, which, didn't that make her as bad a friend as I supposedly had been to her? And at least I wasn't putting someone in friend-ship exile just because I was angry at them!

I threw my phone on the bed, frustrated. I didn't mind apologizing, but I didn't think I could handle the rejection if I called and it went straight to voicemail on the first ring again, because she was pressing the Ig-nore button on her phone.

I scrolled up through my old texts with Harper leading up to our fight, hoping that maybe just think-ing about her hard enough would make a new message appear. As I read, I got a funny, hollow feeling in the pit of my stomach, like the kind you get when you lean over the side of the pool to hoist yourself out of it and your insides feel all jumbled up.

**Harper (4:45 p.m.):** SOS! EMERGENCY!

**Lily (5:45 p.m.):** ?????

**Harper (5:47 p.m..):** Things have gotten 😭 😭 😭 and double plus insane. Can we meet up? Ferris wheel your house my house I don't care. I NEED YOU ASAP.

**Lily (5:47 p.m.):** PuppyGirl! What's going on??

**Harper (5:48 p.m.):** Ugh I can't even over text. Can we meet in 15? Near the pier? My sister can drive us if you want to get picked up.

**Lily (5:49 p.m.):** Oof! Whatever it is sounds awful. I really really want to meet but I can't bc band practice.

**Harper (5:51 p.m.):** . . . Band practice?

**Lily (5:52 p.m.):** Yeah! Well, we're not like a band, band–yet. I play the ukulele and sing, Jane is on harp and Drew plays the water jug. Guess what we call ourselves?

**Harper (5:53 p.m.):** Lily can you call me for a second? I really, really messed up, and I could really do with some Gawkward Fairy love right now.

**Lily (5:53 p.m.):** We're the Jug Judies!

**Lily (5:53 p.m.):** Oh Harper I'm so sorry I wish I could.

I clicked my phone shut, but not before the words began to blur on one last text, sent from Harper the day we ran into each other in the park:

> **Harper (8:00 pm):** Did our friendship just run out of minutes?

How had I been so blind that I couldn't see that Harper had really, really needed my help? Had I really been so scared of her finding out about the wings and Beth-Lynne that I'd transformed myself into a doll who says cheerful phrases when you pull a string? She'd continued to type away at her keypad, trying to access the old me—the actual me—long after I'd stopped responding with anything meaningful or real. She'd been waiting for her BFF Gawkward Fairy godmother to swoop in and save her from that horrible situation at Murphy's Ranch—god, did I even *know* what had actually happened there? Had I ever asked?—the same way Harper's Empathy Charms had saved me, a total stranger, all those years ago.

In fourth grade she'd rescued me from a fate worse than social death and she'd been with me ever since. She had been the one to counsel me about Pathways and listen to all my irrational fears when I was so scared to go to a new school. She was the one who had tried to warn me about the horrors of Nicole and NAMASTE, even when she knew that I was so brainwashed that I wouldn't be able to hear it. She was the one who made me promise not to compromise who I was just to placate someone else. And how had I repaid her? By forgetting her birthday, by insulting her, and even worse, by not making her a priority in my new, sparkly life. I was a monster. I was an animal. I was a disgrace to the title of Best Friend.

Well, all that was going to change. I mustered up my resolve, picked up my phone, and flew into my Contacts. I was ready to throw myself from the gates of the Capital. It was time for Major Action Taking. I scrolled down and pressed that big red CALL button. If it wasn't too late, I might not even have to reconcile with my greatest fear: leaving a voicemail.

I decided to ban myself from Internet stalking. Seriously, I was going to take a time-out. Or a "cleanse," as Rachel would say.

Still, whatever I called it, a crucial problem remained: I'm basically the Sherlock Holmes of the Internet. I can tell you what it means when two people follow each other (mutual crush) or when two people un-follow each other (totally done). I know what it means when someone's photo "like"s suddenly go down by one (the dreaded accidental "like" of a creeping ex, or possibly their new significant other using their account), and I know what it means when someone subtweets a passive-aggressive Beyoncé lyric (she hopes her ex sees it and regrets his loss, but he doesn't).

And I knew what it meant when I saw Derek Wheeler's new Facebook status of "It's Complicated with Kendall Donahue" (because I'm not an idiot), or his stupid Robert Frost quotes about "the roads not taken" (we get it, you're soooo original and also terrible at paraphrasing). Not that I even cared anymore—Derek had shown his true colors with that SchoolGrams video. But then on top of everything, in the four days since the F³ relaunch party, there were approximately one million photos on Instagram and Tumblr and Facebook of everyone having such a good time, and I just couldn't.

"Those Pathways kids dress like middle-aged corporate hippies," I declared while walking with Stephanie on a Wednesday after-school trip to Melrose. She was in search of this perfect denim jacket she had seen in the Kill City window over the weekend, but which her mother said was illegal to wear since it had the American flag on it. ("But it's not like I'm going to burn it," was Stephanie's argument. Seemed like sound logic to me.) "You should have seen them—they all look like middle-age Burning Man attendees in teenage bodies. Of course their quote-un-quote 'fashion' party would be covered on the Internet. The Internet loves weirdoes."

Steph laughed and I instinctively felt my hand beginning to wander back to the pocket of my frayed shorts, in search of the iPhone I'd started leaving at home during school. It was an odd sensation at first not to have it, like Phantom Limb Syndrome, but I'd actually begun to enjoy the perks of an off-the-grid existence, such as the fading desire to capture every single cute moment and put it on Twitter or Instagram or the pleasant realization that my attention span is longer than thirty seconds. Sunsets, it turned out, didn't need filters. Food actually tasted better when I ate it before it got cold as I tried to find the best angle to photograph it from. Who knew?

Across the street, I saw a little girl in a tutu was holding her mom's hand and "blessing" cars with a stick, and I felt a not-so-little rush of familiarity.

"So . . . did Lily look good when you saw her?" I had grilled Stephanie in about a billion different ways since she told me she'd run into my former bestie (god, was that what I was going to have to start referring to her as now?) on Sunday, but elaboration wasn't really one of her strong suits. Most of the time, stuff fell into one of two camps for Stephanie: dope or sick. It wasn't all that dissimilar to the way she and Jessica used to describe the world together.

Stephanie shrugged, pushing up her oversized sunglasses and chewing the straw of her iced chai. "Yeah, she seemed okay. Maybe a little. . . ." She paused, as if to search the storefront signs across the street for the word she was looking for. "Busy."

"Busy? Busy how? Good busy?" I couldn't even pretend to play it chill.

We approached a park bench and Stephanie gracefully jumped onto it and into a crouching position, observing the midafternoon scene like a large, somewhat lazy cat. "Hey. I know what you're going through, kind of," she said, motioning for me to sit down. "It drives you crazy, doesn't it? Wondering where they are all the time, who they're with, what they're doing."

"It sucks," I confirmed, taking a seat beside her and throwing my head back. "It's like, I want her to start calling me again, but not because I want to talk to her. I want her to call me and then I want to not pick up the phone, and I want that to keep happening until she somehow understands what I'm going through."

Stephanie nodded, pulling down her glasses again. "I felt the same exact way when Jessica and I broke up."

Suddenly, an urgent, keening sound blasted through the air and I jumped, startled. The little girl with the imaginary wand accidentally set off a car alarm.

"Sorry. Wait, what about you and Jessica?" I asked, refocusing.

"Come on," Stephanie stared at me, like she was

waiting for me to tell her I was putting her on. "You *did* know we were dating didn't you?"

I shook my head, stunned by my own obliviousness. God, I was such an idiot! I replayed the last ten years of my friendship with those two, looking for signs I might have missed, but my brain was too overloaded with feeling absolutely humiliated and hoping I hadn't offended the one friend I had left. (Well, besides Tim. But Tim was less like a friend and more like . . . something else.)

Stephanie rolled her eyes and smirked at me, yanking her red beanie to one side. "A-ha! What are you, new?"

I shook my head, mystified by my own lameness. "I guess . . . it never crossed my mind." How often had I seen those two hair-cream twins run down the hall holding hands, giggling secrets to each other? And as we got older, the smaller, tender gestures: Stephanie tucking back in a tag that had flipped up from the collar of Jess's tennis dress; Jess nonchalantly tucking an errant wisp of blond hair loosed from Stephanie's bun back behind her ear. At the time, I thought they had just become good enough friends that they shared one brain between their two bodies, like the opposite of conjoined twins. But now that I thought about it, it was totally obvious. "Well, what happened to you guys?"

"Same old boring thing that always happens." Stephanie sighed, her hands on her scratched-up knees. "I got jealous that she was spending so much time with some guy. She said she was confused and needed some space to do some growing. Then we kind of . . . made our issues public. Accidentally."

"The SchoolGrams video?"

"Yup. You're not the only one who's Internet famous."

"Stephanie, wow. I really didn't know. I'm sorry if I

ever seemed insensitive about it. I just figured you'd had some big BFF breakup and didn't want to talk about her."

"It's okay." For once, Stephanie's blissed-out Cali vibe seemed a little strained. She laughed hollowly. "I mean, it was less okay when she told me she'd asked her mom to transfer to a boarding school in France. Just 'cause, you know, she really felt that France was the best place for her to 'get her thoughts together.'"

"Wow." We were both quiet for a minute. "Wait. Does Jessica even know French?"

"Absolutely one hundred percent not," Stephanie laughed, then loosened up with a long, drawn-out sigh. "We still email sometimes. She seems to like it there. It turns out French boys have a thing for girls who *sometimes* like other girls."

"Uh, so what she means is, French boys are exactly like every other kind of boy on the planet?"

"Apparently," Steph's eyes were unfocused as she stared straight ahead: Even though she was with me on Melrose, she was a million miles away. "I couldn't believe it when she wrote that, actually. For me, I always knew that I liked girls. *Only* girls. I mean, I came out to my parents when I was like, eight or something. I told them that I wanted to grow up and marry either Jessica or Chloe Sevigny."

"Oh my god!" I laughed, trying to imagine the tightly-wound Mr. and Mrs. Adler reacting to their pre-tween daughter's declaration of lesbianism, especially when Stephanie's mom was the head of the local church youth group *and* the PTA. "I bet they loved that."

"Actually, they did." Stephanie seemed to shake out of her trance. She cracked her neck—first to one side, then another—with a loud popping noise that made me wince and worry about permanent spinal damage. "My mom said that I was blessed to know my heart at such a young age . . . and my dad just asked if Chloe was that actress from *Big Love*, and if so, I had 'great taste.'"

Stephanie yawned and stood up from the bench in an exaggerated stretch. "Come on," she said, reaching her arm out to me. "I could use, like, a million shots of espresso," she said. "Let's go."

I wanted to say something insightful about everything Stephanie just told me, especially since she'd been so brave to open up to me like that, but my mind was like an old computer that needed extra time to process all the information it had been given. "Okay . . . well . . . hey. Thanks for telling me, Stephanie," I said solemnly.

She laughed her easy laugh and slung a flanneled arm around my shoulder. "Oh, Harper, you're probably the only person who didn't know."

When I got home, I allowed myself my one web session of the day (quitting cold-turkey is dangerous!), and found a mysterious email in my Inbox.

| To: | Harper.Carina@BH.com |
| --- | --- |
| From: | Timothy.Slater@BH.com |

| Subject: **Signs** |
| --- |
| Meet me where the ferris wheel meets the water. Today, 6 pm sharp. No excuses! |

I looked at the time on my laptop. 4:50. I quickly sent my own response.

| To: | Timothy.Slater@BH.com |
| From: | Harper.Carina@BH.com |

**Subject: ????**

Hey Tim,

????????

-H.

I waited and waited, but no response came.

Was it weird that I felt a little thrill over Tim's messages?

If I hustled—and if Rachel agreed to drive me—I could possibly make the six p.m. deadline. I threw on whatever was within reach around my messy room—okay, so I may have had that floral crop top paired with my Alice + Olivia black pleated skirt ready to go in my closet. I checked myself in the mirror and at the last minute I took out the pink plastic barrettes that I decided made me look too much like a kid.

Rachel smirked when I charged into her room. "Going somewhere, baby doll?"

"You need to drive me to the pier," I said matter-of-factly. "It's a surprise."

"For me?" Rachel was faux-thrilled. "How lovely."

"Come *on*, Rachel! This is important."

"You're so lucky I'm nursing a broken heart right now. Otherwise I'd simply be too busy for your childish stunts." Rachel put her shoes on and followed me down the stairs.

"Thank you, thank you, thank you!" I trilled, never so happy in all of my life to have a big sister.

"Yeah, yeah, yeah. Just remember: You owe me."

★

I blew Rachel a bunch of air kisses and told her I'd text her when I was ready to come home (I know, I totally caved on my tech-diet. But this was important!). I waited for Tim on the shore by the Ferris wheel, just where his email told me to. It was almost the exact same spot where, less than a month ago, Lily and I had pledged our undying friendship to each other.

That memory ached like a leg muscle cramp in the middle of the night. But there were no potassium-rich BFF bananas in sight, no friendship-fixing electrolytes that could make the pain go away. I would just have to survive on a diet of terrible metaphors. Tasty.

"Harper?" A voice emerged from underneath the boardwalk, and was then followed by the sight of a small figure walking toward me. Not Tim. A girl.

It took me a minute to recognize her without her wings.

"Hi" might not seem like the bravest word in the world. Anyone can say "hi." You could go up to someone you don't like or even *know* right now and say "hi," and basically the worst thing they will do is roll their eyes and pretend they didn't hear anything.

No, "hi" isn't such a hard thing to say. Or at least, it shouldn't be. And yet. . . .

"Hegh!" I said, walking toward Harper on the beach. I cleared my throat and tried again. "Hiyam?"

"Lily?" Harper started toward me, took half a step, then settled back on the balls of her feet, resolved and confused all at once. "What are you doing here?"

"I . . . I called Tim," I said, forcing myself to speak normally. It helped if I didn't try to make eye contact, so I addressed Harper's Free People sandals instead. "Actually, I asked him to get in touch with you . . . to tell you to meet him here."

"Oh," she said as I stared at her left foot, which was busy scratching her right shin. "So . . . Tim's not coming?"

I shook my head, still forcing myself to focus on the small details, which could tell you so much. Harper's toenails were lacquered in a bright, hard red: Rachel must have convinced her to get a gel pedicure.

"Oh," said Harper's feet, wiggling and then turning to go. "Okay, well . . ." I watched them take one, two, three steps before I found my voice again.

"Hey!"

"What!" The sandals made an indentation in the sand, like snow angels. "What could you possibly say right now that I'd want to hear?"

"I'm sorry Harper," I said. "I'm really, really sorry . . . about everything."

She pursed her lips and studied me silently. I was purposefully not wearing my wings today, and not only because they were basically just threads of fabric at this point. I'd also dressed more "conservatively" than what I'd started to think of as my Pathways Uniform: all bright colors and beaded accessories. Today I was just wearing a dark blue blazer with a poppy colored patch pocket over a T-shirt, and old, beat-up Adidas sneakers. Though it was still kind of a kooky outfit compared to Harper's effortlessly chic skirt and flowered top ensemble.

"I'm sorry about the way I've been treating you ever since I started Pathways," I said, looking her right in the eyes this time. "And for flaking on your PuppyBash. And I'm sorry for not planning a real birthday party and for dragging you along to my thing."

I took a deep breath, because the next part was hard. "And I'm sorry . . . I'm sorry I was talking about you to Nicole. I've been an awful friend. Full stop. I got really caught up with Nicole and NAMASTE, and I guess it was just really exciting to feel like I finally fit in somewhere. That I was expressing myself, and that everyone liked it so much that they wanted to be just like me. I've never felt like I had anything that anybody else wanted, you know? Except a lot of that stuff you heard me say on Saturday . . . that wasn't me. That was Nicole."

I forced myself to keep looking Harper in the eye, which was difficult because of how bad I was tearing up. I needed her forgiveness so badly I felt like I was burning up inside and my eyes felt like they were being rubbed with sandpaper.

"The thing is, Lily, I just don't believe you." Harper cocked her head, and I felt the familiar squeeze of anxiety in my stomach. "The things you said were really mean, and really specific. I would never even think those things about you let alone say them out loud to a group of mean bullies who I was trying to impress. Don't you see, Lily? This is exactly what we promised each other we wouldn't do!"

"I know that now! It was just all very confusing! Please, give me another chance!" Part of me was still a little frustrated that Harper refused to acknowledge the tricky situation I'd been caught in that had made me feel guilty about our pact in the first place. I *hadn't* changed what I wore to fit in! But I realized now that BFF pacts didn't extend to just your accessories. It was about staying true to ourselves, yes, but that meant letting others stay true to themselves as well, no bullying people for not wearing wings—which, now that I thought about it, was CRAZY-PANTS.

And, oh god, Beth-Lynne . . . I sighed to myself out of sheer memory-based embarrassment.

"Hmmm?" Harper had turned around, luckily missing my gasp of humiliation for poor Beth-Lynne.

"Harper, you've got to believe me," I begged. "I will make it up to you a million times over. I . . . I am going to drop out of NAMASTE." I didn't even know that myself until the words were out of my mouth, but as soon as I said it, I knew it was true, and I marveled at how simple it was all going to be from now on. I was done with Nicole and her faux-dictatorship. *Viva la revolución!*

Harper seemed to be weighing my outburst against some internal scale. "But you missed everything," she said finally as the wind picked up. "You missed my first kiss. You didn't even *ask* about it. That's not what a friend does. That's definitely not what a *best* friend does.

"And then there was this video, and it was a whole thing. . . ." Harper hugged her skinny arms around herself and stared off into the ocean. "That night at Murphy's Ranch . . . I acted like a total moron, and the *one* person who could make me feel like I wasn't the worst person in the world didn't even seem to care! Lily, I *pretended* to be *drunk*. On camera. In front of the *cops*. And as nice as Tim Slater is, and as chill as Stephanie is, and as . . . eccentric as Rachel is—they're not you. They don't know how to make me feel better just by being themselves. They don't know how to reassure me that that one big slipup won't make me a pariah for life."

"What?" I said, surprised at my own stupidity. Harper and I had needed the exact same things from each other the entire time. I had to come clean. "Harper, I had no idea . . . I'm so sorry. The thing is . . . part of the reason I've been so . . . so . . . ."

"So . . . zombie-ish? So creepily cheerful?"

I sighed. She wasn't wrong. I collected my thoughts and started again. "Part of the reason I've been so *not myself* is because I did something—a couple of things— that were bad. Harper, I know I said I wasn't sure if I broke our pact, and at first, I really wasn't. But then, I did something . . . I did something that I'm really not proud of. And I guess I was too embarrassed to talk to you afterward, because I knew you'd see right through my fake-happy act into what a gross monster of a person I'd actually become."

"What do you mean? Lily, I could never think you were a gross monster! No matter what you've done!" Harper said, a glimmer of her old, sweet, concerned self shining through the disappointment in her eyes.

"Well, you know how I've been wearing my wings, like, every day since school started?"

"Yeah. . . ."

"Uh, well, that wasn't exactly my idea."

"Let me guess. Nicole?"

"Yup. She told me on Day One that I couldn't be in NAMASTE unless I wore my wings. Because my wings were *me,* they made me who I am. At first I thought, well, maybe it's not so bad—I do like the wings and I did wear them by choice the day we met. But you know me—I'd never wear those things every single day, they're more of a good luck charm." Harper nodded thoughtfully. "So when I came to school without them, thinking she couldn't possibly have literally meant I need to wear them *every single day,* she freaked. I really wanted to join NAMASTE and keep hanging out with Jane and Drew and especially Nicole, this girl that everyone in school seemed to just worship and fear but in a good way, like in the way that you'd be kind of afraid to meet your favorite actor or something. So I kept wearing them, even though I didn't want to."

"Oh, Lily—"

"Oh, that's not even the bad stuff, yet, like how I totally fell for Nicole's self-help NAMASTE nonsense, even though at some level I recognized that she was just using my fairy wings as a way to see how many people she could get to fall in line before taking it mainstream. Making it part of her 'personal brand.' I mean, even at Jane's fashion launch party, everyone was wearing wings and talking about 'expanding our merchandizing opportunities' to like, energy drink companies. It was gross. It wasn't what my wings were about. But I was way too blind to see that I was just being used."

I had to hand it to Harper: She could smell a caveat coming a million miles away. She folded her arms. "So all you did was let other girls borrow your style . . . what's so wrong with that?

I gulped, feeling like I had been running a marathon. Why was this part so much harder!

"There's more," I said, knowing that if I didn't keep going I might lose my nerve before I told Harper the other, much worse thing I did during my shameful NA-MASTE brainwashing days. "You know Beth-Lynne?"

"Yeah . . . you asked about her the other day, too. Why?"

"Well, it turns out that new fancy school she goes to is Pathways."

"No way! Somehow I can't picture her there . . ."

"Exactly. She's kind of in a different part of the school all together, with the tech and science labs. I don't know how I could have missed her for the first few weeks though—she kind of sticks out like a sore thumb, you know in her jeans and flannel that she always wears, which is obviously totally fine—I mean, who am I to talk, look at the way I looked compared to everyone else at Hollywood Middle, for instance, you know?" Harper was looking at me in the expectant-slash-encouraging way she does when I start to ramble nervously. "Right, anyway. So, Beth-Lynne goes to Pathways, which I found out because, one day, she came up to me and said hello when I was hanging out with Nicole in the hallway." I paused, thinking about how to phrase what happened next.

"Okay. And . . . ?" said Harper, nudging me along.

"And at first everything was totally friendly, but then she said something totally innocent about my wings, you know, just commenting on them, and Nicole stepped in and said Beth-Lynne was, like, making a joke about them. Which she was, sort of, but not to be mean. And then Nicole said something about her clothes . . . well, you know what Beth-Lynne's style is like, and, all I can say is if you thought what Nicole said about *your* shoes at the party was mean . . . Anyway, she went on and on about how not only was Beth-Lynne's outfit—which included Uggs, mind you—environmentally irresponsible, but her style was basic and boring and so she must be basic and boring, too."

"Poor Beth-Lynne," said Harper. And then, under her breath, "I can't believe that *bully.*"

"Yeah, it was bad. But what was worse . . . the worst thing about it was . . . I started to believe what Nicole was saying. That Beth-Lynne was against what NAMASTE stood for, and if I didn't say anything to stand up to her, it meant I *also* went against everything NAMASTE stood for."

"Oh, no," said Harper. "Lily, you didn't. . . ."

"I did," I said. "I said everything Nicole said and worse. I'm a terrible person, Harper. I made her *cry.* In front of the *whole school.* And I didn't even run after her or apologize or anything, because that's how much of a monster I've become."

"What? Hey, no. Let me repeat: You are *not* a monster. Yes, that sounds like a bad scene and Beth-Lynne *definitely* didn't deserve any of that. I mean, she and her family save innocent *puppies* in their spare time." And with that, I let the tears flow. I couldn't help it. "Hey! Listen to me. Are you listening to me?"

"Yes," I cry-mumbled.

"Okay. What you guys did to Beth-Lynne wasn't great. And it sucks that you felt you had to let parts of yourself be coopted by an older, cooler girl in order to fit in. But you know what?"

"What?" I sobbed, really losing it now.

"The only thing I hear from you right now is that you made some mistakes—because you're a human being, FYI—and that you *know* they were just that: mistakes. And you feel bad about them, and want to make them right. You can always apologize to Beth-Lynne, and while she may not send you flowers and write you a thank-you note, she'll probably understand and be pretty cool about it. And I *know* you won't stop trying until you make all of this right. *That's* the Lily I know and love! The Lily that stood out as so special on that first day in gym class a million years ago. The Lily who is my *best friend*. Nicole, she does all this stuff and doesn't feel guilty about it, because *she's* the monster. *You're* the Gawkward Fairy—even when you're not wearing your wings—which means that no matter what you do, your light and your kindness is going to win out in the end."

"Really?" I said, trying to wipe off my face with my blazer sleeves. "But, what about our pact? I totally broke it. I didn't stay true to who I was, and I let you down, and I let my grandma down . . . I let everyone down!" I started to bawl again.

"Psh, a temporary slip. I know that you don't actually feel that you need to wear anything to be you. I notice that you're not wearing your wings now, for instance!"

"Only metaphorically," I said, cracking a smile.

"Oh, well, of course," said Harper, returning my smile.

"I'm sorry I wasn't there for you when you needed me. I should have been there right by your side at the Ranch, pretending to be drunk with you and telling Derek that he better treat you right or I'd come after him with every superpower in my repertoire. I guess I just assumed that you were okay without me. Because you're always okay. But I know now that that's not fair to you. As you said, we're all human beings . . ."

"Yes, even us superheroes are still human beings at heart."

"Exactly. So. Forgive me?" I said, letting one last tear fall down my cheek. Harper let out a big mock sigh. "Ohh, I suppose. *On a temporary trial basis.*" She gave me a sly wink.

"Well, maybe I can get off early for good behavior? Or maybe a bribe will help?" I reached into my blazer pocket and pulled out my secret weapon: two jagged pieces of gold attached to two delicate chains. Our broken heart BFF necklaces. After Harper left me alone in the bathroom, the first thing I did was gather up her half and make sure it was clean and safe inside my bag.

"My necklace! You saved it. Thank you." Harper fished her half out of my hand and fastened it around her neck.

When I'd imagined my reunion hug with Harper, I pictured it like one of those slow-mo, on-the-beach moments with some terrible jazz playing in the background. Maybe I would twirl her and promise never to leave her again while the ocean surf sprayed on our feet.

In reality, it was just a comfortable, familiar bestie hug, the kind I'd been missing worse than I'd realized for the past several weeks. Then, suddenly we both seemed to catch on to how cold it had gotten, because we both started shivering.

"Shall we?" Harper said, nodding toward the boardwalk.

"Definitely," I said, and we both started walking homeward.

"Hey Lily," Harper said in the waning light after a few moments of silence. "Guess what?"

"What?" Our feet made crooked crisscrosses through each other's shoeprints.

"I actually really liked your friends Jane and Drew. They seem cool and nice. I'm happy you found people who really like you at Pathways, and that you're finding out what you like to do and who you are. That's important. I'm sorry if I ever seemed like I was jealous of that part of it. I'm actually so proud that you're in a band."

"Hey, thanks! You know, I'm actually really proud of us, too. I mean, it's so silly but I guess at this point it's the only extracurricular I'm involved with. Well, besides NAMASTE . . . for now."

"Can you just tell me one thing?" Harper asked slyly when we got to the boardwalk, which was lively as usual and filled with the scents of all kinds of delicious treats. I could feel my mouth begin to salivate over the idea of food—any food—as long as it was deep-fried and not macrobiotic. "Can someone please, please explain to me what you guys actually do in this cult of yours?

Like, what does NAMASTE actually do?"

I opened my mouth with the answer ready, but in that moment it must have flown away. Maybe it was the owl of Minerva that had stolen the words from me, on her way to warn the next poor schlubs who would be too late to save themselves from Pathways' mind-meld.

Instead I laughed. "You know?" I said, throwing my arm around Harper's shoulders. "I have absolutely no idea."

Going back to school on Monday was difficult. Everything was the same, but completely different all at once. Lily and I were friends again, but after everything that happened, things still felt a little tense between us. And while I appreciated that Tim had played the go-between to set us up together, I still found myself irrationally annoyed that he'd more or less tricked me.

Per usual, I was definitely not in a rush to get to history, where I knew Kendall and Derek, the "it's complicated" couple, would be cozily snuggled up together in the back. I made sure to come in at the last possible moment (but not too late to get detention—it's an art, really), and slid into my seat with my eyes looking straight ahead.

"Hey," said an all-too familiar voice. I could feel Tim on the edges of my peripheral vision, tapping a pen cap on the edge of his desk. "Harper, what's up?"

"Hi, Tim." I bent down and pulled a pen and piece of paper from my bag, explicitly not making eye contact with him.

"What's up? What happened with you and Lily? You haven't answered any of my texts." His tapping increased in tempo.

"I've just been pretty busy, that's all," I said curtly.

"Can you please stop tapping your pen? It's driving me nuts."

He stopped, clearly stung. "Sorry."

When I didn't turn around again, he poked me with the tip of his pen. "Hey, are you mad at me? Because—"

"I'm not mad," I hissed, turning on him suddenly. "Why would I be mad? I'm just annoyed because . . . because . . ." I floundered. In truth, I had no idea why I was so pissed off. "Because you're always, like, *inserting* yourself into my life."

This time, Tim was so surprised that he dropped his pen and had to make a grab for it as it rolled away toward the floor. As soon as he sat back up, class had officially started. I could feel him looking at me throughout the entire period with those hurt, quizzical eyes, and I had to really suppress my Empathy Powers so as not to turn and tell him directly, in front of the whole class: *I'm upset because I spend so much time worrying about what other people feel that I literally have no idea what I'm feeling. About anything. Ever.*

I felt so on edge for the entire fifty-minute class, and when the bell rang I practically jumped out of my skin from a combination of surprise and relief. I decided I couldn't risk Tim trying to catch up to me in the hall, so I decided to just keep freezing him out and stall a while to make him leave first. As everyone else filed out, I pretended to be busy on my phone, while Tim just sat there, relentlessly giving me those puppy eyes.

"Okay, well. See you later, I guess," Tim said, finally getting up from his desk when the second-period bell rang. As he passed me, I smelled that woodsy-clean scent of his again, and I furiously swiped at my phone to overcompensate for the fact that my hands were shaking. I watched him walk away from me and didn't take another breath until he disappeared down the hall.

"Hey, Carina."

I looked up. Derek Wheeler waltzed back into the classroom, slinging his backpack into Tim's empty seat behind me. He yanked on my braid, like a fifth-grader demanding attention, when I refused to acknowledge his presence. He tugged again and I looked over reluctantly, but my scowl turned into an *O* of surprise when I saw his T-shirt.

"Hey, Derek," I said, as neutrally as I could, while scanning the room to look for signs of Kendall. I was in the clear. "Is that your D.A.R.E. shirt from . . . fourth grade? You still have it?"

"Yeah, well," Derek smiled, wrapping his finger around my braid. "I remember you said you liked it."

"I said I remembered it, not that I liked it or that you should bring it out of retirement." I pried my hair out of his hands. "I mean, god, hasn't it disintegrated from all the combined stink particles and subsequent hosings?"

For a moment, Derek look embarrassed. He flicked his hair to the front of his face as if it were a shield that could protect him from ridicule. "I actually bought it new, yesterday," he shrug-mumbled behind his hair. "When you mentioned it the other night, it kind of got me thinking how much I loved that shirt."

I just looked back at him and nodded, completely perplexed as to what was going on.

"Anyway." Derek shook back his fluttering mane like a surly pony. "I've actually been meaning to talk to you. . . ."

"So talk," I said.

"About the other night."

"Sure." Was I still nodding? I had to forcibly stop my head from moving in an agreeable motion.

"I'm sorry I let Kendall take that video of you. You were so good at pretending to be drunk and I honestly thought it would make for a funny scene in my movie, but then she uploaded it to SchoolGrams without telling me. I felt really bad about it, and, uh, I didn't know how to approach you about it."

Huh. I must have missed the part in my horoscope that said October would bring me a record number of apologies.

"It's just that . . . you kind of intimidate me," Derek went on after a pause. He pulled his dark, wiry eyebrows together in what looked like an attempt at deep thought.

"Sorry?"

"You just come off as so, I don't know . . . put together. Like you have everything figured out and live this, like, perfect TV commercial life."

"Uh." I said. *TV commercial?* What commercials was Derek watching? My life was as put together as a telenovela soap opera. Minus the murder and secret love children, but still. "Thanks for that, Derek, but now that everyone's seen that video the most obvious comparison for my life would be the nightly story on *TMZ*."

Derek laughed. "See? You can make me laugh, and I don't even think girls are funny."

*Wow.* And he actually said this like he was proud of it.

"Okay, well, good talk, Derek," I began gathering up my things, still totally overwhelmed by this turn of events. "But you should probably get out of here before Kendall sees you talking to me."

At the mention of her name, Derek rolled his eyes and stuck out his tongue. Despite his dreamy physique, I realized he was still just a little kid.

"Kendall and I are *not* dating. She doesn't own me. Plus, the other reason I wanted to talk to you is ... uh ... well, I wanted to give you this." Before I could move, Derek jerked into me and fastened his lips onto mine.

For a moment I was too stunned to do anything. All I could think about was how chapped his lips were, and how he really needed to moisturize his stubble area. Plus, his hair obviously hadn't been washed in a while and he gave off a patchouli-scented funk.

"Mmph!" I said after I somehow regained my full senses, my arms pin-wheeling out until I hit Derek in the chest. "Mrrrph!"

"What's wrong?" Derek pulled back, and I had to do everything in my power not to wipe my lips in disgust.

Suddenly, I heard a cough behind me.

"Sorry." It was Tim. "I just forgot my notebook," he said stonily, standing in the doorway. Had he seen everything? "Didn't mean to interrupt."

"No problem man," Derek smiled, clearly supremely pleased with himself. Tim gave us one more angry glare then turned on his heels, stalking off without even pretending to come in and retrieve his imaginary lost notebook. Every single one of my nerve endings wanted to run after him, but what would I say? I didn't know how to explain how I felt about him, so here I was taking the easy route with a guy I had absolutely zero complicated feelings for.

"Derek," I said gently, reaching into my pocket and leaning in toward him.

"Yeah?" He leaned in, too.

"Here's some ChapStick. Please . . . for Kendall's sake . . . use it." The last thing I saw as I ran out the door was Derek's look of total confusion. I knew I'd treasure it forever.

I texted Lily immediately.

**Harper (10:00 a.m.):** SOS HELP!

**Lily (10:00 a.m.):** I'm here! What's up my love?

I considered leaving my wings at home the next day, but in the end I couldn't do it. I needed them for one last appearance as LilyFairy, the freshman representative of NAMASTE.

It was the day of our NAMASTE council meeting, the first one since Nicole had given her speech out in the Lane. Without my diaphanous appendages, I would be just looking for trouble, and I wanted to be as in control as possible. Nicole had already made it known that she thought the "best me I could be" was the one that dressed exactly as she decreed. But with Jane and Drew and even Nicole now sporting their own versions of my persona, I was beginning to feel like one of those characters from Dr. Seuss. You know, a Star Bellied Sneetch, or one of the Sneetches with no stars, who then gets a star, but then all the other Sneetches get stars and now the stars aren't as special anymore.

I was walking around aimlessly during my morning free period when I heard a familiar, welcome voice.

"Why, hello young sprite, you seem to have lost your way!" I looked up from my texts with Harper (I hadn't realized how much I had missed talking to her like a normal person!) and saw Drew smiling goofily up at me from his usual spot on the grass. He wasn't wearing his wings, and instead had his guitar slung to his back. Bold move. "Where are you off to on this fine Monday morning?"

"Oh, you know. Fighting crime, saving the world. The usual."

"Sit down." He patted the grass. "Rest awhile." I took a seat and texted Harper one last time

> **Lily (10:16 a.m.):** BRB I promise!

before turning my attention to Drew. "Want a macaron?" he asked, pulling out a tin from his knapsack.

"Only if you're sure you won't tell anyone how you're contributing to the plight of those overworked sugar granules."

Drew laughed and stretched out with the ease of a guy who spends most of his free time in downward facing dog and handed me a honey-flavored macaron. And then a bright pink pistachio one. And then a coconut. Before long, half the box was gone.

"Oh, my sweet lord," I moaned, spraying crumbs everywhere. "My belly is going to explode. I am literally in my third trimester of a sugar baby."

"Just make sure you deliver before our first show this weekend," Drew said, patting my tummy. "We could use the extra audience member."

My laughter died in my throat as I saw who had materialized behind Drew and was now regarding him with the cocked hip of a gunslinger. Nicole's hair, her follicular mood ring, was jet black and gelled down flat against her head. She glared down at us with dark, kohl-rimmed eyes, and her face was completely pale save for a slash of dark red lipstick.

She looked nothing like the bohemian girl I had met on my first day of school, and I wondered if her new Goth look was any more "true" to her real self than that nu-hippie persona had been. Maybe, I thought, *none* of this was part of the real Nicole. Maybe she was like a chameleon who changed colors, but instead of using her outfits to blend in to the background, she used her plumage to stand out.

I looked at her wings, which today were so black they were almost blue, like a dark angel's. She had taken my fairy wings, which used to be my escape, *my* fantasy, and turned them into just another part of her ever-evolving "look."

"What are you doing?" Nicole said to Drew, who was unfortunately still holding the macaron box on his lap.

"They're gluten-free, Nicole." Drew said, exasperated. "And . . . vegan. And made with agave syrup."

Nicole shook her head, the wings shuddering with the motion. "I meant, where are your . . ." Nicole mimed a bird flapping with her arms, her ankh rings glaring and casting sunlight into my eyes.

"I left them at home?" Drew looked confused. "Was I . . . you don't expect us all to wear them every day, right?"

"Here," I said, tugging down a strap. "You can wear mine, Drew."

Nicole seemed to notice my existence for the first time. "I appreciate your concern, Lily," she said, her voice icy. "But Drew needs to own up to his lack of personal responsibility." She shook her head again. "I'm sorry, Drew, but if you mess up one more time you're out of NAMASTE."

"You can't do that!" I said. I knew how much NAMASTE meant to Drew. "Don't you have, like, a three-strike policy? It's not fair to kick him out because of one mistake!"

Nicole pursed her lips coolly. "Get ahold of yourself," she said, as if I were a bawling baby instead of a high schooler talking in a reasonable tone. "That's not the attitude we're looking for in a NAMASTE representative. Your behavior is rather . . . normative."

"I think you mean 'normal,' Nicole. 'Normative' means something completely different. And what's so wrong with being normal?" My voice was cracking, but I stood up and drew myself to the tallest height I could be. "There are worse things in the world then being normal! Like being judgmental and making everyone feel bad about themselves!"

The words were out before I could stop myself, but instead of looking upset, Nicole just kind of shrugged and smiled lightly, as if I had just told her I liked her shoes. "It's so sad when conformists try to pretend they're something they're not. In the end, they always show their true colors," she said, addressing Drew. "I guess for some people, cafeteria hierarchies and America's patriarchal beauty standards are still more important than what's on the inside."

But Drew's smile just became even more serene. He clasped his hands together and, without standing up, gave a mock-bow from the waist. "Nicole, I want to thank you for this humbling experience. You've really made me think and reflect on who I want to be and how to be a better person. Also? I quit."

Nicole rocked back on her heels, swaying like a charmed snake. "Don't you *dare* talk to me like that, Andrew! When I found you, you were just a wannabe musician working part-time in the Grove!"

"So?" Drew shrugged nonchalantly and stood up, his tall frame towering over both of us. "Who cares, Nicole?" He turned toward me as smoothly as if he'd just complimented someone on their alpaca poncho. "So, Lily, we still on for band practice tonight? And the show on Saturday?"

I had a hard time tearing my eyes away from Nicole, who was almost shaking with fury. I started to back away slowly, the way I do with the bigger and more ferocious charges at PuppyTales.

"Sure," I said. "I'll see you! Oh, and Nicole? I quit too. I don't think it's a good idea to wear wings every day, not while they're still so 'trendy.'" And then, without another word or glance, I fled.

# Harper

I wish I could say everything went back to normal after my fourteenth birthday, that Lily transferred to Beverly Hills High and Tim fell in love with me and Jessica left her Nutella-scented lifestyle in France and flew home to be with Stephanie. That we all lived happily ever after. But, spoiler alert: Life never works out like that.

Tim was still icing me out in an intense way. He had switched seats with Josh Davis in history and took the bus home, and whenever I passed him in the hallway, he shoved on his Beats and ducked into the closest bathroom. When I wasn't watching him run away from me, I was catching him fake-laughing with some Kendall-y girl near his locker, refusing to meet my gaze or answer any of my subsequent texts.

But at least some things work out. Just like Lily promised, I did get a do-over for my birthday: a brand-new, supersized PuppyBash do-over the Friday after we made up, which Lily helped me plan and everything. And I have to say, it was one for the books—and not only because Lily had arranged the best surprise ever: She'd managed to pull some strings with both the Jacobys and my parents and get me permission to be a foster mom for the most adorable three-legged pug for one week while Mom was away on business! Don't tell anyone but I'm secretly planning on never giving that little puppy back. . . .

Lily also had another big plan for the party: She was going to apologize to Beth-Lynne. She asked me to talk to the Jacobys beforehand to make sure Beth-Lynne would be there. It actually took a lot of convincing—Beth-Lynne was still pretty upset and her parents were a little worried about forcing her to be at the same party as Lily, who they now thought of as this big Nicole-level bully—but I set them straight, and they agreed to bring her.

So, all in all it was a successful birthday re-do . . . except for the fact that a certain nerdy, comic-drawing someone whom I've known all my life ignored all my calls and invitations and didn't show up.

Then, on Saturday night, I agreed to see Lily's band play at Art Rebel. I had no idea what to expect, and though I didn't tell Lily, I was secretly kind of dreading it a little bit. The last time I'd been to Art Rebel was my birthday, which had been an epic disaster to end all epic disasters, so it's not like I had great associations with the place. But Lily had been on my case all week about going, and it was kind of hard to say no to her, especially when she'd done so much for me the past few days. Like listen to me cry about the Derek fiasco, and even a little bit about how I was worried that I'd irreparably hurt Tim, who, despite my constant attempts, refused to accept my apology. I'd finally admitted to myself that he was the guy I liked, the one I had liked all along. I had just been too confused and scared about hurting Lily's feelings—and still kind of was, to be honest—to realize that I'd been falling for him ever since school started.

"Hey, you made it!" a voice called from across the floor.

Lily was unmistakable even amidst the mish-mash of people stuffed into the room. She had on a lace baby-doll gown in teacup blue and white tights—not leggings—that fit into her soft, embroidered pink boo-ties. Her hair was up in two big buns on the side of her head, which she held in place with two blue strings of ribbon. But most important . . .

"You're not wearing your wings!" I shouted, trying to make myself heard above the din.

"Nope!" Lily wrapped me in a giant hug and then began dragging me by the hand to the stage. "Come on, let's get you settled in the front row so you can see everything! And you can come say hi to Jane and Drew before we go on!"

"Oh, Lily, I just got here," I said, eyeing the closest exists. I did like Jane and Drew, but the last time Lily tried to mix me in with her new friends, it hadn't gone so well.

Lily deposited me at the front of the stage where Drew was working the mic. He was wearing an odd-fitting suit in dark material and no socks.

"Hey Drew!" Lily said happily. "You remember Harper, right?"

"Oh, totally," he said. "Thanks for coming!"

"Wouldn't miss it for the world," I said. I was so distracted trying to figure out what was weird about his suit that I couldn't help myself from staring.

"Black tie," he said, forcing me to look up from his pants to his face.

"Sorry?"

"My suit," he said. "It's black ties. Get it?"

Oh! Another necktie suit. Clever. He was wearing this one with tweed slippers, like the kind you'd wear at home, but boy did they look comfy.

"Ha! That's really cute!" I said. "Did you make it yourself?"

"Drew makes all his clothing himself with a sewing machine," Lily chirped proudly, then looked over my shoulder. "Hey, Stephanie! Hey, Jane!"

"Hey guys," Stephanie said, squeezing through the crowd along with Jane, who had a fancy camera hung around her neck. Seeing our reactions, Stephanie made a face and looked down at her outfit. "Before you say anything, I *know*."

"I love it!" I squealed, clapping my hands. Stephanie, the ballerina-twin-turned-skateboarder, was now standing in front of me wearing the most adorable shift dress I'd ever seen. It was white and starched, and had little blue anchors that almost matched her galumphing white snow boots. Her blond hair, usually shoved into a beanie, was today done up in elaborate French maid braids.

"Don't say it, I'm begging you," Stephanie said.

"Don't say what?"

"That I look like Swiss Miss." She stuck her thumb out at Jane, who seemed oblivious to our conversation as she snapped photos of the life-size American Girl doll that Stephanie had become. "Jane made me wear this get-up."

"I told you, once your friend Jessica sees these photos of you, she'll be begging her parents to switch her out of that ski school," Jane said. Apparently after meeting Stephanie at her house, Jane had decided she'd found her new F³ muse, and the two of them had been taking photos after school almost every day this week.

"Can you believe she almost didn't let me dress

her for the show?" Jane rolled her eyes conspiratorially. Even though she was dressed like a slinky cat goddess otherwise, Jane had on a pair of suede chestnut moccasins that looked vaguely familiar.

"Lily, Jane! We're about to go on! I need my other Judies!" Drew plugged in the microphone, and Lily gulped and nodded. Jane stopped taking photos and joined Drew backstage for a final sound check.

"Are you scared?" I asked Lily, peering into my friend's eyes and putting my hands on her shoulders. "Nauseous? Headachey? Do you need Tylenol? A pre-rock show nap?"

Lily laughed and put her hands on top of mine. "I'm fine," she said. "Promise. After enduring the first month of high school, how hard could it be to get up and sing in front of hundreds of people? Plus," she added slyly, pulling out something from underneath the front of her dress, "I have my good luck charm." She opened up her hand to reveal her half of the BFF necklace.

"Yay, me too!" I said, hugging my best friend. "I'm so excited for you! You're going to be a singer! My little Lily is all grown up!"

"A real adult lady singer!" Lily exclaimed in a nasally voice. "Why, I never! Next thing you know, we'll be getting the vote."

A sound like a loud train whistle screaming through a long tunnel blew from the stage.

"Okay, that's my cue." Lily looked pale but brave. "I love you so much, Harper. Wish me luck!"

"You don't need luck," I said. "You've got talent. And magic!"

Lily wrapped me in the biggest hug ever before bounding up to the stage. "Welcome, everyone!" she called into the microphone. "My name is Lily Farson. This is Jane Cooley and Drew Sawyer, and we're the Jug Judies! But before we get started tonight, I just wanted to say hi to one awesome girl in the audience tonight. Beth-Lynne, are you out there?"

There was a murmur from the center of the room, and suddenly a blushing, mortified Beth-Lynne stood completely still, like maybe we'd go away if she didn't move, the way it worked in *Jurassic Park*.

"Now, Beth-Lynne, I said some pretty mean things about your shoes last time I saw you, but I want you to know . . . that's not me." Lily was on the verge of tears, and the audio feedback whined. "I need to let you know . . . I would never judge someone by how they express themselves, because I know what that feels like. Well, actually, they say you can't know what it's like till you walk a mile in someone's shoes, so for tonight, my friends and I have tried that out."

No . . . she couldn't have! Suddenly Steph and Jane and Drew and Lily's footwear all made sense . . . they were all wearing different kinds of Uggs in solidarity.

"You know what? These are pretty freakin' comfortable!" Lily shouted. "Beth-Lynne, do you maybe wanna come up onstage and help us sing?"

Beth-Lynne, a big smile on her broad face, couldn't rush to the front of the room fast enough, to where Lily was waiting with outstretched arms. Lily grabbed Beth-Lynne with one arm and then launched into Nancy Sinatra's "These Boots Were Made for Walking" with her other hand on the mic.

Lily looked amazing up there, the bright lights creating a sparkly, fairylike halo around her face. I clapped and whistled as loud as I could, and Lily winked at me. I winked back, and watched her face turn from smiley-happy to surprised-excited as her gaze moved from mine to a spot just beyond me. I started to turn around to see what she was reacting to, but before I could—

"Hey, Harper."

I turned. Time stopped. I know, I know, that's a cliché, but wow, how else do you express that thing where it's like you're watching a movie of your own life, and suddenly the camera just zooms in on that crucial detail that you otherwise would have missed?

"Tim," I said, not even sure if my voice was working, let alone whether I was even moving my mouth. There he was, in a white V-neck and jeans and totally perfect in every way. "You're here."

"Looks that way." He still didn't look happy, but at least he was talking to me. "Let me guess, Lily told you to wait by the stage."

"No . . ." I said, confused, but then I remembered how she had just dragged me up to the front. "Oh, maybe. You?"

"Yeah." He pinched the back of his neck and shook his head. "I should have known she'd meant for me to run into you." He looked up. "I guess, I deserve it, after playing match-maker with you two."

"Oh." From about a million miles away, I heard Lily's voice over a cacophony of cheers, jug xylophones, and ukulele strums. I didn't know what to say. "I don't know what to say," I said.

Tim smiled wryly, showing off one of his dimples. "Dog got your tongue?" I groaned, and rolled my eyes at his lame pun. Some of the tension seeped out of my body, and I could see that Tim was relaxing a bit, too.

"I want you to know, that whole Derek kiss was

nothing!" I strained my voice to be heard above the crowd. "I think he's totally gross, but like, pathetic, too! I just felt bad for him. He reminds me of how I used to think about you!"

Tim snorted, his hands folded across his chest.

"Not that I think you're gross or pathetic!" I babbled. "I mean, maybe before, when we were growing up! But come on, you were like my little brother! And now, you're like . . . someone I don't want to be related to, because that would be gross in a completely different way!"

If there was a bubble caption above Tim's head like in one of his comics, it would have read:

"I guess I just wanted to say that . . . I missed you!"

Tim cocked his head to one side, straining to hear. "You what?"

"I *missed* you!" I shouted.

"Did you say you *WRIST* me?" He cupped a hand over his ear as the music rose in a crescendo.

"I MISSED YOU!" I screamed, jumping up and down. "I MISSED YOU! I MISSED YOU! I MISSED YOU!"

I landed, panting, only to realize that the song had

ended, and the entire audience was looking at me. From the stage, Lily had shielded her eyes from the stage lights and was trying to peer out at us.

"Sorry!" I squeaked. "Everything's fine! Nothing to see here!" Onstage, Lily grinned, Drew counted down—"Three, two, one!"—and the Jug Judies launched into another song. With the audience happily entranced by my best friend's music, I turned back to Tim.

"Hey, no shouting," he said, pulling me into our very first kiss. "I heard you the first time."

**Lily (12:09 pm):** I love you moar than all the fro-yo in the world!

**Harper (12:10 pm):** Oh yeah? Well I love you moar than you love singing to sold out audiences!

**Lily (12:11 pm):** I love you so much I'm going destroy everyone in your life that matters and force you to depend and love only me.

**Harper (12:11 pm):** That sounds beautiful. I love you.

**Lily (12:12 pm):** I love you moar.

♥ ★

In late 2014, HelloGiggles.com and Penguin Books for Young Readers held a contest for teen writers to submit essays about their own besties to celebrate the publication of *A Tale of Two Besties: A HelloGiggles Novel*. We are pleased to share the winning essay by fifteen-year-old Megan Phelps: "M+M: A Bestie Story."

## CALIFORNIA

On the day we met in 2009, my soon-to-be bestie, Margot, was racing Matchbox cars down the driveway with her grandmother. I was sitting in my parents' house, bored and strangely attuned to the sounds of the neighborhood, especially sounds that were right next door. I decided to investigate by running outside and casually playing on the wooden swing in our front yard—an awkward excuse to introduce myself. After a few minutes, my mysterious neighbor called me over, her French accent effortlessly cultured.

"This is my granddaughter, Marguerite," she told me, introducing Margot by her full name. I was nine and Margot was eight at the time, though it never occurred to us to be bothered by this age difference. I joined their game, playing for hours and stopping only when my mom called me home for dinner. You know that feeling when you click with someone instantly? When just being around them makes you feel more known? That was what happened that summer day with Margot. I met my soul-mate best friend.

We played every waking hour of the remainder of her visit that summer, tiptoeing to each other's houses as soon as the sun rose to plan our adventures. When we were together that summer (and for years to come), it was hard to imagine anything else. We spent our time splashing in the ocean and people-watching, throwing impromptu dance parties, singing together and sewing, making jewelry and sculptures in the sand, and cooking—we especially liked making raspberry sorbet, telling each other it could fix anything.

When Margot finally had to go back home to Montana, I was crushed, but she promised she'd return—and she did, often. These visits continued for years, each more fun than the last. Every time Margot left, I felt alone. But during our time apart, we remained close. We wrote each other long, detailed letters. We sent each other packages filled with things that reminded us of the other: magazine clippings, leaves and pressed flowers, artwork, photos. We sent each other questionnaires and quizzes and drawings that said "I miss you."

Thoughout all this I would beg my mother to let me visit Margot's home in Montana. I needed to explore the areas of her world that I'd never seen. Then one day, my mother finally said yes.

## MONTANA

"Get down!" Margot commanded, though her blue eyes were calm and unworried. We'd just hiked to the highest point in all of her small hometown. I felt cool raindrops fall as I watched streaks of lightning pierce through the big Montana sky, which had begun to darken with puffy storm clouds. Within a few tense seconds, a thunderous boom sounded, and that's when Margot yelled—a lightning storm at this height in this sky could be disastrous.

After a minute or so spent crouching on the damp trail, we hurried down the hill. She linked her arm through mine with a kind of ease that only besties share. A brook gurgling and the raindrops on the leaves overhead were the only sounds we heard for a while.

When we broke the silence, Margot chattered about the storm and the moon, which had begun to shine brilliantly through the clouds.

As I gazed up at the sky, the rain left drops like glistening jewels on my glasses. I turned my head to look at my friend, familiar and comfortable, noting the blonde strands of hair that the wind had blown onto her face. I marveled at the fact that it was the same face I had seen rounded with laughter in California so many times for so many years. The joyful face I had seen sprayed by the salty ocean after hours spent playing under the San Diego sun. The carefree face painted scarlet with raspberries after we had made sorbet, dusted with flour after we had baked *gâteau au chocolat*. The familiar face I had lightly kissed in greeting—first the left cheek, then the right—in that sophisticated European way that she had taught me after her summer trips to France.

But there was something more now. This was also the face I had seen stained with tears that came one after the other, each one filled with a deep grief, after she'd found out, the winter before, that her dad—her great and amazing dad, whom Margot loved as much as anything in the world—had died in a horrible skiing accident.

It was New Year's Day when we learned of her dad's death, Margot was visiting her grandmother for the holidays. The night before, on New Year's Eve, Martinelli's in hand, she'd toasted, "May your troubles list be shorter than your New Year's resolutions!" I remember remarking later to my mother, my eyes swollen and my heart sore with empathetic grief, "Margot's worries list is a lot longer than her New Year's resolutions."

Margot flew home the next day to Montana with her grandmother as a chaperone. I felt helplessly detached from her, over 1,100 miles away. She mourned; I cried for her. She mourned; my appetite lessened. She mourned; I missed her sorely and selfishly. She mourned; I wrote her a letter every day for two months—my feeble attempt to lessen her pain.

I had met her dad a single time. I had never been to Montana at that point, but he had come to San Diego once. He was picking up a surfboard that he had stored in Margot's grandparent's garage, and Margot introduced me to him. I felt shy, but saw his blue eyes—just like Margot's—and felt at ease. The conversation ended after ten minutes. And yet I felt as though I knew him. He was a nature-loving guy who loved wolverines and skiing and, even more than anything, he loved his spunky, cheerful daughter. I knew because of the daily postcards he sent her during her visits to California, and because of the way he sounded when he called her on the phone to check in. He made the joke "Do you want a little toast with that butter?" And now he was gone.

I felt so deeply connected to Margot that when I learned of his death, I was filled with raw sorrow and grief, unlike anything I had experienced before. I had always known logically that death happened, but my sense of it was very vague. For Margot, the experience was exponentially more painful—to a depth I still can't fathom. It was her first experience with death as well. And I felt more bonded to her and more protective of her because of it.

"Hey, Megan?" Margot asked, nudging me softly. "You OK?"

"Yeah," I replied. I felt slow and filled with bittersweet nostalgia. She had her arm around me and pulled me in a little closer, smiling, though the Montana summer air was warm and the rain had only intensified the stickiness of the sweat on my skin.

Margot stopped for a moment. She cleared the leaves from a small patch on the ground and etched "M + M" into the dirt, the code name we had affectionately given ourselves when we were younger and had never let go.

I responded approvingly, touched by the gesture, and we continued our walk back to her house.

It only took a few moments to get back to her house, and without hesitation, Margot put on music and looked back at me with a mischievous grin. We danced until we couldn't any longer, twirling ourselves and jumping up and down in a far sillier way than we would want anyone else to see.

When her mom reminded us of all the adventures we had planned for the next day, we climbed into the bunk beds in her room, tired from the day of travel. She listened to music as I read a book I had found on her shelf. After a few minutes, Margot looked down at me from the top bunk, her face flushed with warmth.

"I'm glad you're here," she told me, smiling.

"Me too," I responded, and she smiled broader. I pulled the sheet that covered me closer.

"Goodnight," Margot whispered, turning out the light. "Sleep tight."

"Goodnight," I whispered back, my eyelids growing

heavier with each word. "Don't let the bedbugs bite."

Before I drifted off to sleep, I remembered the letters we had written each other when we were younger, before we had been allowed into the digital world. She would tell me stories of all the things she had done and the friends she had made. Though we live 1,100 miles apart, the letters reminded us of our bestie-hood and made the distance seem infinitely shorter.

In the letters I kept, I had counted at least fifty-five times that Margot had written some form of "I love you." She would always decorate these notes with colorful pens and write on the back of the envelope, "sealed with a kiss," and amend it by saying, "and the sticky envelope glue."

Her letters highlighted all the things I had learned from Margot that summer and in the six years of our friendship:

1. *Be adventurous, daring, and independent.*

2. *Don't take yourself too seriously.*

3. *Listen to music, all the time.*

4. *Most importantly, love with all your heart, and when in doubt, make raspberry sorbet—it makes everything better.*